# OUT OF PRACTICE

# What Reviewers Say
# About Carsen Taite's Work

**Leading the Witness**

"…a very enjoyable lesbian crime investigation drama book with a romance on the side. 4.5 stars."—*LezReviewBooks.com*

"Riveting. …The character of Catherine Landauer is absolutely fascinating and Taite does a phenomenal job of drawing her out. …Definitely recommend."—*C-Spot Reviews*

**Practice Makes Perfect**

"This book has two fantastic leads, an attention-grabbing plot and that sizzling chemistry that great authors can make jump off the page. While all of Taite's books are fantastic, this one is on that next level. This is a damn good book and I cannot wait to see what is next in this series."—*Romantic Reader Blog*

"This is possibly the funniest of Taite's books with good use of banter and witty dialogues. The main characters are well portrayed and even though the romance is very slow-burn, it's realistic and angst-free. The chemistry is sizzling and the intimate scenes are well written. …Overall, a very good start of a series full of fun, romance, and donuts. 4 stars."—*LezReviewBooks.com*

**Pursuit of Happiness**

"I like Taite's style of writing. She is consistent in terms of quality and always writes strong female characters that are as intelligent as they are beautiful."—*Lesbian Reading Room*

"I can't believe I'm saying this, but I think Meredith and Stevie are my new favourite couple that Taite's written. …They're brilliant, funny, and the chemistry between them is out of control."
—*Lesbian Review*

**Love's Verdict**

"Carsen Taite excels at writing legal thrillers with lesbian main characters using her experience as a criminal defense attorney."
—*Lez Review Books*

**Outside the Law**

"[A] fabulous closing to the Lone Star Law Series. …Tanner and Sydney's journey back to each other is sweet, sexy and sure to keep you entertained."—*Romantic Reader Blog*

**A More Perfect Union**

"Readers looking for a mix of intrigue and romance set against a political backdrop will want to pick up Taite's latest novel."
—*RT Book Reviews*

"A sexy soldier. …Yes, please!!! …Character chemistry was excellent, and I think with such an intricate background story going on, it was remarkable that Carsen Taite didn't lose the characters' romance in that and still kept it at the front and centre of the storyline."—*Les Rêveur*

**Sidebar**

"*Sidebar* is a sexy, fun, interesting book that's sure to delight, whether you're a longtime fan or this is your first time reading something by Carsen Taite. I definitely recommend it!"
—*Lesbian Review*

**Letter of the Law**

"Fiery clashes and lots of chemistry, you betcha!"—*Romantic Reader Blog*

**Without Justice**

"Another pretty awesome lesbian mystery thriller by Carsen Taite."
—Danielle Kimerer, Librarian, Nevins Memorial Library (MA)

"All in all a fantastic novel. ...Unequivocally 5 Stars."
—*Les Rêveur*

**Above the Law**

"...readers who enjoyed the first installment will find this a worthy second act."—*Publishers Weekly*

"Ms. Taite delivered and then some, all the while adding more questions, Tease!! I like the mystery and intrigue in this story. It has many 'sit on the edge of your seat' scenes of excitement and dread (like watch out kind of thing) and drama...well done indeed!"—*Prism Book Alliance*

**Reasonable Doubt**

"Another Carsen Taite novel that kept me on the edge of my seat. ...[A]n interesting plot with lots of mystery and a bit of thriller as well. The characters were great."—Danielle Kimerer, Librarian, Reading Public Library

"Sarah and Ellery are very likeable. Sarah's conflict between job and happiness is well portrayed. I felt so sorry for Ellery's total upheaval of her life. ...I loved the chase to find the truth while they tried to keep their growing feelings for each other at bay. When they couldn't, the tale was even better."—*Prism Book Alliance*

**Lay Down the Law**

"Recognized for the pithy realism of her characters and settings drawn from a Texas legal milieu, Taite pays homage to the prime-time soap opera *Dallas* in pairing a cartel-busting U.S. attorney, Peyton Davis, with a charity-minded oil heiress, Lily Gantry."
—*Publishers Weekly*

"Suspenseful, intriguingly tense, and with a great developing love story, this book is delightfully solid on all fronts."—*Rainbow Book Reviews*

**Courtship**

"Taite (*Switchblade*) keeps the stakes high as two beautiful and brilliant women fueled by professional ambitions face daunting emotional choices. ...As backroom politics, secrets, betrayals, and threats race to be resolved without political damage to the president, the cat-and-mouse relationship game between Addison and Julia has the reader rooting for them. Taite prolongs the fever-pitch tension to the final pages. This pleasant read with intelligent heroines, snappy dialogue, and political suspense will satisfy Taite's devoted fans and new readers alike."—*Publishers Weekly*

"Carsen Taite throws the reader head on into the murky world of the political system where there are no rights or wrongs, just players attempting to broker the best deals regardless of who gets hurt in the process. The book is extremely well written and makes compelling reading. With twist and turns throughout, the reader doesn't know how the story will end."—*Lesbian Reading Room*

**Switchblade**

"Dallas's intrepid female bounty hunter, Luca Bennett, is back in another adventure. Fantastic! Between her many friends and lovers, her interesting family, her fly by the seat of her pants lifestyle, and a whole host of detractors there is rarely a dull moment." —*Rainbow Book Reviews*

**Beyond Innocence**

"Taite keeps you guessing with delicious delay until the very last minute. ...Taite's time in the courtroom lends *Beyond Innocence*, a terrific verisimilitude someone not in the profession couldn't impart. And damned if she doesn't make practicing law interesting."—*Out in Print*

**The Best Defense**

"Real Life defense attorney Carsen Taite polishes her fifth work of lesbian fiction, *The Best Defense*, with the realism she daily encounters in the office and in the courts. And that polish is something that makes *The Best Defense* shine as an excellent read."—*Out & About Newspaper*

**Nothing but the Truth**

Author Taite is really a Dallas defense attorney herself, and it's obvious her viewpoint adds considerable realism to her story, making it especially riveting as a mystery. I give it four stars out of five."—Bob Lind, *Echo Magazine*

**Do Not Disturb**

"Taite's tale of sexual tension is entertaining in itself, but a number of secondary characters...add substantial color to romantic inevitability"—Richard Labonte, *Book Marks*

Visit us at www.boldstrokesbooks.com

# By the Author

Truelesbianlove.com
It Should be a Crime
Do Not Disturb
Nothing but the Truth
The Best Defense
Beyond Innocence
Rush
Courtship
Reasonable Doubt
Without Justice
Sidebar
A More Perfect Union
Love's Verdict
Pursuit of Happiness
Leading the Witness

**The Luca Bennett Mystery Series:**
Slingshot
Battle Axe
Switchblade
Bow and Arrow (novella in Girls with Guns)

**Lone Star Law Series:**
Lay Down the Law
Above the Law
Letter of the Law
Outside the Law

**Legal Affairs Romances:**
Practice Makes Perfect
Out of Practice

# OUT OF PRACTICE

*by*
Carsen Taite

2020

# OUT OF PRACTICE

ISBN 13: 978-1-63555-359-8

This Trade Paperback Original Is Published By
Bold Strokes Books, Inc.
P.O. Box 249
Valley Falls, NY 12185

First Edition: February 2020

Credits
Editor: Cindy Cresap
Production Design: Susan Ramundo
Cover Design By Jeanine Henning

# Acknowledgments

I can write anywhere—coffee shop, car dealership, waiting in line at the DMV, but my favorite place to write is at my desk in my home office next to a cozy little dog bed where Lambchop and Chewbacca are nestled together waiting for their pet dog Mollie to come home. Unfortunately for us, Mollie is frolicking at the Rainbow Bridge and we who are left behind will have to make do without her until it's our time to say good-bye to this mortal life. I discovered exactly how hard making do was while I was in the middle of writing this book. Mollie was at my side for every one of the books I've written, and it's hard to comprehend doing this without my little superdog sitting on my shoulder, nestled at my side, or gnawing on the pages to remind me that a good dinner can be more important than a higher word count. I love you, Mollie, and I miss you every single day.

Thanks always to Rad and Sandy for making this publishing house a home. To my intrepid editor, Cindy Cresap—thanks for all the work you do behind the scenes to make my work shine. Jeanine, thank you for the beautiful set of covers for this series. Ruth, your tireless efforts to make us all shine are most appreciated, and I treasure our friendship.

I've made so many good friends during my writing journey. Georgia, I love our daily word count check-ins, but the thing I'm most grateful for is your friendship. Melissa, thanks for always being available to talk about all the things. Paula, thanks for being available whenever I needed to dish about all things bridal, legal mumbo jumbo, and *everything* else. And special thanks for reading all the versions of this story up until the day it was due. You're one hundred percent the best pal ever!

Thanks to my wife, Lainey, for always believing in my dreams even when they involve sacrificing our time together. That you are always available to brainstorm book ideas and plot points is a total bonus. I couldn't do this without you and I wouldn't want to.

And to my loyal readership, thank you, thank you, thank you. Every time you purchase one of my stories, you give me the gift of allowing me to make a living doing what I love. Thanks for taking this journey with me.

# Dedication

To Mollie, the fiercest, most devoted, loyal,
loving little dog on the planet. We miss you big time.
And to Lainey, the best dog mom ever.

## CHAPTER ONE

I'm not a hundred percent sure what's in a mai tai, but I'm ordering five of them as soon as the plane touches down." Abby Keane made the announcement to her law partners Campbell Clark and Grace Maldonado as she shoved her passport into her purse. "Are you sure you two are going to be okay on your own?"

"Absolutely." Campbell shooed Abby to the door. "Besides, we agreed—now that the firm is up and running, we all start taking vacations. Real ones. No phone, no computer. Lots of drinks. Although I have to say that if you come back all sugared up from drinking fruity beverages with tiny umbrellas, we might not be your friends anymore. What say you, Grace?"

Grace cocked her head like she was giving the question serious thought. "We'll take a vote when she gets back. I've had my eye on her office for a while."

Abby grinned at her friends, not at all worried they would ditch her under any circumstances. Early this year, they'd all reunited at their five-year law school reunion and, upon finding out they all hated the careers they'd chosen working for big law firms, decided to quit their jobs and form the law firm of Clark, Keane, and Maldonado. The transition had been challenging, but they were starting to see some success. In any case, they were having a much better time working for themselves than they had doing the bidding of irrational, egotistical big firm law partners.

One of the conditions when they'd started the firm was that they each take actual vacations, not the poor stand-ins they'd had in their last jobs, where weekend getaways were guaranteed to be interrupted by sketchy emergencies designed to get them to feel indispensable and beholden all at the same time. No, they'd cover for each other to make sure that everything was handled while the others were gone so that when they returned, they wouldn't face the usual nightmare of reentry. In deference to their equal partnership, they'd actually drawn straws to decide who would get to go first, and Abby had won. She'd spent two weeks scouring the internet for options and finally landed a resort that promised to be the perfect locale. Remote, yet devoted to providing their guests with every luxury. The reviews used words like lush, pampered, and lavish. She'd booked a first class ticket because she figured she'd earned it, and spent the last two weeks tying up loose ends.

Abby's phone buzzed to let her know the car service was almost there. "I left a list of pending matters with Graham," Abby said, referring to their office manager. "And he knows how to get hold of me if there are any emergencies and you can't reach me on my cell."

"Which there won't be," Grace said. "At least none that we can't handle. Now go. You're the first one of us to get one of these vacation thingies. We're relying on you to report back and tell us what it's all about."

Abby grabbed her bag. "There's a tiny part of me that feels bad about leaving you alone, but the rest of me is dreaming of endless sun and lots of fruity drinks." She gave them each a hug and headed to the door where Graham was waiting to say good-bye.

"Ms. Keane, your chariot awaits," he said with a flourish of his arm and a bow.

She smiled. She'd miss his odd formality and she'd miss hanging with her friends, but it had been her decision to take this trip alone. She'd packed several books—real hold-in-your-hand-paperbacks—and magazines, and she was looking forward to turning her brain off for an entire week.

Her ride was only a few minutes away from the airport when her phone rang and her mother's picture appeared on the screen. For a moment, she considered not answering, but Donna Wheeler was a persistent woman and Abby didn't want to be bothered once the vacation officially started. "Hey, Mom, I'm almost at the airport."

"Are you sure it's safe for you to be traveling alone to such a remote place?"

It was a constant wonder how she'd become so independent when she had a mother who would never imagine traveling alone or doing anything else for that matter without a partner by her side. Plus, she likely equated "remote" with some kind of jungle full of hungry wild animals. "I promise. I thoroughly researched this place and it's loaded with security, and it's only a couple of hours from Puerto Vallarta. Beyoncé stayed there just a few months ago," she added, knowing the pop culture reference would be soothing to her TMZ-watching mother.

"Really? Then I suppose it's okay. Do you think she'll be there during your stay?"

Abby suppressed a laugh. "If she is, I promise I'll try to get you an autograph." She glanced out the window. "Hey, we're pulling up to the gate. I have to go. I'll call you when I get back."

"Have fun. Send pictures. Text often."

Abby stowed her phone, feeling a tinge of guilt in advance because, aside from a quick "Hey, I arrived safely," she had no plans to call or text anyone, especially her mother, while she was gone. There was a time in her life she would've felt guilty for not inviting her mother along, but she knew from experience her mom would spend the entire trip on high alert, trying to find them both someone to hook up with. A mother does not a good wingwoman make.

As the car came to a stop, Abby shoved away her guilt and gathered her stuff.

"See you in a week," the driver called out after he loaded her luggage onto a cart.

A whole week with no clients, no opposing counsel, no work at all. The idea sent her brain into a tailspin, but she took a deep breath and leaned in. She was going to have a blast doing absolutely nothing.

❖

*Honeymoon apparently used to mean the month (moon phase) after the wedding when the bride's father loaded the happy couple with all the mead (honey beer) they could drink. Honey was believed to be an aphrodisiac, and a month of drunken lovemaking would hurry along the next logical phase of the couple's life: baby-making.*

*Times have changed. Despite the proliferation of craft beer and microbreweries, no one's rushing out to buy a growler of mead, let alone newlyweds rushing away from the chaos of their nuptials to find a little alone time. And while raising a family is a worthy goal, it's not for everyone and certainly not the first thing on the minds of most fresh-minted married folk.*

*Which leads us to ask—what is a honeymoon and how do you make the most of it?*

Roxanne stopped typing and cocked her head at the sound of the gate agent calling her boarding group, which happened to be the very last one. She offered a silent curse to the travel coordinator at the magazine who'd booked her flight, tucked her laptop in her bag, and joined the herd of passengers queuing up to board the flight to Puerto Vallarta.

She'd packed light, as she usually did when she traveled for business, which put her in contrast with the rest of the passengers boarding the flight, most of whom toted travel pillows and snacks in addition to their allowed carry-on items. Truth was she hadn't had a lot of time to prepare for the trip. The staff writer for *Best Day Ever* bridal magazine who usually handled honeymoon features had fallen ill at the last minute, and the editor had asked her to step in for the already booked trip. The online version of the magazine already licensed her popular wedding blog, *The Bride's Best Friend*, so the gig was a perfect fit for both of them, and Roxanne hoped the feature spread would garner the attention she needed to land something bigger.

After being shoved in the back several times, she barely resisted the urge to turn around and smack the woman behind her with the too big purse and oversized suitcase. When they finally crossed from the Jetway to the plane, their already slow procession ground to a halt in the middle of first class, while they waited for the million passengers ahead of them, who'd apparently packed as much crap as the woman behind her, to board the plane.

When the line finally started moving, Roxanne stepped forward only to immediately trip and land square across the aisle seat of one of the first class passengers. She grabbed the headrest to regain her balance and came face-to-face with a ravishing beauty. "I'm so sorry."

"Are you okay?" the woman asked.

"Aside from being embarrassed, yes." Roxanne zeroed in on the champagne flute the woman was holding in her outstretched hand. "Did I spill your drink?"

"No worries," the beautiful brunette said, tilting the glass toward her. "I could lie and say you're the reason it's empty, but the truth is I polished this off seconds ago."

Ah, the ease of first class. Not only were these passengers already lounging in big, cushy seats, but the flight attendants were tending to their every need with little regard to the herd of people waiting to find space in the back of the plane. Champagne woman's easy smile and relaxed posture was evidence the price of the ticket might well be worth it. Roxanne sighed. One day she too would spare no expense when she traveled, but since she wouldn't be taking this trip if it weren't being comped, she would make do with a tiny seat in coach and the sandwich she'd stowed away in her bag. "Well, that's a relief."

"If you're sitting nearby, maybe we can share a toast to start the trip."

Roxanne was caught off guard. Was champagne woman flirting with her? Right here in the aisle of a packed airplane?

"Hey, some of us are trying to get to our seats."

She couldn't pinpoint exactly who'd yelled, but Roxanne could feel the tension from the rest of the passengers behind her. She raised her shoulders. "Rain check?"

"Definitely."

With one last reluctant glance at the woman whose lap she'd landed in, Roxanne strode down the aisle. Once in her aisle seat, she shoved her small carry-on under the seat in front of her and opened her iPad. Her sister, Valerie, had texted a series of emojis consisting of a plane, a rocket ship, a palm tree, a drink, and a red heart. She typed back, *Love you, sis. I'll text you in a few days after I leave the first resort.*

*As if. You know you'll never last more than a few hours off grid.*

*There's only one way to get the full experience. I'm doing it for my readers.*

*We'll see. I have a twenty that says I'll hear from you later today.*

*I'll take that bet. Gotta go, sour-faced flight attendant heading toward me.*

Roxanne put the iPad in airplane mode and nodded politely to the attendant to head off a scolding, but she kept it open in her lap. While she scrolled through her apps looking for the articles she'd saved to read on the plane, out of the corner of her eye she spotted Champagne standing in the aisle. She was much taller than Roxanne had been able to ascertain while she'd been seated. Of course, it was hard to tell much when sprawled across someone's lap. What she had been able to tell was that Champagne was smokin' hot, and seeing her now, reaching up into the overhead bin with her well-toned arms, only confirmed her initial assessment.

"I think you're going to have to put that away before we can take off."

Roxanne reluctantly tore her gaze from Champagne and looked at the elderly woman in the middle seat. She smiled. "It's all good. Laptops have to be stowed, but these," she held up the iPad, "are perfectly fine." She glanced at the white-haired man seated by the window, already snoring. "Is that your husband?"

"Yes." Middle Seat rolled her eyes and thrust out a hand. "Millie Lawrence, pleased to meet you."

Roxanne shook her hand and introduced herself. "Where are you headed?"

"Same place as you, I imagine, Puerto Vallarta. Our kids bought us this trip for our sixtieth wedding anniversary."

"Wow, sixty years. That's amazing."

Millie shot a look at her still snoring husband. "It's a lot of work is what it is, but there's no one I'd rather do it with than my Albert." She patted his arm, but he didn't budge. "He likes to think he doesn't snore." She rolled her eyes again. "He always has."

Roxanne grinned while an idea for a blog about anniversaries started churning in the back of her brain. "Do you have anything special planned to commemorate the big day while you're in PV?"

"Our son made us a reservation at a nice restaurant near the resort. It's supposed to be a popular place for honeymooners, but a lot of people celebrate anniversaries there too. Maybe you've heard of it? *Aguas Danzantes*. It means dancing waters."

Millie waited with an expectant expression, and Roxanne nodded. *Aguas Danzantes* was next door to the Blue Wave resort, one of the places that Roxanne planned to check out while in PV. "I actually read about it in a magazine last month."

"I bet it was *Best Day Ever*."

Roxanne wondered if the shock showed on her face. "You know, you're right. Into bridal magazines, are you?"

Millie waved a hand. "Not me, dear. My granddaughter is getting married in the fall, and she can't stop reading everything she can get her hands on. She's constantly showing me new dress styles, articles about where to have the honeymoon, what kind of cake to serve, the best favors for the guests. But I bet you know all about those things if you're getting married too." She looked down at Roxanne's ringless hand and then back up at her face. "Sorry, I didn't mean to assume. When you mentioned you'd read about the restaurant in *Best Day Ever*, I just thought…"

Roxanne could feel the warmth of a blush forming, and scrambled for a response. "Oh, no. I mean I did read the review, but the magazine was my sister's. She's getting married next year."

Millie nodded approvingly. "All the details wear me out. Albert and I got married in front of a JP and then drove to Galveston for a long weekend at his boss's beach house. Nothing fancy, but I suppose it had staying power."

"Staying power is important." It was on the tip of Roxanne's tongue to mention that she was traveling to PV to research an article she was writing for *Best Day Ever*, but she quickly changed her mind. The key to the perfect write-up about PV as a honeymoon paradise was keeping her identity secret. Like a restaurant reviewer, she'd sample the experience, and then the magazine would send a photographer along later to capture all the moments. If the resorts found out she was writing an article, they'd likely put on a show that regular honeymooners might never experience.

Luckily, she was saved from her impulse to divulge when the flight attendant came over the loudspeaker to detail the safety procedures. Millie watched dutifully, and Roxanne enjoyed watching her drink in the information as if she were hearing it for the first time. There was something refreshing about Millie's naiveté. It was definitely a stark contrast to the bored expressions and often outright disregard the other passengers had for the in-flight warnings, although she could hardly blame them since her own mind started to wander as the monotone voice droned on. What had it been like having a wedding in front of the JP? Why the JP? Were Millie and Albert naturally no fuss folks, or maybe Millie's parents hadn't approved, and they didn't have money for anything more than the marriage license?

It was fun to ponder the questions, consider the possibilities. Weddings were so completely individualized, and everyone had different opinions about what made them special. The story idea that had jumped into her head a few minutes ago came back, and she jotted a few notes on her iPad and filed them away for later before she read over her notes for the trip ahead. She was headed to PV to do this honeymoon feature, and she was determined not to get distracted by shiny new ideas or hot women in first class.

❖

Abby informed the customs agent she was in Puerto Vallarta for purely recreational reasons, but he'd stamped her passport before she could finish her sentence. Once she was on the other side of the counter, she pulled up the travel documents she'd saved to her phone and consulted the instructions about where she was supposed to meet the transport to the resort. Graham had meticulously highlighted all the important information she'd need immediately upon arriving in PV, and she quickly located the portion that said a driver would be waiting with the name of the resort on a placard. She looked up and glanced around but didn't see anyone waiting for incoming travelers. She turned back to ask the customs agent if he could point her in the right direction, but there was a long line in his queue, and she decided to try to find her way on her own. When she turned back toward the airport exit, the woman who'd sprawled across her tray table earlier was standing right in front of her.

"Need some help?" the woman offered, her blue eyes bright. She held her hands up, palms forward. "I promise I'm not going to spill any drinks on you."

Abby grinned. "You say that now because neither one of us is holding a drink, but how do I know you're not planning on some drink spilling later when I'm least expecting it?"

"Fair enough, but I'd like to point out that you were so deep in thought just now that I could've easily snuck up on you. Besides, didn't you promise me a toast?"

Abby took a moment to appraise the woman. Blond and blue-eyed, dressed in casual travel wear and carrying only a small suitcase, she sported a carefree vibe that said I travel all the time, follow me. Abby had traveled plenty, but most of it was for work with her former law firm and involved traveling in packs with other associates on trips that had been meticulously planned by an administrative assistant. "Actually, I could use some help. I'm supposed to meet up with a driver from my resort, but I don't see anyone waiting. I'm thinking maybe they queue up somewhere besides right here."

"Good instinct. Most of them are outside by the taxi line. I'm headed that way if you'd like to tag along."

"Sure, but on one condition."

"Name it."

"Funny you should say that. I was about to say we should exchange names. I like to know who I'm dealing with, especially when they've already been in my lap."

The woman smiled and her eyes brightened. "Seems reasonable." She stuck out her hand. "I'm Roxanne."

Abby grasped her hand. It was soft, but her handshake was firm. "Nice to meet you Roxanne. I'm Abby," she said, noting Roxanne hadn't offered a last name, leading her to respond in kind.

"Now that we've been properly introduced, shall I lead the way?"

"Please." Abby watched as Roxanne picked up her one bag, and she felt a little silly about the two large suitcases and carry-on she'd carted along, but it had been easier to throw everything in her bags rather than taking valuable time before the trip trying to figure out what she'd wear in advance.

Roxanne started walking and looked back over her shoulder. "You need some help with all that?"

"I'm good." Abby stowed her carry-on on top of one of the larger bags and pulled one with each hand, determined not to look foolish in front of the cute girl. Cute. No, that wasn't the word. Pretty. Fun. Flirtatious. Yep, those all worked. Oh, and she had a nice butt. Abby started to scold herself about staring at the stranger's ass, but stopped. She was on vacation for the first time in years, and if she wanted to ogle a cute, pretty, fun girl, then dammit, she was going to.

The moment she'd made the resolution, Roxanne looked back again. "Everything all right back there?"

Roxanne wore a big grin and Abby was certain she could see into the part of her brain that was completely focused on trying not to stare. After a minute, Abby decided there really wasn't any point in pretending, and she very deliberately swept her gaze over Roxanne's entire body, feeling warmer by the second. She stopped when she met Roxanne's eyes and let a slow smile spread across her face. "Everything is absolutely okay."

A few minutes later, they were standing outside near a line of vans. Roxanne scanned the area. "Did the resort give you any ideas about what kind of vehicle to look for?"

Abby shook her head. "I was expecting someone with my name on a placard, but other than that, I'm clueless." She felt her face redden at her lack of detail, and she rushed to add, "I picked the place, but I didn't do the actual booking." She wasn't used to not having all the answers, and now she felt a little silly for leaving all the arrangements to Graham.

Roxanne contemplated her for a moment. "Did your booker give you any paperwork?" At Abby's nod, she held out a hand. "Let's see it."

Abby extracted her phone from her pocket, pulled up the detailed email from Graham, and handed it over. She watched while Roxanne skimmed the screen and scrolled through the rest of the email. When she looked back up, she was grinning again.

"What is it? Did I miss the bus? Did I pick the absolute worst resort? I did a lot of research on this, but you know how the internet is."

Roxanne handed her phone back to her. "I hope you picked a good one because I'm headed there too."

Abby blinked, unsure if she'd heard Roxanne correctly. "You're staying at the Azure. With me?" She felt the heat in her face again. "Well, obviously, not with me, but..."

"Yep. We're both headed to the same place. How about we find our van together?"

"That sounds like a perfect plan." Abby immediately started rearranging all her preconceived notions about her plans for this trip. Reading books and magazines, sunbathing with her AirPods in, listening to the podcasts she'd downloaded—all in perfect solitude. The allure of having Roxanne at the same resort made the idea of solitude a tad less appealing. She watched Roxanne scan the waiting drivers for their van, and admired her toned physique and easy confidence. The attraction was immediate and strong. She'd like to spend more time with this woman, solitude be damned.

Of course, Roxanne might have different plans. Maybe she was here for some alone time as well and didn't want the company.

Roxanne pointed to a white Mercedes van. "Pretty sure that's the one." She glanced at her phone. "Yep, matches the description to a tee. Shall we?"

Abby picked up her luggage and followed her to the van. Henry, the driver, introduced himself and handily stowed their bags before offering them a glass of champagne from the tiny fridge in the passenger compartment. Abby decided this was perfect synchronicity since she'd promised Roxanne a toast. Once they were settled, she tilted her glass toward Roxanne. "To a wonderful vacation." A couple of beats of silence passed before Roxanne finally clinked her glass against hers, and Abby was certain she'd seen something flutter in Roxanne's eyes when she'd said the word vacation and it wasn't excitement or pleasure. She took a sip of the champagne and plunged in. "So, how did you come to pick this particular resort for your vacation?"

Again with the look. Roxanne took a drink of champagne before answering, and Abby couldn't help but feel like she was stalling. Finally, Roxanne set the glass down. "I did a lot of research. It's an occupational hazard."

Abby started to say research was an occupational hazard of her job too, but stopped short when she heard Campbell's voice in her head. *Don't talk about work. Don't think about work. Work doesn't exist while you're in paradise.* She elected to glide over the remark and raised her glass again. "Looks like our research really paid off because this is starting off really well. And I can't wait to see where things go from here."

"Me too."

Abby took another sip of champagne. This vacation was shaping up to be even better than she could've imagined.

## Chapter Two

By Roxanne's calculation, they were still about twenty minutes from the resort when they finished off the bottle of champagne, and she was starting to feel that giddy, bubbly feeling that came when she drank too much too fast, but Abby was clearly in the mood to let loose, and Roxanne found her vacation mood infectious. She was going to need a nap when she got to her cabana.

In an effort to stay awake and sober for the rest of the ride, she cast around for innocuous topics of conversation. Asking about Abby's work would only invite questions about her own, and now that she was within miles of the resort, her anonymity was more important than ever. She'd ask about the resort itself—that was safe.

"I'm guessing you haven't been to Azure before. I understand they don't do a lot of advertising. How did you find out about it?"

"In a roundabout way. I was talking to my…friend Campbell about where I should vacation, and Braxton Meadows overheard us. He insisted I check this place out. Apparently, he rented the entire resort for a corporate retreat last year. Can you imagine? 'Hey, we're going to work in paradise. Don't forget to pack your swimsuit.' Like anyone would get any work—"

Roxanne grabbed her arm. "You know Braxton Meadows?"

Abby's face closed up. "Um, kind of. He's an acquaintance of Campbell's. I don't really know him personally."

"He's amazing. I saw his TED talk and it was truly inspiring. His new app, Leaderboard, is fantastic, and he's helped so many young entrepreneurs with his foundation. I'm a big fan." She stopped gushing long enough to notice that Abby had a weird look on her face. "Did I say something wrong?"

Abby shook her head. "Not at all. I think I should've eaten something before I gulped two glasses of champagne."

"Me too. The peanuts in coach barely made a dent in my alcohol shield. At least you were in first class."

"True. I had a hot cookie." She held up her hands and bowed her head. "Okay, I had two. You'd think that would prepare you for anything."

They both laughed and the mood lightened again. Roxanne breathed a sigh of relief. Moments later, they pulled off the road and onto a long narrow drive marked with only a small sign that read Azure. She recognized the discreet signage from the photos the magazine had provided, and even though she was here for work, she felt a twinge of excitement about this adventure. The boutique resort had only fifteen cabanas, but their overall amenities rivaled those of the much bigger resorts closer to PV. Horseback riding, spa treatments, yoga on the beach, and world class dining. She planned to try it all because not only did she need the full experience if she was going to write a proper article, she was here on *Best Day Ever*'s dime. Since the magazine was paying plenty for her to be here taking advantage of all the resort had to offer was more than a pleasure, it was her duty.

"Do you vacation by yourself often?" Abby asked.

Roxanne started to say this wasn't a vacation, but it kind of was in that she was simulating a vacation in order to be able to give the magazine's subscribers the inside scoop. The only way it would be more authentic would be if she were here on an actual honeymoon. As if. She didn't want to lie to Abby, but the truth was she couldn't remember the last time she'd been on a real vacation. Maybe that time she, her sister, and her parents had spent a long weekend in San Antonio right after she'd graduated from high school. They'd stayed at a motel not on, but not too far from, the famous River Walk, and strolled the trails along the river for a couple of days. Even though they'd been traveling on a budget, her parents made sure they made the most of the experience, and she savored the memory. Certainly someone like Abby who flew first class and stayed in expensive resorts wouldn't be impressed with a simple road trip, she settled on a half truth. "Not often. Frankly, I'm kind of a workaholic." She winced, hoping that wasn't the kind of information that would scare a pretty girl away. "Vacations are something I always put off."

Abby nodded. "Amen to that. This is the first one I've had in a while." She grimaced. "I think the last time I traveled for pleasure was a trip to Europe after college graduation."

"Sounds like we both deserve a break." Roxanne started to ask where she'd graduated from and what she did for a living, but didn't want to invite similar questions, so she hatched a plan. "Let's make a deal. While we're at Azure, let's pretend that there is no life outside. No work, no career, no obligations. Neither one of us will discuss our professional lives back home. I mean the resort encourages guests to go off the grid anyway, so we may as well pretend there's nothing outside the resort walls. What do you say?"

Abby raised her empty glass. "I say that's the most excellent idea I've heard in a long time, and I'll drink to it as soon as I have some dinner in me."

"Speaking of dinner, would you like to join me?" As the words tumbled out of Roxanne's mouth, she wondered if she was making a mistake. She wasn't here to have fun, but how was she supposed to test this playground for couples if she wasn't in one, even a faux one?

"I'd love too."

Too late now. Oh well, this way she could have the best of both worlds. She'd get to spend some quality time with an interesting woman and get a second perspective on the resort for her article. It was a win-win. Before she could overanalyze it, the van pulled up at the resort. "How about seven—that should allow us both time for a well earned, post-champagne nap? I'll meet you in the main dining room."

"Perfect."

"Señoritas, let me get your bags and I'll meet you right outside," the driver said as he opened the door. He held out a hand and Abby stepped out first, and then turned and waited for her. Roxanne grabbed her tote and started to step out of the van, but her shoe caught on the rubber tread and she pitched forward. Henry caught her, but the contents of her bag spilled onto the driveway. With Henry's help, she managed to get her feet back on the ground and brushed off the fall.

"Seriously, I'm not always such a klutz. I blame the lack of cookies in coach." She laughed, expecting Abby to join in, but Abby wasn't even looking at her. Her eyes were focused on the scattered contents of her bag, and Roxanne immediately zeroed in on what had captured her attention. Five bridal magazines were fanned out on the pavement, having landed from the fall like they'd been set out for display with the latest copy of *Best Day Ever* right on top. She wrenched her gaze from the magazines to Abby's face, and she didn't like what she saw. The friendly smile and sparkling eyes were replaced by clear signs of distaste including a furrowed brow and pursed lips. Holy shit.

Nothing she could do about it now—the bridal cat was out of the bag. Her only choice was to not make a big deal of it. She reached down and scooped up the magazines along with the rest of her fallen effects, doing her best to pretend like packing a bag full of wedding magazines was what every modern single woman brought on vacation. When everything was gathered, she edged away from Abby. "Okay, well, I guess I'll see you at dinner."

She wasn't sure if Abby responded since she sped away before the last words left her lips, unable to bear the disappointed look on Abby's face. Unlikely now that Abby would show up for dinner, which was probably just as well since this wasn't a vacation for her no matter how she wanted to pretend it was. She was here to work, and if she worked hard enough and long enough, one day she'd have the kind of success that allowed her to take first class vacations to luxury resorts for fun instead of work. But right now, that wasn't her life and she had no business hanging out with women for whom that lifestyle was nothing more than an afterthought. But damn, she was bummed to miss sitting across the table and staring into those caramel eyes.

*What the hell just happened?* Abby watched Roxanne dash away, the images of way too many Stepford brides wearing way too much lace burned into her mind. What kind of woman carries around a sack of bridal magazines?

The kind who's obsessed with weddings, obviously. No, the kind who's obsessed with marriage. As Roxanne's form faded into the distance, all Abby could think was *bullet dodged*. Oh, and nice ass. But mostly bullet dodged.

A moment later, a woman dressed in a crisp uniform met her by the side of the van. "Señorita Keane, my name is Juanita Perez, and it will be my pleasure to assist you during your stay. We have your bungalow ready. Would you like a tour of the property now or later, after you've had time to settle in?"

Abby wanted to see the entire place, but she also wanted a nap. "How about a full tour tomorrow? I'd love some time to relax."

"Perfect. Please follow me. Henry is already on the way with your bags."

As tired as she was, the breathtaking scenery on the way to her bungalow captured Abby's attention. Lush tropical gardens gave way to a spectacular view of the turquoise ocean lined with pristine white sand. She followed Juanita along a path lined with patterned stepping stones, but it wasn't until they were standing right in front of the bungalow door that she was able to make out the structure.

"Is it not okay?" Juanita asked.

Abby pulled her gaze from the foliage surrounding the bungalow. "It's beautiful. I love the way it's nestled in the flora. I don't think I would've even seen it if you hadn't led me here."

Juanita's face relaxed into a smile. "If you think this part is beautiful, just wait until you are inside."

She unlocked the door and handed the key to Abby, who stared at it for a moment. She couldn't remember the last time she'd been at a hotel that used real keys instead of electronic key cards. It felt...quaint. Definitely contributed to the whole off-grid experience. She shoved the key in her pocket and followed Juanita inside.

Everything inside was light and bright and airy. Palm leaf shaped fans whirred overhead, gently lifting the gauzy curtains on the windows. Abby strode over to the window to look outside and gasped.

"See what I mean?" Juanita said.

Abby could only nod. The entire opposite wall of the living room area was lined with floor to ceiling windows, and outside those windows was a breathtaking view of the crystal clear ocean, not fifty feet from where they stood. She closed her eyes and opened them back up again a few seconds later, hoping this view wasn't a dream. It wasn't.

"The entire stretch of beach is privately owned by the resort. If you would like a canopy and chairs set up for your use on any of the days you are here, merely let us know at dinner the night before and it will be ready for you by eight a.m. Meals are served in the dining room back at the hacienda, where you came in, but if you'd prefer to eat in your room, we can accommodate that as well." She pointed to an old-style rotary phone sitting on a wicker table. "Simply dial one and the kitchen staff will bring you what you need. The kitchen is staffed around the clock."

Abby's mind flicked back to Roxanne's dinner invite, and she felt a twinge of longing. She'd been excited at the prospect of spending more time with Roxanne right up until it looked like she was on the marriage prowl. Maybe room service was the best way to avoid what would surely be an uncomfortable situation. "I may take you up on that."

"I know you said you were tired. If you don't have any questions right now, I'll leave you to settle in. You can call me tomorrow at this number to arrange your tour." Juanita handed her a card, and then she walked to the door. "Have a wonderful evening, Ms. Keane."

When she was gone, Abby kicked off her shoes, grabbed a bottle of water from the fridge, and slid open the back door and stepped outside. To the left of the bungalow was her very own infinity pool, shielded from view by an eight-foot privacy wall. She sank into the poofy cushions on the lounge chair and dangled her feet in the water, instantly feeling the stress of work, travel, and beautiful, bride-seeking strangers fall away. This. This was the reason she was here.

She fished her phone out of her pocket. She'd made a pledge to turn it off and not turn it back on until she stepped off the plane in Dallas on her return trip, with the exception of one text when she arrived to let her friends know she'd made the trip safely. Deciding a text wasn't enough to convey the gloriousness of this place, she called instead. Grace answered on the first ring.

"Did you make it?" She sounded worried.

"Safe and sound. Take everything we read about this place and add fifty percent."

"Good. You deserve it. Now go and enjoy it. Campbell and I have everything under control."

"I know and I will…"

"I hear a 'but.' What's up?"

"I'm not sure. I rode in from the airport in a van with this other woman, Roxanne."

"Cool name. I'm liking this already."

"Settle yourself. Anyway, I was definitely feeling a flirty vibe, but then I find out she's got a bag full of bridal magazines."

"Let me guess, you ran like a frightened gazelle."

Abby both loved and hated that Grace knew her so well. "It wasn't my best performance, but yeah, I did get away as fast as I could."

"Maybe her sister's getting married and she's helping plan the festivities. Maybe she's looking for good cake recipes. Maybe she's a kleptomaniac and she stole them from the airport bookshop."

"Maybe she's looking for a bride."

"Of course you would go there first. Think about it, Abby. Why would she come to a honeymoon paradise to look for a bride? I mean you're probably the only other person there who legit isn't celebrating their recent nuptials. Seems like she'd have better luck finding her soul mate at one of those single only resorts. Speaking of which, why did you of all people pick a place guaranteed to be devoid of available women?"

Abby scoffed at the dig. "You act like I plan my life around getting laid."

"I've seen you in action."

"Touché. But seriously, I purposefully picked a place where I could be assured of solitude."

"For all you know, she's there for the same reason."

Abby wasn't buying it. "Maybe she's looking for a place to spend her own honeymoon."

"Maybe you could stop speculating and ask her."

Abby balked. "Oh, no. I think we're done."

"Abby, you can talk about substantive things with a woman without it leading to an engagement. I may not be an authority, but I promise I know this one thing. You're going to be there a week. Are you going to hide in your room the entire time?" Grace asked.

"I'm not hiding."

"Sounds like you're hiding. And from a hot woman no less. She is hot, right?"

"Yes. Super hot."

"And she seemed interested?"

"Hey, she's the one who invited me out."

"Then quit overanalyzing it. She could've picked up those magazines by accident. She could be…anything. But you'll never know if you don't give her a chance. Besides, it's a vacation. You're supposed to do fun and relaxing things. Go have some vacation sex. If you come back with nothing more than a bunch of pictures of towel animals on a perfectly made bed, then we're going to vote you most likely to end up a spinster."

"Are you supposed to be lecturing me on my vacation?"

"I'm not supposed to be lecturing you at all because you're supposed to be enjoying your vacation instead of talking on the phone."

"But—"

"No buts, unless they're cute ones. Go find the girl and have fun. That's an order and I have no doubt Campbell would agree. Love you, bye."

Abby stared at her phone, but it was real. Grace had actually disconnected the call. It was just her and her thoughts, wondering what came next. First up, a nap. She sank farther into the deck chair. This truly was paradise and Grace was right. She'd be a fool not to take full advantage. A few minutes later, as she drifted off to sleep, her last thought was wondering what Roxanne was doing right this very minute.

Roxanne told the restaurant host she'd only needed a table for one and tried not to grimace at his surprised look. She wanted to say, "Yes, I'm pretty much the only single person at the resort, but since I'm only here to write a review, quit looking at me like I'm a cipher who can't get a date." But instead she decided it was better not to draw attention to her solitary situation. She dutifully followed as he led her to a two-top close to the kitchen, because who needs a quiet table when you clearly can't get laid?

She made a mental note about the lapse in service but decided to keep an open mind. She ordered a margarita and perused the menu which was more extensive than she would've thought considering Azure was an all-inclusive resort. When the waiter returned with her drink, she smiled her approval and ordered a ceviche for her first course. He nodded his approval and left her to sip her drink.

"I don't think you can call it a vacation unless there's a tiny umbrella in your drink."

She recognized Abby's voice and rushed to hide her surprise. *Don't get too excited. She's probably on her way to her own table, far, far away from you.* Roxanne set her drink down and looked up, barely holding back a gasp at the sight of Abby dressed in a blue and white print maxi wrap skirt and angled crop top that hinted at sculpted abs. Abby was standing less than a foot away, and Roxanne scrambled to catch her breath. "Maybe I tucked the tiny umbrella away for a rainy day."

Abby grinned. "I see what you did there." She pointed at the empty seat. "May I join you?"

"That was the plan, after all."

Abby slid into the chair. "I'm sorry I'm late."

"I'm a little surprised you showed up at all." Roxanne picked up her drink and swallowed deep to buy time. Why did she have to bring up what had happened earlier? Couldn't she just let things be? Abby was a beautiful, sexy woman. Maybe she hadn't given her enough credit. For all she knew, Abby showing up late for dinner had nothing to do with the bridal explosion that had happened when they'd arrived.

"I'm going to be honest with you," Abby said, placing both hands on the table. "I almost bagged on you."

"It was the magazines."

"Yes. I mean, not really the magazines, but I don't think I've ever seen someone with so many of them at once unless they were, you know…"

"A bride?"

Abby nodded. "Or someone who wanted to be."

Roxanne started to say she could think of a dozen other reasons for someone to be toting a bunch of bridal magazines around, like being a wedding blogger for one, but she didn't want to risk losing her anonymity. Not even if it meant risking Abby's attention. She didn't want to lie either, so she scrambled to find a half-truth. "I found them at the airport." Truth—her sister had handed them to her when she dropped her off at the airport, but Abby's eyebrows were raised and she felt the need to add some fluff to the story. "A woman left them sitting on a chair when she went to board the plane and I didn't realize they were bridal magazines until I'd already grabbed them. I figured I'd run into her on the plane and return them or ditch them later, but no such luck." She stopped talking when she saw the tension in Abby's face relax. No sense letting a little lie spin into a much bigger one. "Let me guess, you're not a fan of weddings."

"What's not to be a fan of? There's cake and dancing and pretty flowers. I mean, I can think of a dozen better things to do, but I don't hate going to weddings." Abby paused and grinned. "As long as I'm not the one getting married."

"I see." Roxanne wasn't sure that was true. She couldn't remember ever having discussed marriage with a first date, and this was going sideways fast. Abby's flippant dismissal of marriage spurred a desire to defend the institution, but doing so would doom this date for sure. Thankfully, she was saved by the waiter's return.

"Good evening, ladies," he said. "May I tell you about our specials?"

Abby nodded eagerly. "Yes, please. I love specials." She turned to Roxanne, "Don't you?"

Roxanne couldn't help but smile at Abby's infectious enthusiasm. "Absolutely. The more specials the better."

Larry the waiter rattled off a number of seafood dishes, complete with details about the sauces and garnish. Abby stared at him with rapt attention while he talked, but Roxanne was barely listening. Her attention was fully focused on the way the light caught the highlights in Abby's hair. When Larry finally finished his novel-length descriptions and left them alone, Roxanne put her menu down. "I'm having one of those amazing dishes he listed, but I don't have a clue which one."

"Me too. I adore seafood," Abby said. "And speaking of weddings, I went to one last year where they had a raw bar before dinner at the reception." She clutched her hands to her chest. "Swoon."

"So you're a live and let live kind of person when it comes to putting a ring on it?" Roxanne wanted to bite back the words. Why was she so obsessed with this talk of weddings? Perhaps it was because if Abby found out what she did, this flirtatious banter would go nowhere fast. But she didn't want it to. Did she?

Abby frowned. "Not a fan of the institution. It's like a business arrangement with too much emotion attached. Those almost always go south." She lifted her shoulders. "But hey, if that's what other people want to do and they're throwing a great party, that's cool by me."

"I bet you're one of those people who crashes a wedding to find a date."

"I can't say as I've ever actually crashed one, but I can attest that weddings are a great place to meet women."

"Better than out-of-the-way resorts?" Roxanne asked, purposefully injecting a flirtatious tone in her voice to match Abby's.

Abby raised her glass and tilted it toward her. "I'm not sure about that. Can I get back to you later?"

Roxanne heard the unmistakable invitation, and it was a tipping point. She was here to work, but what better way to assess the hospitality of the resort for couples than to indulge in some flirtatious fun during her stay? It wasn't like she had to worry about it turning into something more since Abby was making it abundantly clear she wasn't interested in anything long-term, which was just fine with her. She raised her own glass. "Here's to meeting beautiful women in faraway places."

Abby clinked her glass to hers and they sealed their toast. Abby's eyes met hers over the rim of her glass and they were dark and smoldering. Roxanne's body reacted instantly with a warm surge of heat, and suddenly dinner wasn't remotely on the list of things she wanted or needed, but something else was. Make that someone. "You know, I got a thorough briefing while you were off in your room taking a nap. They have room service here."

"I like room service."

"My place or yours?" Roxanne tried not to wince at the corny line, but Abby seemed unfazed.

"I do have a beautiful view of the ocean."

Roxanne resisted adding that every bungalow had the same view. She didn't want to risk inviting Abby back to her place because she was pretty sure she'd left her laptop open and the wedding magazines were scattered in a pile on the bed. "I'd love to see that view."

Abby stood and reached for her hand. "Come on then."

Roxanne grasped her hand and followed. She hadn't had a one-night stand since her freshman year of college, and sex with a stranger hadn't been remotely part of the plan for this trip, but it seemed all her careful planning was out the window for now. Telling herself this would be the perfect opportunity to check out the resort from a lover's angle, she followed Abby through the dining room, stopping only to tell the host they'd changed their minds about the dining room for tonight. He gave them a knowing look as they walked away, and Roxanne grinned back at him. Hooking up with Abby was the perfect cover. Oh, and it was certain to be fun too.

## CHAPTER THREE

A bby led the way along the stone path, clutching Roxanne's hand. Part of the reason she'd picked this resort was the intimacy and seclusion, but for solitude's sake, not for a potential rendezvous. She certainly hadn't planned on meeting someone she'd want to sleep with, let alone on the first day. But Roxanne was next level hot, spurring her to shove away any concern about what might happen tomorrow. *It's just a week. We'll have some fun and go our separate ways.*

But would they? They'd flown in on the same flight, which probably meant Roxanne lived in Austin or nearby. What if they ran into each other at home, shopping at the Domain or someplace more common like the local H-E-B. She could see it now. "Hey, do you think this tomato looks ripe? Oh wait, didn't we have sex in sunny paradise for a week?"

*Whoa. Way to get ahead. Let's have sex tonight and see what happens. No need to worry about the future until it happened.*

When they reached the door, she fumbled for her key and slid it into the lock. She started to turn the knob, but Roxanne touched her wrist.

"Wait."

"Wait?" Abby asked. Not the reaction she'd been hoping for.

"Are you sure this is what you want?"

It occurred to Abby that they hadn't defined the "this," but she knew exactly what Roxanne was talking about. She ran her hand up Roxanne's arm, gently caressed her neck, and drew her forward. Her lips tasted like berries and she lingered, letting soft touches serve as a prelude for more. "Don't you?"

"You are an incredible kisser," Roxanne murmured against her lips.

"Is that an answer?"

"I think it might be."

Abby pushed open the door and walked them both inside. She eased her hands around the hem of Roxanne's blouse, searching for skin. "Something more definitive?"

Roxanne arched into her touch. "Oh, most definitely."

Like a switch went off, slow went out the window. Abby pulled at the fabric between hers and Roxanne's skin. "Clothes are overrated. Don't you think?"

Roxanne pulled away with the teasing grin. "Indeed. How about you lose that top?"

Abby reached back, untied the halter, and tossed it to the floor, enjoying the sound of Roxanne sucking in a breath.

"Don't stop there," Roxanne said.

"Oh no," Abby said. "It's your turn now." She motioned to Roxanne's shirt with a lifting gesture. Roxanne didn't hesitate, shedding her blouse faster than Abby had, and throwing it in a ball where Abby's had landed. This time it was Abby who sucked in her breath at the plunging bra. She stepped closer and traced a finger along the edge of the satin. "Red is my favorite color."

"Good thing I wasn't wearing the purple one."

"I'm very flexible."

Roxanne pressed a hand to Abby's chest. "And you're blinded by lust."

"You say that like it's a bad thing."

Roxanne leaned close, her lips a whisper away from Abby's. "Do you want to discuss your favorite colors of lingerie or do you want to get naked with me?"

Abby answered by capturing Roxanne's lips between her own, but this time the kiss was fierce instead of soft, with each of them vying for dominance. Roxanne pressed hard with her tongue and

Abby groaned at the wave of heat that spread to her core. When they finally broke for air, Abby gasped. "You. You are an amazing kisser."

"Takes two," Roxanne said.

Abby merely took her hand and led Roxanne to the bedroom. They both kicked off their shoes and scrambled out of the rest of their clothes, and Abby was pleased that Roxanne seemed as excited as she did about forgoing a big lead-in. She pulled a very beautiful, very naked Roxanne into her arms and ran her hands down the smooth skin of her slightly curvy hips. "Lights on or off?"

"My place has a dimmer switch in the bedroom," Roxanne said, her lips sliding into a slow smile.

Without breaking contact, Abby reached behind Roxanne and felt for the switch, returning the smile when the light faded into a low glow. "Nice," she murmured. She slipped her hand around Roxanne's waist, reaching lower to cup her ass. "You feel so good."

"You have no idea." Roxanne reached for her other hand and placed it between her legs. "See for yourself."

Abby drew a single finger through Roxanne's slick folds, and the sensation sent a surge of arousal that weakened her knees. She pulled Roxanne closer to steady her balance and pressed her lips to Roxanne's until they parted to allow her in, and then she used her tongue to mimic the strokes of her finger—a slow, lingering, steady path to climax.

Roxanne moaned against her mouth, arching closer as if seeking release. Abby broke the kiss long enough to whisper in her ear. "Are you ready to come?"

She nipped at Roxanne's neck while she waited for her answer, keeping the rhythm with her fingers, two now, against Roxanne's clit. She could feel how close Roxanne was to coming, how her body begged for release. As much as she wanted to prolong the ecstasy, she didn't want to deny her what she so clearly needed. To make the choice easier, she ran her tongue along the crest of Roxanne's ear as she asked again, "Ready?"

Roxanne turned and captured her tongue in her mouth, kissing her fiercely before releasing the touch. "Not yet," she gasped, trailing her fingers up Abby's thigh until they rested over her very own wet hot center. "Let's get in bed and take our time."

With Roxanne's hand between her legs, Abby barely registered the words beyond "not yet," but she knew she was being told to slow things down, and the prospect was both exciting and unfamiliar. Bed. Roxanne had suggested bed, and a vision of her being able to stretch out over Roxanne—or under her—sent a wave of arousal through her body. "Yes, let's."

Roxanne pulled back the covers, slid onto the bed, and invited her in. Abby took a moment to admire Roxanne's gorgeous body reclining against the crisp white sheets, her blond hair fanned out on the pillows. She knelt between Roxanne's legs, eager for the electric press of flesh between them, but determined to follow Roxanne's lead and draw out the tension for as long as possible. She started at her breasts, teasing them to perfect points, before slowly kissing her way down to the inside of Roxanne's thighs, pausing at the apex to drink in the scent of her before lowering her lips to her hot, wet center. Lost in the heady blur of arousal, Abby had no idea how long she lavished Roxanne with her tongue before she began bucking wildly against her touch.

"Almost there. Don't stop," Roxanne panted, her voice a hoarse whisper.

Abby answered by drawing a finger along the inside of her thigh while she continued to lick and thrust with her tongue. The featherlight touch was apparently Roxanne's undoing. Her entire body arched off the bed and Abby could feel the orgasm course through her, but she didn't break contact even when Roxanne sagged back against the bed, clearly spent.

Again, she didn't know how much time had passed before she felt Roxanne's fingers in her hair, gently tugging her closer. She eased her way up along Roxanne's side and cradled her in her arms. Roxanne still hadn't said anything, and she started to worry something was wrong. "Are you okay?"

Roxanne turned in her arms until they were face-to-face. Her eyes were still dark and smoldering, and she took a deep breath and slowly exhaled. "Okay is not the word I would use. Amazing. Blown away. Those are better words. You are incredible."

It wasn't the first time a woman had told Abby she was good in bed. She took pride at being good at everything she did, and sex had always been just one more thing on the list, but the earnest tone in Roxanne's words carried more weight than all the compliments that had come before, and she braced against the twinge of discomfort they ushered in.

Roxanne started awake and immediately felt disoriented because she was on the wrong side of the bed, but a quick look around revealed why. Abby appeared to be blissfully asleep, her face buried in her pillow, her sandy brown hair a tangled mess. Every tingling moment of last night's sex came flooding back, and Roxanne's libido stirred. She wanted to reach out and caress Abby's bare shoulder, but the rays of light starting to poke their way through the blinds told her she'd likely stayed too long already. A woman spooked by a bunch of bridal magazines probably wasn't fond of waking up to the one-night stand. Key word: night, which it was no longer.

Roxanne eased out of the bed and tiptoed around the room gathering her clothes. Each article she retrieved—her blouse from the floor, her bra from the top of the lamp, her pants from the chair—conjured a vivid memory of the passionate night, and she couldn't help but smile as she thought about the draft of her article. *The generously sized bedrooms in the bungalow are well suited for honeymoon play, providing lots of furniture upon which to toss unnecessary and restrictive garments.* Yep, the editor would love that particular insight.

Fully clothed, she took a moment to cast one last look at Abby in repose, sleeping peacefully. No one would imagine she was the same tiger who'd jumped her last night, and Roxanne enjoyed knowing that little secret. She blew a kiss in Abby's direction and slipped out of the bungalow, taking care to be extra quiet. She was about ten feet from Abby's door when she ran smack into Juanita who seemed to appear out of nowhere dressed in another crisp, neat uniform, emblazoned with the resort's logo, in sharp contrast to her own wrinkled, day-old attire.

"Good morning, Señorita Daly, are you on your way to breakfast?"

The mention of food made her stomach growl, and Roxanne remembered that in the rush to get naked last night, she and Abby had completely forgotten about dinner. She was famished, and the idea of a full-on breakfast buffet almost tempted her to head straight for the dining room. Almost. "In just a few. I need to stop at my bungalow and check a few emails."

Juanita waggled a finger and made a tsking sound. "Surely emails can wait until you are no longer in paradise. Rest from work is good for the mind and body both."

Shit. She wished she hadn't made it sound like she was working. "No worries. I just promised I would let my sister know that I made it here and am settling in." She edged away. "I'll see you around." She started off before Juanita could trap her into more conversation, but not before she noticed the knowing look Juanita shot in the direction of Abby's bungalow. Oh well. She hadn't done the walk of shame since college, but she'd walk back to her place buck naked every day if the sex with Abby was always this good.

Once she was safely in her bungalow, she decided calling her sister wasn't such a bad idea after all even though she'd take some flak for all her assurances she was going to stay offline the entire trip. She snagged a mango from the fridge and put her phone on speaker while she peeled the perfectly ripe fruit. Val answered on the first ring.

"Either, you hate it there and you're ready to come home, or something incredible happened. Those are your only two choices, and if it's not one of those, then hang up and go back to enjoying paradise."

"Try none of the above."

"Then spill?"

Roxanne took a deep breath and blurted out, "I met an incredibly hot woman and we spent the last ten hours having sex."

"Holy Hannah! I knew this trip wasn't all about work. I'm so proud of you I can't even stand it. What's her name? Where does she live when she's not slipping around paradise seducing the likes of you? What does she do for living?"

"Whoa," Roxanne said. "Slow down. Her name is Abby." She paused for a moment and bit into a piece of mango while she stalled to fill in the information Val wanted. "She's fantastic in bed."

"Duh. I think ten hours kind of proves that. But I want to know more."

"There isn't anything more. I mean, we didn't do a lot of talking."

"Right. That's good. So are you going to see her again? Well, of course you are since you're both staying at the same small place. I'm thinking a candlelit dinner on the beach. Oh wait, there's sand. Never mind. How about one of those tandem kayaks? I mean, I'm not picky, but since I'm living vicariously through you, I figured I should have some input."

Roxanne stared at the piece of mango in her hand, no longer hungry as Val's rush to coupledom caused a pit in the center of her stomach. "I don't know. We'll see how it goes."

"That's nice and vague."

"Look, Val, just because we had sex doesn't mean we're going to spend every waking minute together."

"Okay."

Val drew out the word, and Roxanne recognized the doubt in her tone. "She doesn't seem like she'd be into anything more than what just happened."

"For two people who didn't talk much, you sure seemed to nail that down fast."

Roxanne told her about Abby's visceral, negative reaction to the bridal magazines.

"Not definitive. Besides, you're not looking to marry her, right?"

"No, but one-night stands aren't really my thing either." She sighed. It was pretty clear she didn't know what she wanted, which was another unfamiliar place for her to be. "All I know is I'm not interested in pursuing someone who might not be interested. Last night was great, and I'm content to let it stay that way. Pushing things will only end badly."

"Then don't push. Have some fun and see where it goes. People never know how they really feel about something until it smacks them in the face."

There was some truth to what Val said, but she wasn't certain who was getting smacked in this scenario, her or Abby. To stave off further discussion, she promised she wouldn't write Abby off yet. They exchanged a few more words and she signed off, promising not to call again unless the resort was under attack by zombies and she needed to be airlifted out. She put the rest of the mango in the fridge and took a quick shower. After toweling off and slipping into shorts and a tank top, she considered her options. She could indulge in the breakfast buffet or hide out and order room service and eat solo on the deck. The latter sounded like perfection, but since she was here to work, she needed to experience every aspect of the resort. Decision made. She'd go to breakfast, and then head back here to write up her notes so far. The deadline for the copy was due the day after she returned so she'd need to draft parts of the article each day to stay on top of it, and she only had two more days here to pack everything in before she headed to the next resort on her list. When she'd agreed to the whirlwind schedule it had seemed like a great idea to only spend a few days at each resort. Of course, she hadn't counted on meeting Abby.

The pull to spend more time with Abby was strong, and she wondered what Abby was doing right now. Still sleeping? Enjoying a room service breakfast? What would a tall, leggy, woman like Abby eat for breakfast? Yogurt? Fruit? Coffee no cream? Or would she want to carb load in preparation for a day full of activity?

Roxanne glanced over the activity schedule for the day. Options included kayaking, a hike through a nature preserve, and snorkeling. She'd need to get a move on if she was going to pack all of these in before she was scheduled to leave day after tomorrow. It would definitely be more fun to do these things with Abby. There was no law that said she couldn't mix business and pleasure...

Before she could change her mind, she grabbed her room key and headed out the door, retracing her steps back to Abby's door. She knocked, and then shifted from one foot to the other, waiting for Abby to answer. After counting to five Mississippi, she raised her hand to knock again, but stopped midair. *Give it a rest, Daly. You had a great night. Don't push it.* Resigned to the fact her inner voice was right, she turned to walk away when the door swung open.

"There you are."

Abby stood in the doorway wearing a fluffy terry cloth robe with the resort crest, and based on how much skin was showing, probably nothing else. Roxanne focused her attention back to Abby's face, pleased she hadn't greeted her with "what are you doing here?" Roxanne smiled tentatively and accepted Abby's invitation to come in. "I couldn't bear to wake you earlier. You're kind of cute when you're sleeping."

"And here I thought you were having second thoughts."

"Oh, I might have had second thoughts, but only about having seconds." Roxanne shook her head. "Did that sound as corny out loud as it did in my head?"

"Yes, but it was sweet." They stood for a moment, staring at first and then each of them looking away. Roxanne decided to take the lead and deflect the potential for discomfort. "So, here's the deal. Last night was amazing, but I get the impression you're not looking for anything more and neither am I."

Abby nodded slowly, her eyebrows slightly raised like she was waiting for the other shoe to drop. "Fair assessment."

"But we're here in this gorgeous place and there are a ton of cool things to do. Things that I personally think are more fun with someone else than by myself." She thrust a piece of paper at Abby. "I made a list. Want to see how many things we can check off?" She waited a moment before adding, "Unless you'd rather just sit on the beach or lie by the pool. Not that there's anything wrong with that."

She watched while Abby skimmed the list. When Abby finally looked up there was a question in her eyes.

"What?"

"I don't see horseback riding on here. Juanita said they have some openings today. Is it too late to offer amendments?"

"Not at all." Roxanne snatched the paper back and made a mock note to the list. "Okay?"

"Perfect."

"Oh, and one more thing."

"What's that?"

"We're here for fun, so let's keep it light. No talk of work or anything outside of this place."

"What happens here stays here, and if it didn't happen here, it didn't happen?"

"Exactly."

"I can agree to that."

Roxanne figured she would, but now that she'd secured the agreement, she wasn't sure it was what she wanted. Too late now. She'd look pretty silly if she acted like whatever this was was anything other than a paradise tryst. She pressed on. "I think we should have a huge breakfast to fuel for the day ahead because I have lots of stamina. You're going to need all the energy you can get to keep up with me."

"Like I hadn't noticed."

"You're hilarious."

"And hungry." Abby pointed to the door. "Lead the way. I'm prepared to eat my way through a breakfast buffet to shore up for all the activities you have planned for the rest of the week."

Roxanne started to say she was leaving day after tomorrow, but, taking a page from her sister's advice, she changed her mind. Live in the moment. Mentioning they only had a short time would put all the focus on what they'd miss out on instead of what they might enjoy. Besides, something in her wanted to see if Abby even stayed interested after a full day of all Roxanne, all the time. For her part, she was excited about sharing this adventure with Abby and couldn't wait to see how it turned out.

## Chapter Four

A bby dipped her fingers in the jar of lotion and warmed it in her hands before smoothing it over Roxanne's very tan and very naked back. They were taking a break from the constant stream of activity to have a picnic on the beach. Juanita, with a knowing smile, had arranged for a canopy, luxurious loungers, and a feast of local foods complemented with a bottle of a delicious red wine. "How are you so tan after only two days in the sun?" She pointed at her own face which was two shades short of lobster. "Let me guess, this never happens to you."

Roxanne laughed. "True, but I come by it honestly. I may be blond, but my mother's Mediterranean and natural tint is in my genes. Trust me, by the end of the week, you'll be as tan as I am."

"If you say so." She reached into her bag, grabbed the SPF50, and handed it to Roxanne. "In the meantime, do you mind?"

Roxanne frowned, and Abby immediately sensed something was wrong. "Did I say something wrong? Do you have some personal belief system that doesn't allow you to reciprocate in the lotion department?" She smiled, hoping the levity would wipe the pained look from Roxanne's face. They'd had a blast the last couple of days. They'd sampled tequila, paddled kayaks, ridden horses. Left to her own devices, she would've spent the entire week sitting by her personal pool with a book in one hand and an umbrella drink in the other, but instead she was having a grand adventure. Campbell and Grace would be so proud.

And the sex had been exciting, without any of the awkwardness repeated encounters usually held for her. Different from her usual fare. She'd felt a connection to Roxanne that made it seem easy and natural to wake up in each other's rooms and share meals. She attributed the newfound feeling to vacation sex since she'd never felt like this in real life. Which made sense since this wasn't real life. Her fantasy getaway with Roxanne would only last until the end of this week, and then they would go back to their separate lives—she to her law practice and Roxanne to whatever she did. Abby let her mind wander for a second while she imagined what Roxanne's life was like outside of the vacation bubble. Did she have family in Austin? Did she live in a house or apartment? What part of town? What was her favorite restaurant, bar, coffee joint? They'd found so many similarities within the confines of Azure, Abby wondered why they'd never run into each other in Austin. Of course, she'd only moved there from Dallas a few months ago. Her thoughts drifted to the possibility of seeing Roxanne back home, and she was surprised that the idea of not seeing her again left her feeling sad. Should she break their rule about not discussing the outside world to tell Roxanne she'd like to see her when they got back to Austin? "I was thinking," she said. "Maybe we could—"

"I leave tomorrow," Roxanne said, her words falling like thick bricks blocking out the feeling behind Abby's lost declaration. "I've been meaning to tell you, but we've been having such fun, I didn't want to ruin it by thinking about it coming to an end."

"Wait, what?" Abby said, trying to wrap her head around the revelation. "You're not staying for the whole week?"

Roxanne shook her head. "Just the long weekend. I'm on the first shuttle out in the morning." She reached out a hand and pulled Abby in close. "But we have the rest of today and tonight, right?"

Abby tried not to tense up, but she couldn't help it. She'd been about to propose breaking the rules and taking whatever this was to the next level, sharing more personal information, time together outside of paradise. Her desire to be closer seemed awkward now that Roxanne was the one who was pulling away. And here she'd been worried Roxanne was one of those women who was obsessed with finding a mate.

*Don't be such a dumbass.* She could almost hear Campbell and Grace saying the words. *Just because she's going home early doesn't mean you can't see each other when you get back to Austin.* True. Why should she let temporary disappointment cloud the opportunity to get to know Roxanne better on their home turf? Pushing aside her reluctance to get personal, Abby decided she was ready to take the plunge. "Yes, we have until tomorrow, and I would like to make the most of that." She cleared her throat and started to say more, but Roxanne beat her to it.

"Perfect." Roxanne lifted her hand and brought it to her lips. "We'll always have this wonderful memory. It'll be the perfect souvenir when we go our separate ways."

Separate ways. This was the time for Abby to interject that she'd prefer that their ways cross again, soon if possible, but the moment had passed and she couldn't muster the words to ask for what she wanted, so she told herself she mustn't have wanted it very badly. This was better. They'd spend Roxanne's last day having fun, and she'd have stories to take home along with memories of her bonus vacation fun. It was all good.

But if this was supposed to make her feel good, then why did the prospect of spending the rest of her vacation alone make her feel so sad?

*Azure's allure is its ability to anticipate your every need. The staff far outnumbers the guests, but they've perfected the art of being attentive without being obtrusive. I ate all the mangoes in my well-stocked bungalow fridge on the first day, and not only did more mangoes appear within twenty-four hours, but fun little mango treats started showing up throughout the rest of my stay illustrating just one of the many ways Azure tailors their luxury experience for each guest. Honeymooners will appreciate the*

*balance of ample intimate space, including private decks and pools, with a host of activities, like horseback riding and parasailing, for when you're ready to come up for air. Have a special excursion in mind to surprise your new spouse? A few whispered words to Juanita, the concierge, and dreams become realities in this Fantasy Island paradise.*

Roxanne typed the last few words and added in some notes about particular shots the photographer should capture before shutting down her laptop. She should be pleased to have accomplished as much as she had in just a few days at Azure, and from the perspective of a couple no less. She was pretty sure *Best Day Ever* would be happy with the result, but the whole experience was falling flat now that she faced the reality that she wasn't really on vacation and she wasn't free to just enjoy the ride with Abby. Tomorrow morning she'd be headed back to PV for another whirlwind resort experience sans the pretty girl with the great laugh. Not to mention the fantastic sex.

Speaking of which, it was time to meet Abby for dinner, which she hoped would be a quick bite before retiring to Abby's bungalow. Early this morning, she would've taken it for granted, but Abby's cooled enthusiasm at her announcement she was leaving tomorrow hadn't escaped her attention, and now she hoped she could rekindle their spark even if it was only for this final evening.

She glanced once more at her itinerary for the next day before changing into a red jumpsuit with a plunging neckline she hoped would focus Abby's attention solely on her. When she arrived at the restaurant a few minutes later for her date with Abby, Nick, the host greeted her enthusiastically.

"How are you doing, Señorita Roxanne?" He waved an arm the length of her body. "The sun agrees with you."

"Thanks, Nick. I'm having a fantastic time." She peered around his shoulder, looking for signs of Abby.

"She's not here."

"What?" She hoped she'd misunderstood his answer to her silent question.

"Señorita Abby is not in the dining room this evening. That is who you are looking for, yes?"

She didn't want to admit it, but clearly, her emotions were on full display. "I was, but perhaps you can show me to a table for one."

"That won't be necessary."

Roxanne turned at the sound of the familiar voice to find Juanita standing behind her, wearing a sly smile. "Hi, Juanita, what's up?"

"Please follow me."

Juanita didn't wait for her to reply before turning in the opposite direction and walking briskly away. Roxanne shrugged at Nick and rushed to follow. She had no idea where they were going, but a tingling sense of anticipation circled around her nerves, tickling a response. They stepped carefully along the trail to the beach and Roxanne gasped when she spotted row after row of lit candles in a semicircle around a canopy. Abby rose from her chair and Roxanne spotted her timid smile in the candlelight.

"I'll let you find the rest of the way on your own," Juanita said before disappearing back along the trail.

Roxanne stood in place for a moment, stunned by the romantic gesture. Was this the same woman who'd been spooked by a stack of bridal magazines? Things sure had changed in a couple of days' time. For her, it wasn't a big stretch. She'd always imagined that one day she'd find the one and it might come in the least expected moment, kind of like pitching headfirst into a dream girl's lap on an airplane, but was Abby really her final destination?

She shook her head. Clearly, she'd become too emerged in the world of fairy-tale wedding bliss to tell the difference between reality and fiction. This moment on the beach with Abby was super romantic, but also incredibly unreal. Tomorrow she would board the shuttle and ride off in the morning light to the next destination on her list, and then the one after that—each one an oasis, insulated from the real world.

Abby stepped toward her. "You don't look happy to see me." She motioned toward the spread. "I figured since it was your last night, you should have an excellent experience to cap it off. Too much?"

Roxanne studied her face for a moment, looking for some magic clue to tell her what she should read into Abby's gesture, but all she saw was earnest anticipation and infectious excitement, which made her hesitation seem silly. "It's perfect. I'm a little blown away that you would do all this for me."

Abby took her hand and led her to the table. "Well, to be perfectly honest, it's long been a dream of mine to own a private island that I could whisk away to on a moment's notice and indulge a life of luxury on the beach."

Roxanne pointed at the bottle of Dom in a bucket next to the table. "I'd say you've got this down. All except the island part."

"True, but I'm resourceful. Making islands where none exist." Abby poured them each a glass and handed one to her. "To making dreams come true."

Roxanne tilted her glass toward Abby, wishing she could read her mind. Was all this talk of islands a way of saying she wanted to keep her distance despite whatever this was brewing between them? This back and forth was making her crazy, but she knew it was up to her to take control. She had a choice. She could think about tomorrow and how there was no way any of the other places she would visit on this trip could possibly measure up since Abby wasn't there. Or she could enjoy tonight, and if it went as well as the rest of the time they'd shared, she could summon the courage to tell Abby she wanted to see her when they were both back in Austin.

She took a sip of the expensive champagne and let the cool bubbles fizz away her doubts. "To making dreams come true."

❖

Roxanne woke to the sound of an obnoxious horn. Who in the world was playing the trumpet in the middle of the night? She opened her eyes but quickly shut them again against the onslaught of sunlight streaming into Abby's bedroom.

Sunlight. Shit. She shot up in bed and glanced around for something, anything to tell her what time it was, but by the time she found Abby's Rolex on the dresser, she already knew it was late. Way late. Seven fifty. Her shuttle was supposed to leave at eight a.m. She'd planned to get up early, go back to her bungalow, shower, and finish packing, but now she'd be lucky to cram the rest of her stuff in her suitcase and jog after the shuttle, hoping it would slow down long enough for her to jump on. She took a deep breath and tried to focus.

"What are you doing?" Abby's hand stretched across the covers, beckoning her back to bed, her eyes still closed. "It's early still."

Roxanne reached down and kissed her adorable sleepy face. "Early in vacation time, but not for someone who's on a schedule. I'm sorry, babe, but I have to go." This was it. The moment to tell Abby she wanted to see her when they were back home. That the few days they'd shared had been the most meaningful she'd ever had and she wanted to see where it led once they were back to real life.

Abby sighed. "Have fun. See you later." A moment later, her breaths fell into the rhythm of sleep. Roxanne stared at her sleeping form. Apparently, Abby was non-fazed by their impending separation. Well, maybe she should take a page from her book. She hurriedly dressed and had her hand on the door to leave when she remembered the decision she'd made the night before. A waiting bus and a sleeping Abby meant she wouldn't be able to get into a discussion about why she really had to leave and her desire to see Abby again at home, but she wasn't without options.

She scrambled around the bungalow until she found a pen and a scrap of paper. She scrawled her phone number and wrote *Text me when you're stateside and let's find a beach where we can pick up where we left off.* She signed it with a simple *R*. She held the paper at arm's length for a moment while she wavered about leaving it for Abby to find or crumpling it into a tiny ball. When the voice in her head told her she needed to get going, she carefully placed the note on top of the bookmark in the paperback novel on the nightstand, and blew a kiss at Abby's sleeping form as she slipped out the door.

❖

Abby heard a knock on her door and rolled over in bed. It took a moment for her to realize there was something wrong and another to realize what it was. She stretched a hand across the bedsheet and came up empty. She was alone.

*Knock. Knock.*

Well, she was alone except for whoever was at the door, eager to get her attention. She rolled out of bed and shimmied into the hotel robe. "I'm coming," she called out as she weaved her way across the room, still not quite awake. She flung open the door, fully expecting to see Roxanne on the other side, but instead—

"Good morning, Señorita Abby."

She rubbed her eyes. Henry, the driver who doubled as a waiter at the resort, stood in front of her holding a large tray. "Morning," she mumbled as her sleepiness morphed into irritation he wasn't Roxanne. "Can't a person sleep in around here?"

"Señorita Roxanne asked me to deliver this nice breakfast to you this morning. She said these were all your favorite foods."

Abby instantly felt bad for snapping at him, and her stomach started growling at the smell of bacon. And French toast. And a French press full of the dark roast she loved. "Thank you, Henry." While he set up the food in the kitchen, she reached into her purse for some tip money, but he waved her off.

"Señorita Roxanne took care of everything."

Abby looked toward the door, half expecting Roxanne to walk in, ready to join her for this feast, but then she remembered that Roxanne was leaving today. Surely she wouldn't have left without saying good-bye. "Is she still here?"

Henry shook his head. "She left on the early shuttle." He took his time arranging the food and coffee, but instead of feeling annoyed, Abby almost wished he would stay. She could use a little human interaction to ease back into the solitude staring her down for the rest of the week.

Ironic since she'd come here seeking quiet and the freedom of being completely on her own, but she'd been on her own for less than a few hours and already she was getting antsy at the prospect of spending a few days without Roxanne and her super ambitious list of activities. Henry tipped his hat to her as he left, and when the door shut behind him, she felt more alone than ever. She surveyed the breakfast feast and decided that though the tray was full of her favorite things, she'd trade them all for more time with Roxanne.

So much for vacation flings.

## CHAPTER FIVE

*S*unny *beaches, swim-up bars, world class cuisine—the choices in PV are abundant and you won't go wrong with any of these three resorts. It's more a matter of your preference, and the choices range from social to solitude. Do you want to make new friends or spend one-on-one time with the friend/soul mate you just pledged to spend the rest of your life with? The decision is yours, and I have no doubt you'll be happy, whatever you decide.*

*Enjoy your honeymoon,*
*BBF*

Roxanne stared at the screen and her mostly honest assessment. All three resorts were stellar, but Azure was the clear standout and she knew exactly why, but mentioning her three-night stand with a woman she'd probably never see again seemed antithetical to the whole happily ever after theme.

She shut down her laptop, shoved the last bit of clothes into her suitcase, and leaned hard to get it to shut. A week in paradise was probably fun if you actually got to stay put in one place and enjoy it, but aside from her time with Abby, she'd been on the run, sampling every activity available at the three resorts she'd visited. On top of that, she'd eaten more food in one week than she usually ate in a month, and her suitcase wasn't the only thing straining at the seams.

She checked out on the television screen and left her room key on the nightstand. When she reached the lobby, she headed directly to the bell stand to catch the shuttle but stopped when she heard someone calling her name. Surely, it couldn't be…She turned and quickly masked her disappointment when instead of Abby, she saw Millie from the plane ride to PV with her husband, Albert, in tow. "Hi, Millie," she called out, happy for the distraction. "Are you two headed to the airport?"

"We are indeed," Millie said enthusiastically. "We had a great time, but there's no place like home, right?"

Home. Roxanne sighed at the thought a night in her comfy bed in her little house. She might not have room service or fancy drinks with those little umbrellas that Abby liked, but she did have a nice outdoor deck and she could grill like nobody's business. Idly, she wondered what Abby's house was like and whether she liked to cook outside before she realized it didn't matter since she was probably never going to see her again. It had been four days without a text or call. She'd picked up the phone to call Azure and ask for Abby's bungalow several times, but as each day passed, she lost her nerve. Bottom-line, they weren't looking for the same things, and the radio silence was a clear signal Abby wasn't missing her, which meant she should get over her. The sooner the better.

The shuttle was crowded with departing guests, and Roxanne was tucked up against Millie listening to a full-scale recap of the couple's week. Albert merely nodded at Millie's account, clearly used to never being able to get a word in. When she finally paused for breath, Roxanne asked, "Where did you two spend your honeymoon?"

Millie laughed. "When we got married, we barely had two nickels to rub together. We borrowed a friend's condo in Galveston and spent a week romping on the beach and grilling burgers for dinner every night. Nothing like this place, although those were happy times. We focused on each other instead of a million different activities and restaurants and casino games."

Roxanne made a mental note to include something about the quiet, off the grid nature of Azure and how it could really benefit a relationship. Which only made her think of Abby again. She pushed the thought away. "Sounds refreshing. There are resorts that cater to a quieter pace, fewer distractions."

"True, but why would I pay a fortune to get some peace, when I can get that on my own? Problem with people nowadays is they look at simplicity as a novelty instead of just finding it in the everyday."

Apparently, Millie was a sage. Roxanne agreed with her, but she doubted her readers would see their quest for getting back to nature as a fad. Still, there had to be some way to work Millie's wisdom into the article.

She napped the rest of the way to the airport, jerking awake when everyone around her started moving. "It's time to go, dear," Millie said with a gentle pat on her shoulder. "Back to reality."

That about summed it up. The airport was crowded, but she, along with Millie and Albert, sailed through check-in and made it to the gate well before their flight. When it was time to board, she glanced around the Jetway, holding out a ray of hope that Abby might suddenly appear and board the flight with her. She allowed herself a quick fantasy reel where Abby gave up her first class seat to join her in coach, or a miracle where she received an unexpected upgrade. They'd spend the flight getting reacquainted, sharing real info this time instead of vague references to a real life outside of paradise.

On the plane, after the obligatory safety instructions, she waited until Millie and Albert were napping and pulled out her laptop and spent the flight time typing up the rest of her article. It was good overall, but she had a feeling her editor would notice a strong bias toward Azure, and although she was prepared with lots of reasons to back up her preference, she knew the truth. Azure would always be special because that's where she'd met Abby.

When the plane touched down in Austin, she turned on her phone like everyone else. While she waited for the cell signal to cycle back to life, Millie tapped her on the arm.

"I hate to bother you, but do you think you could help us get our bags back down?"

Roxanne smiled and slipped her phone in her bag. "Of course." She reached into the overhead bin and hefted the two carry-ons down just in time for the line in front of them to start moving. When they reached the end of the Jetway, she paused to check her phone again while Millie and Albert scurried off to make their connecting flight to Dallas. She'd just pulled her phone out of her bag when she heard a voice behind her.

"Tell me you weren't just on that flight."

She whirled to find Abby standing directly behind her. As much as she'd thought about seeing Abby again, she wasn't sure how she was going to explain why she'd stayed in PV instead of flying back to the States. She guessed she should've been prepared to run into Abby here, but they'd never discussed exactly what day Abby was flying home. She may as well come clean. "I was." She cleared her throat while she decided what to say next, but Abby beat her to it.

"I have to say, I imagined this playing out differently," Abby said. "We would've spent the rest of the week at Azure together, working through your crazy long list of activities during the day, and at night..." She sighed. "I'd even planned to see if we could get you an upgrade to first class so you'd be much closer when you decided to fall into my lap again." A dreamy expression flashed across her face and then quickly faded. "But I guess you had other plans."

This was it. Time to tell Abby why she'd really been in PV. After all, she wasn't at the resort anymore, trying to hide her identity. "I can explain. It's silly really and I probably should've told you from the start." She stopped as the phone in Abby's hand buzzed.

"Finally," Abby said. "I always get such crappy signal at this airport." She stared at her phone, and her frown deepened as she scrolled through the display. And she kept scrolling.

"Is everything okay?" Roxanne asked, suddenly worried that Abby was dealing with some kind of post vacation personal tragedy.

"Um, I'm not sure." She looked up. "I mean yes, I'm okay, but there's something I need to deal with."

"Oh, okay. Well, maybe we can talk later." Roxanne started edging away, since it was clear Abby was immersed in whatever was happening on her phone. "Do you still have—"

"Thanks," Abby said, cutting her off, her phone already to her ear.

She strode away and Roxanne watched her go trying to get some glimpse of the woman she'd shared the best time of her life with in the all business version of Abby who'd just brushed her off for a freaking phone call. She almost wished she hadn't given Abby her number, and she could hear her sister saying "bullet dodged." Val was probably right. Some people were completely different in paradise, but this was the real world, and like Abby, she should get back to work and quit dreaming about pretty women in bikinis who were amazing in bed.

"Clark, Keane, and Maldonado."

Abby glared at her phone. "Graham, can't you see it's me on the caller ID?" she said, irritation filling her tone. "A simple hello would do."

"Greetings, Abby. I trust you had a wonderful vacation."

She suppressed the urge to growl. "I did, but I'm sure you know I'm calling because you and Grace have been blowing up my phone. Put me through to Grace and if she's busy, interrupt her."

"Someone needed an extra margarita before heading home."

She started to retort, but Grace picked up the line.

"Finally. Where are you?"

"Getting in the car from the airport. What's going on?"

"Your client, the wedding dress guy, is freaking out. Big time. His siblings shut the doors of all their stores, and brides are rioting."

Abby laughed at the mental image of brides in white dresses carrying picket signs outside of Barclay's Bridal stores. Of course, they wouldn't have dresses or they wouldn't be picketing in the first place, right? "Seriously?"

"Seriously. Look, I don't get it either, but it's happening. Tommy says they have a container full of dresses sitting on the dock in Houston, and the shipper won't unload without payment and he can't pay them because the rest of the family has decided to thumb their noses at all their creditors. He's freaking out and he's headed to the office right now."

"Welcome back to the real world," Abby muttered. She could feel her neck starting to seize up and all the relaxation she'd enjoyed over the past week started slipping away.

"Sorry, pal. I would totally handle this for you, but I have a big hearing tomorrow and Campbell is holding down the fort."

"No worries. A week away is better than I've gotten in a long time. I know I should be grateful."

"I can't wait to hear all about your trip, especially the mysterious blonde."

Abby's heart sank when she remembered the way she'd left things with Roxanne at the airport. Hell, she'd promised to call, but she didn't even have Roxanne's number. And what had Roxanne even been doing at the airport today if she'd left the resort days ago? Too many thoughts to process, especially when she was about to have to focus on work. "Rain check? Let's have drinks when your hearing is over, and we can dish together."

"Fair enough. See you in a few."

Abby spent the rest of the ride scrolling through her jammed email inbox, flagging messages that she'd need to address right away and noting which ones could wait until later. Mixed in with the rest were several emails from Tommy, each one escalating in tone, detailing how his siblings, Sadie and Phillip, had joined forces to unilaterally close all of the one hundred and twenty Barclay's Bridal stores, including the flagship store in Austin. She had to admit it was a big deal to close a business so abruptly, but it wasn't unheard of, especially since the business had been struggling since Tommy's parents had passed away the year before. She suspected Tommy's heartburn came more from sentiment about letting go of their legacy. She sympathized with her childhood friend, but businesses were like any other kind of relationship—prone to breakup. She'd set his mind at ease that she'd look after his interests in the dissolution, and then get back to her overflowing inbox. Satisfied with her plan, she spent the balance of the ride to the office daydreaming about the margarita Graham had teased her about, and resolved that one or two of those would be happening later.

Things changed the minute she got to the office. Grace and Campbell were waiting for her in the lobby. After a big hug, they ushered her back to the conference room where the remains of a box of Kate's Donuts were the centerpiece. Campbell shoved the box her way. "I can't even," Abby said, patting her stomach. "I ate my weight in seafood and guacamole the past week."

"You might need some sugar when you hear what we have to say," Grace said.

"Seriously?" Abby leaned back in her chair, determined not to let this little wrinkle kill her post vacay vibe. "Businesses close all the time. I got this. I'm sure Tommy's freaking out because it was his parents' legacy, but as soon as he gets here, I'll talk him down. The twins were never interested in the wedding dress business, and frankly, I'm surprised they waited this long to make a move. We'll go over the paperwork to make sure everything was done correctly, and we'll issue a statement." She brushed her hands to indicate this was an easy mess to clean. "It's all good. I promise."

Grace tapped on the screen of her iPad and turned it toward her. "Check out these headlines."

Abby scrolled through the search results. *Say No to the Dress, Barclay's Bridal Denies Brides Their Custom Frocks, Brides without Dresses Leave Wedding Messes.* Photos showed groups of women with their faces pressed against the glass of various

Barclay's locations. She pushed the newspapers to the side. "Okay, so maybe this is attracting a little attention. It'll blow over. There have to be dozens of other places where women can get wedding dresses. It's not like these dresses were couture."

Grace shook her head. "You're hopeless. Even I know how important a bride's dress is to the big day."

"Has Campbell been making you watch *Say Yes to the Dress?*"

Abby turned toward the voice. Campbell's girlfriend, Wynne Garrity, was standing in the doorway. She smiled and motioned for her to join them. "Come on in. Apparently, we're having a bridal therapy session even though none of us are planning on getting married anytime soon." She looked from Wynne to Campbell. "Unless I missed something while I was gone."

Wynne pointed at Campbell's left hand and held up her own. "I promise no one put a ring on it in your absence. But thanks to my recent introduction to the wonders of reality TV, I'm very well acquainted with all things bride. The dress is everything."

Abby shook her head. "I promise this is all a big dustup over nothing. By the end of the week, it will be business as usual. Companies go out of business all the time, and customers move on."

Campbell wagged a finger. "Mark my words, this is a huge deal, and you need to get out in front of it. Besides, what if Tommy wants to stay in the wedding industry? How do you think all of this is going to affect his reputation?"

Abby still wasn't convinced, but she decided to play along. "Fine. Let's work up a media plan and a base-line strategy. Between us, we've got this."

"I'll help out however I can," Campbell said, "But I'm scheduled in depositions the rest of the week."

"Then maybe Wynne should handle this with me," Abby said, turning to Campbell and Grace. "What do you think? Grace, you're busy, and someone needs to keep the place running." The more she thought about it, the more she liked the idea. Wynne had recently left her old firm and was doing contract work while she decided on a new career path. They'd floated the idea of asking her to join the firm, but Campbell had been hesitant about how working together might affect their relationship and the balance of power the three of them shared. Hiring Wynne to assist with this case seemed like the perfect compromise, although now that she'd blurted out the idea, she realized she shouldn't have put either Campbell or Wynne on the spot. "We can talk about it later. Like I said, this whole thing may go away in a few days."

"Wynne, you should totally do it," Campbell said. "If you want to."

Abby glanced at Wynne and tried to deduce from her thoughtful expression whether she was even interested. "How about this? Tommy will be here any minute. Why don't you sit in on the meeting, and if you're intrigued, we can talk and if you decide you're not interested, no hard feelings?"

"Deal," Wynne said. "Good thing I wore a suit."

The group of them spent the next few minutes talking about initial strategy. They were deep in discussion when Graham burst into the room, a harried look on his face.

"What's up, Graham?" Abby asked, unused to seeing the usually unflappable office manager look frazzled.

"Mr. Barclay is here to see you."

"Okay. We're expecting him." She stared at Graham, certain he had more to say. "What's wrong?"

"He's in his car in the parking lot. There are women with signs blocking his entrance to the building."

Graham held up his phone, and as a group, they all leaned in to look at the photo he'd snapped. A half dozen women wearing bridal veils with their regular street clothes milled around a car, and a couple of them were holding signs. Abby pinched the photo to enlarge it so she could make out the sign in the foreground. *Give me my dress or you'll have a mess.* Ugh. "When did they show up?"

Graham hunched his shoulders. "Apparently, they followed him here."

Abby sighed as the image of white, sandy beaches and turquoise blue water receded from her memory. The idea of a horde of angry brides standing in the parking lot made her think of Roxanne and her stack of bridal magazines, and she wondered what Roxanne was doing right now. She wished she hadn't been so curt at the airport. Maybe they could've exchanged numbers and tried to reconnect, but she'd been super annoyed to find out Roxanne had spent the rest of the week in PV without her, as well as embarrassed that she even cared. She shrugged the thought away. What they'd shared had been a part of the paradise she'd left back in PV. She was back to real life now, and it was time to focus.

Reentry was going to be way harder than she'd thought it would be.

Roxanne waved at the approaching maroon Honda CRV, but when it drew closer, she realized it wasn't Val behind the wheel. She silently cursed her decision not to take a cab home, but Val had insisted on picking her up to hear all about her faux honeymoon in paradise. She leaned her suitcase against a cement pillar and pulled out her phone on the off chance that maybe Abby had texted an apology for her abrupt behavior back in the terminal, but when she glanced at the screen it was loaded with notifications, none of which were from Abby.

*Barclay's Bridal Leaves Brides Undressed*
*Say No to the Dress*

She scrolled through, gulping down the developing story until she reached a text from Rodney, the assistant to Nancy Marshall, the senior editor at *Best Day Ever*.

*These brides! Are you on this?*

The blaring text was followed by a photo of nearly a dozen women dressed in black trash bags carrying signs that said *Is this what I'm supposed to wear now?* Roxanne couldn't help but chuckle at the picture, but she also felt a twinge of regret that she wasn't on the scene getting all this firsthand. She pulled up the address for the nearest Barclay's Bridal store, but before the page could load, she heard a honk and looked up to see Val pull up to the curb.

"Hey, lady," Val yelled out the window. "You lookin' for a ride?"

Roxanne shook her head but smiled. Little sisters were supposed to be embarrassing, right? She grabbed her suitcase, shoved it in the back seat, and climbed into the SUV. "What are you doing right now?"

"You mean besides picking you up at the airport and hoping there's a big bottle of expensive tequila in your bag?"

"Sorry." Roxanne took a breath. "Thanks for picking me up. Yes, I have your tequila. Now, do you have plans right now?"

"Other than dragging you to look at possible venues for the reception, no."

"I promise I'll go with you to all the places, but right now I need a big favor. You know the Barclay's Bridal on Central?"

Sis shook her head. "Not doing it. Mom tried to get me to pick a dress from there, but it's too overwhelming. They have too many to choose from. I got hives."

"Seriously, do you not read the news at all?"

Val pulled away from the curb. "What?"

"You'll see. And don't worry. I'm not going to make you try on dresses."

When they turned on the street to the Barclay's flagship store, Roxanne could already tell something was up. She'd been to the store on a couple of occasions, covering trunk shows from some of the top wedding dress designers. Barclays wasn't the highest end, but they did pamper their brides with champagne, white chocolate petit fours, and lots of oohing and aahing over what beautiful brides they were going to be. They prided themselves on rolling out the red carpet for everyone who entered their store.

But today that red carpet was nowhere to be found. Instead, she spotted the women like the ones who'd been depicted in the online photo marching in front of the store. The full effect of the protest was even more powerful in person, and Roxanne barely waited until Val pulled to a stop before jumping out of the car. She pulled out her phone and went straight into news reporter mode, jostling her way into the crowd of reporters already gathered at the scene. Recognizing a friend from KNOP, she took a place beside her. "Hey, Mary, how long have they been here?"

"Roxanne, long time no see. You back to covering news again?"

Roxanne grimaced inwardly at the question her father often asked, but she couldn't resist a smart-ass reply. "Nope, still covering the same fluff and no circumstance as always." She pointed at the brides-to-be in front of Barclay's. "I see you're on fluff patrol right along with me." She'd met Mary right after college when they'd both started working for the local station where Roxanne had embraced the social beat and Mary chafed against it.

Mary shook her head. "We're short on the metro desk this week. Len's wife is pregnant, and they put her on bed rest until her delivery date, so he's home dealing with the other five kids. Believe me, none of us think a store closing is big news, but it's clickbait and that's what we're all about lately, right?"

Roxanne started to list all the reasons why human interest stories were important to the life of a news outlet, starting with they garnered a large readership, but she was here to get her own story, not convince someone else to see the value in it. "I'm going to see if someone will talk to me. Catch you later. Give Len my regards."

She edged away before Mary could reply. It had been three years since she left the news outlet, much to the dismay of her parents who thought she'd traded respectability for something akin to a tabloid. She'd tried to explain that producing online content for bridal magazines was not only more lucrative, but it served a valuable purpose. They weren't buying. Even Val thought it was a little strange that she spent so much time covering all aspects of other people's path to happily ever after at the expense of having time to find her own, although she'd made time on this trip despite it being for business. For a second, she drifted into a daydream of waking up on the beach next to Abby's long, lean, sexy body. In her fantasy there was no pesky sand or sunscreen to get in the way of their lovemaking, and they'd done it right there with the waves lapping around them, a rhythmic accompaniment to a perfect scene.

But life wasn't like that. Beaches were messy and vacation rendezvous were meant to be left on vacation. She never should've given Abby her number because then she could've written off the lack of follow-up to a mutual desire to keep the fantasy alive.

She shrugged off her disappointment. It was time to talk to some disappointed brides-to-be and get their stories. She'd write her own story later.

## CHAPTER SIX

A bby rubbed her temple with both hands, while she waited for Campbell and Grace to join her at the bar. It had been a helluva few days back and she was ready for a drink. Or a few. No tiny umbrellas this time. Just her usual dirty—make that extra dirty—martini. When Campbell and Grace finally showed up, she was two out of three olives down.

"Somebody needed a drink," Campbell said, pointing to her glass, as she slid in on her left while Grace perched on the other side. She waved the bartender over and pointed at Abby's near empty drink. Abby nodded and Campbell ordered her usual tequila straight up and a Manhattan for Grace. "No offense, but except for the tan, you don't look so hot."

Abby chewed on her last olive. "I can hardly believe that less than a week ago, I was sitting on the beach, sipping fruity drinks and soaking up sun without a care in the world. What happened?"

"Ah the double-sided pleasure of vacation," Grace said, raising her glass. "Which is precisely why I don't take them. They only serve to highlight the restrictions of real life—getting up early, making your own meals, making your own bed."

"Oh, please," Campbell said, "that's ridiculous. You don't like to travel because you decked out your house like it's Wayne manor, but normal people don't live like that. Vacations are supposed to be rejuvenating. You go, you rest, you have fun, and then you come home relaxed, renewed, and full of energy to face whatever life throws your way."

"Campbell, I love you, but sometimes your eternal optimism is annoying." Abby set her glass down, thinking she should probably pace herself. "I don't mean to bitch. I had a good time and I really appreciate you both covering for me. At my old firm, the other associates would've spent the entire week figuring out ways to steal my work while partners called me asking for stuff their secretaries could handle."

"Like we'd try and steal Tommy from you," Grace said. "He's as loyal as they come. What's up with the rest of his family, though?"

Campbell held up a hand. "Slow down, Ms. All Business. We haven't finished with the topic of Ms. Keane's vacation." She frowned and assumed her best courtroom voice. "Isn't it true, Ms. Keane, that you met a woman while you were sunbathing in Puerto Vallarta?"

Abby squirmed in her chair. "Not exactly."

"Do I need to read back your earlier testimony?"

"No. I mean, I wasn't sunbathing when I met her." She squirmed again as a vision of Roxanne in a crimson bikini floated through her consciousness. "Guys, I really don't want to talk about this."

"I'm sensing we have a hostile witness," Grace said.

"Agreed," said Campbell. "Abby, we don't need every last detail, but seriously, can't you spare a few crumbs for the folks who stayed back home and toiled over your work while you basked in the sun with a vacation goddess?"

Abby sighed, knowing her friends weren't going to give up. Not that she'd expected them to, because in the same position, she knew she would've pushed for more. Still, she'd harbored some hope that she could keep the small pleasure she got from the memory of her time with Roxanne private because it was the only souvenir she cared about from her trip. Telling the story meant adding the part about how Roxanne had spent the rest of the week in PV without her, probably with someone else, and that would only tarnish the memory.

The irony almost made her laugh. She'd been so freaked out that Roxanne would be the kind of woman who was looking for a forever match instead of a vacation fling, and here she was the one all hung up on Roxanne instead of the other way around. She looked up to find her friends watching and waiting for her to say something, so she summoned her best version of her player self.

"It's a short story. Here are the facts. Hot woman helped me find the shuttle from the airport to the resort where, as luck would have it, she was headed for a little R and R. We drank champagne, we ate a nice dinner, or rather we went to a nice dinner that we quickly abandoned for my version of R and R. Her bungalow, my bungalow, the beach, the stars. It's all a blur. We stayed offline and kept all personal details to the absolute minimum. It was like a one-night stand on replay and it was fantastic."

Grace sighed. "Only you could wind up in bed with a hot woman within minutes of arriving at a posh resort." She raised her glass. "I admire you, my friend."

Campbell joined in the toast. "Cheers to Abby and Whatshername."

Abby bit off the impulse to say Roxanne's name, but Campbell's next question caught her off guard.

"Now what?"

"Now what, what?"

"Where is she from? Are you going to see her again? What's the story here?"

"Leave her alone," Grace said. "She doesn't even know the girl's name."

"I do too." Abby immediately wished she'd kept her mouth shut, but now that she'd spoken up, she decided she might as well divulge a little to get them off her back. "Her name was, is, Roxanne. We had an amazing few days, but what happens in PV, stays in PV. You know my motto, single and fabulous." She tilted her glass toward Campbell. "No offense. I'm glad you found Wynne, and I wish you both the best, but married life is not for me."

"Slow your roll," Campbell said. "I'm certainly not opposed to the idea of marriage, but I don't know if we're there yet. I mean Wynne hasn't said anything, but she's had a lot on her mind since she left her firm."

Abby reached over and clasped Campbell's hand. "I didn't mean 'married,' I meant, you know, committed."

"You make it sound like a prison sentence."

"I get that it's not for everyone, but I'm living my best life right now." Abby turned to Grace. "You're with me, right?"

Grace raised her glass. "I'm Switzerland. Not looking, but not opposed to falling in love if someone like Wynne shows up on my doorstep."

Campbell shook her head. "People! Doorsteps are overrated. Love doesn't show up on people's doorsteps. You show up on doorsteps and fall in love."

"That's the tequila talking."

"Maybe," Campbell said, draining her glass of the last few drops. "Thanks for the nice bottle of booze you brought back, by the way."

"Yeah," Grace added. "I may become a tequila convert. That stuff is liquid gold."

"You're welcome." Abby took another drink of her martini, while her mind wandered to the memories of Roxanne. She was glad to be home with her friends, her work, her favorite bar. Vacation was nice, but there was a comfort in the rhythm of her life just the way it was. So, why did she feel so completely unsettled since she'd returned?

❖

Friday morning, Roxanne slapped at her phone until the alarm stopped its incessant and annoying tone, and then she lunged out of bed before she could change her mind and go back to sleep. She lurched her way into the kitchen to start the coffee.

Pre-PV, she'd always been up early, ready to tackle whatever the day had in store, but after a few days with Abby, she'd learned to love the art of cuddling in bed and she kind of liked greeting the day tangled in the sheets with a beautiful woman beside her. The thought brought with it a flash of naked Abby rolling over into her arms. Yum.

The image slipped away as she sipped her coffee and started to wake up. Vacation life was not reality. Abby was probably waking up right about now before she headed to her job as a corporate raider, tech guru, or some other equally boring but lucrative occupation that gave her the financial freedom to be able to afford to fly first class and spend a week at Azure. She, on the other hand, had to scratch out a living. She reached for her phone and scrolled through her messages before switching over to her social media accounts. The column she'd written about the protest outside of Barclay's was still trending on an uptick. Surprising, since she'd expected the story would peak and then fade, as most did. Curious, she typed in a few quick searches and found a list of new groups formed for the sole purpose of discussing the plight of brides without dresses in the lead-up to their wedding.

Her phone rang in her hand and she nearly dropped it into her coffee. She looked at the screen but didn't recognize the number. She was tempted to send it to voice mail, but what if it was...No, it couldn't be Abby. Could it? She wouldn't call this early, even if it was her. But maybe this was the only time she had before the demands of her high-powered job kicked in. Before she could equivocate further, she answered the call. She barely had a hello out before a voice interrupted her.

"Roxanne Daly?"

"Yes."

"Hold for Ms. Marshall, please."

She said okay, but the music on the line meant Ms. Curt and Dismissive had already placed her on hold. She racked her brain for any Marshalls she knew but could only come up with one and she didn't actually know her. Nancy Marshall was the senior editor for *Best Day Ever*, the premier publication of Women's Work Publishing & Production, the company responsible for all the wedding programming on GAL, the up-and-coming new female-focused cable network. She laughed at the idea Nancy Marshall would be calling her directly. She was mid-laugh when a piercing voice came through the line.

"Ms. Daly, Nancy Marshall here. Where are you on the coverage of Barclay's closing?"

"Good morning, Ms. Marshall." Holy shit. It really was *that* Nancy Marshall. Roxanne scrambled to think of a response, since Nancy's tone indicated she should be in the middle of a hot story, not a winding down one. "I plan to do a full series on the chain closing, and I have several sources I'm consulting. The story is actually gaining traction, not fading away."

"As I suspected. I'd like to get a team on this right away, with you leading it, of course. Your draft of the PV honeymoon piece was excellent. Let's set up a meeting. Rodney will contact you with the details. Can I count on you?"

Roxanne barely heard the compliment buried in Nancy's charging tone. She felt like she was a confident person, but she hoped that one day she would possess the insane level of confidence that Nancy had just exhibited where she could call people on the phone, command that they do things, and know it would be done. There was no denying this request. Besides, it could propel her career to the next level. "Yes, you can count on me."

When she hung up the phone, she did a little dance to celebrate, and finished the rest of her coffee. She considered breakfast, but the only food she had in the house was a grapefruit of undetermined age that closely resembled a shrunken head. She made a mental note to go to the store later, but right now, her focus was on all things Barclay's, and she took to the internet to do some research.

Barclay's Bridal had been an Austin staple for years, and when they first opened, they hadn't specialized in wedding dresses.

They started as a family-owned dressmaker slash tailor, catering to wealthy clients in Austin. Over time, they'd started to get more and more requests for wedding gowns and began to specialize in wedding attire. The business model changed from a focus on the wealthy to providing ready access to custom dresses for a broader clientele. At their peak, the company had over a hundred stores throughout the country with their flagship store, the one she and Mary had visited the other day, in Austin, and Barclay's became the go-to store for brides across the country. They offered an ample mix of off-the-rack dresses, but they also featured trunk shows from many up-and-coming designers whose careers were made by the exposure they received at the store.

Last year, following the death of the senior Barclays, things started to change. Roxanne clicked through several articles that detailed the changes at the store. Less designer influence and less selection. Customers began complaining about the downturn in customer service and how the "experience" they'd come to expect was sorely lacking. Sales dipped and there'd been talk of closing a few of the stores in lower volume areas, but the sudden closure of all the stores wasn't an act any of the forecasters had seen coming. The closure had been abrupt, like many such business closures were, but unlike when a grocery or electronics store closed, customers couldn't just run down the street and pick up a new wedding dress.

Roxanne jotted down a few questions. *Were finances the reason for the closure? Did the reputation for quality and great service die with the founders?* Based on what she'd read, she couldn't imagine Mr. and Mrs. Barclay would've closed with no notice, leaving brides-to-be without their gowns. She scribbled down a few more notes, and then she checked her email to find a new message from Nancy Marshall's assistant, Rodney, with details for a meeting at *Best Day Ever* tomorrow morning. Yikes. She drained the last dregs of her coffee, thankful she'd got up early because she had a lot to do to be ready to pitch Nancy and whatever team she'd assembled. Her mind was already whirring with possibilities. This could finally be the big break she'd been hoping for, and nothing was going to throw her off track.

❖

Abby spread out her files in the conference room while she waited for Wynne to arrive. She was looking forward to spending some one-on-one time with Wynne, plus she was glad for the company since Campbell and Grace were both out of the office, working other cases. When Campbell had come up with the crazy idea that they all should quit their jobs and start their own firm, she figured they'd spend the first year hustling for new clients, but four months in, they had already developed a good client base. Between landing social media breakout star, Leaderboard, and the loyalty of past clients like Tommy Barclay, the three of them had wound up being busier than they'd been at their old firms, but decidedly happier now that they called the shots.

"You look deep in thought."

Abby looked up to see Wynne smiling at her. "That's how I always look before my second cup of coffee. Join me?"

"Absolutely."

Abby led the way to the office break room and pointed at the espresso machine. "I'd offer you a cappuccino, but your girlfriend purchased this beast and I still haven't figured out all the features. I hate to admit it, but Graham usually makes mine."

"Good news, we have one at home and I've finally mastered the art of cappuccino making. Do you like yours dry or extra dry?"

Abby flashed on an image of Roxanne's delight when she'd brought her cappuccino from the resort restaurant in bed. She'd vowed then and there to learn how to use the machine, and maybe even buy one of her own. "What I'd really like is for you to show me how to make my own once we get this silly dress business sorted out."

"Deal," Wynne said. "In the meantime, I'll be your contract barista."

Abby watched her flip some switches and turn some knobs, and then accepted the steaming cup Wynne handed her way. "This is delicious." Abby sipped her drink. "I'm not usually intimidated by new things, but for some reason, I have an aversion to all the dials and buttons. I guess I got too used to ordering on the fly, but it really would be much nicer to be able to make it whenever I want. Besides, then I can file this under skills to impress all the girls."

"Campbell may have mentioned something about a particular girl from your trip."

"Campbell has a big mouth."

"Sorry, I didn't mean to pry."

Abby instantly felt bad. "No, it's okay. I've never been one to keep secrets when it comes to my social life…Besides, it was a vacation fling, nothing more."

"Got it. No special cappuccinos for vacation-only girl."

Abby laughed along with Wynne, but she felt a twinge of guilt at relegating Roxanne to the same category as all her past flings, but she wasn't sure why. Silly, really, since she wasn't likely to see her again which meant none of this even mattered. It was time to turn off vacation mode and get focused. Back in the conference room, she dug into the Barclay's file.

"I don't know if Campbell mentioned this, but Tommy is an old friend and I knew his parents. I may not be sentimental about wedding dresses, but I do care about supporting whatever he needs as far as the family business. Basically, he wants to know what his options are. The twins, his brother and sister, are kind of jerks, and they've never been keen on being part of the family biz. Tommy's been anticipating a break with them for a while and has already started looking at other options, including an online only site to sell wedding attire, but all this media is going to kill any chance of salvaging the business in any form if it's not contained."

"I'm surprised Tommy was on board with shutting down the business in the first place," Wynne said.

"He wasn't, but he was outvoted. The twins held a meeting when he was out of town. They have completely unrelated business interests and were never really into the whole bridal industry thing anyway. Barclay's started having some financial trouble before their parents died, and they view this as an opportunity for a fresh start. Of course, if they'd really wanted to do this right, they should've filed bankruptcy first, but they probably suspected Tommy would fight them on that front because he's always been convinced bankruptcy means failure. Now, everyone's options are pretty limited. "

"I'm guessing Tommy doesn't get along with the twins."

"It's hit-and-miss. They're younger and weren't raised in the business like he was. Mr. Barclay senior always envisioned his children taking over the business, but Tommy was the only one of them who expressed an interest. Just last year after his wife died, I advised him to give Tommy a larger interest if he wanted to create a legacy, but he held out hope that the twins could one day spark to the business. Of course, he had no idea he would be gone so soon."

"That's rough. I remember reading about his death so close to his wife's. Truly tragic."

"It's been hard on all of them, but Tommy has been devastated. And now to watch while the business he made his life's work be shuttered and then smeared in the news? It's a lot."

"Okay, what's the plan?" Wynne asked. "Revive the business or keep it closed and mitigate the damage?"

"Good question. The plan for now is to provide Tommy with his options, which includes making a plan the twins can live with, hopefully one that allows him to salvage Barclay's reputation long enough for him to spin the current business model into something workable. We'll put together all the contingencies and arrange a meeting. And I think at this point we need to consider bankruptcy as one of the options, and I know only enough to be dangerous. Campbell said you have some experience?"

"I do, although I'm not an expert, but I'm as qualified as anyone to give some advice. The first step is deciding on the long-range goal. There's completely going out of business and then there's staving off the debt to give time to restructure."

"Yes, those. I'm already hearing about lawsuits headed our way, and if bankruptcy can hold those off, I'm all for it. Are you in?"

"You bet." Wynne raised her coffee mug. "Here's to saving the bridal dress business."

Abby clinked her mug against Wynne's. "And the future of Barclay's." She wasn't sure she cared about the bridal dress business, but she did care about Tommy and his happiness. She couldn't imagine how she'd feel if she showed up to the firm one day and found that Campbell and Grace had decided to shut down the business by outvoting her.

Stolen dreams. That's what she was fighting against, and now that she had realized her own dream of being in business for herself, she was even more committed to helping others achieve theirs. And no, her dreams definitely did not include a certain tall blonde who looked particularly good in a swimsuit.

## CHAPTER SEVEN

R oxanne stepped into the sleek glass and steel conference room and tried to act nonchalant, but she was a queasy mixture of excited and nervous. She'd been to *Best Day Ever*'s offices a couple of times, but never to the top floor executive suite, and she was glad she dressed for the occasion in something other than her usual writer's attire of yoga pants and her favorite hoodie.

"Ms. Marshall will be with you in just a moment." The thin, gorgeous, perfectly accessorized receptionist answered another call, and Roxanne took the opportunity to wander around and look at the framed magazine covers on the wall. Online content was becoming the driving force of the various magazines Women's Work put out, but print still reigned supreme and *Best Day Ever* was their crown jewel. Despite the plethora of Pinterest boards and Etsy shops, brides-to-be still loved to gather a stack of magazines and spend hours flagging pages featuring all their favorite things. Maybe someday print would be obsolete, but she hoped not because having a regular column in the print edition was her idea of making it, and she held out hope she would achieve that dream one day.

She heard the sound of the door open and looked up to see Nancy Marshall enter the room flanked by a tall, thin young man with a goatee and another, slightly older man who looked like he'd raided the fashion closet and taken everything he could get his hands on. Trailing behind were several tall, willowy young women, all carrying iPads and green juices. Roxanne suddenly felt underdressed and like she had the words "I ate a cheeseburger and fries last night" tattooed on her forehead, but she hid the dip in confidence beneath a smile. "Ms. Marshall, it's nice to meet you."

Nancy gripped her hand. "Good to meet you too. Have a seat?"

Roxanne followed her lead and took a seat close to the head of the table. Nancy introduced the guy with the goatee as her assistant, Rodney—he was the one who'd called her with the assignment for the honeymoon piece—and Mr. Too Much Fashion as Stuart Lofton, head of visual media, whatever that meant. The juice girls remained nameless and they gathered at the other end of the room where they started typing on their phones, giving the impression they were either bored or live tweeting the meeting. She did her best to ignore them and focus on Nancy. "I think you'll be pleased with the final spread on the resorts in Puerto Vallarta. I just received the photos and I should have the captions turned in this afternoon."

"I didn't bring you here to talk about that."

"Okay." Roxanne wasn't sure what to make of the brisk tone.

"Women's Work would like to take *Best Day Ever* to the next level."

"Next level?" Roxanne felt foolish for repeating the words, but she wasn't at all sure what Nancy expected and she didn't have a clue where this conversation was headed.

"Yes." Nancy motioned to Rodney who sprang to life and fired up his iPad. He displayed a new logo on the screen with a flourish, while Nancy kept talking. "We've been working on the concept for this pilot for a while, and GAL network is on board. All we need now is the talent. I know that we've discussed expanding our licensing agreement to link your blog to other platforms, but I'm thinking bigger picture."

"Bigger picture." Roxanne suppressed an urge to bite her lip. "What exactly did you have in mind?"

"Television. An hour a week. All things bride. Occasionally featuring celebrity guests with their grand, splashy plans, but primarily focused on ideas that normal, everyday brides can incorporate into any-sized budget. A perfect combination of aspirational and practical. Rodney?"

He started a slideshow and turned it toward her. Roxanne watched the presentation, impressed with the level of planning that had gone into developing the concept. When the slideshow concluded, she turned her attention back to Nancy. "Very thorough and a great concept."

"It is for the most part, but like I said, we've been stumped on one portion of the planning." She paused and Roxanne was unsure about whether she was expected to fill the void, so she merely nodded. "The host. We've met with some top talent, but nothing has quite been the right fit."

"I'm sure you'll find the right person," Roxanne said.

"Actually, I think we have." Nancy motioned to Rodney, who fired up the iPad again. "Take a look."

Roxanne watched the screen fill with a familiar scene—the front of the downtown Barclay's store, with a crowd of protesting brides-to-be. And there she was in the thick of it. But how? She hadn't taped the interviews. She glanced back at everyone else in the room, but they were all staring at the screen raptly watching her talk to a bride-to-be named Emily who'd ordered a wedding dress based on a picture she'd drawn of her dream dress when she was only twelve. Emily detailed how she'd scrimped and saved to purchase the dress and her final fitting had been scheduled days before, but when she showed up to try on the dress, Barclay's was closed for good.

Roxanne watched as Emily teared up and she did too, moved by the emotion in her voice. She couldn't deny there was an extra level of emotion in the video footage that didn't always come across in her blog posts.

"You were the only one there who captured the feelings," Nancy said, her eyes never leaving the screen as they all watched the video play on.

It was true. While the rest of the reporters on site had been peppering the women with questions about their plans, Roxanne had given them a forum to talk about their very personal wedding prep stories. She glanced at the stats under the video. It had gotten more hits than her most popular blog post, tenfold, and it was quickly going viral. "Who posted this?"

"One of the reporters from KNOP," Nancy said. "You didn't know?"

"I had no idea."

She tore her gaze away from the screen to find Nancy observing her with a smile on her face. "You'll be perfect for the job. Frankly, your talent has been wasted behind the scenes. Your blog is great, but these interviews are next level. The difference is the personal touch. You made every one of these women feel like you actually cared about their plight."

Roxanne resisted pointing out that she actually did care about how they felt, or she wouldn't have been talking to them in the first place, but she decided pushing back while getting a compliment wasn't good strategy. Besides, a bigger concern was edging in. "I appreciate the interest, but I'm a blogger, a columnist. Being in front of the camera is not my thing. *The Bride's Best Friend* was designed to be anonymous, so it's never about me and all the focus is on the bride. Wouldn't you rather have a big name launch this concept?"

Nancy's stare was intense. "Trust me, it *is* your thing. It's my job to know. We'll start filming right away. We'd like to have the premiere episode ready in a few weeks and we'll use this story to launch the series. In the meantime, we'll boost the attention to your blog with a combination of video spotlights to tease the new show. Stuart will be the producer, and he'll be in charge of all the details."

Nancy pointed to the tablet screen where an image of her standing in the middle of the brides-to-be or BTBs as she'd started calling them was frozen mid-action. Roxanne was pretty sure that the next screen showed the BTBs throwing bouquets made of dead flowers at the front doors of Barclays. She'd gotten caught up in the excitement and apparently never noticed Mary's crew was filming her in addition to the action shots.

She stared at the screen with a critical eye along with the rest of the group, her mind whirring with changes she would've made to her wardrobe, makeup and other little details if she'd known she was being filmed. When the clip ended, she looked up to find everyone in the room staring at her. She shifted in her chair, certain Nancy was about to tell her that after a second look, they'd reconsidered their offer.

"It's the raw energy," Rodney said.

"She exudes empathy," Nancy added. "All the other reporters were there to get a story, but she was there to get their stories."

"Rough around the edges, but there's a lot to work with here."

Roxanne shifted in her seat, uncomfortable at being talked about like she wasn't in the room, and focused on the man who'd made the last comment, Stuart Lofton, her new boss. He was pointing at the still shot of her on the screen, and she was pretty sure he was referring to her outfit. She rushed to defend herself. "I'd just landed from a trip to Puerto Vallarta, and I wanted to get in on the story right away. I assure you, vacation attire is not my go-to work wardrobe choice." She wasn't sure why she was defending her attire since she wasn't entirely convinced she wanted this gig in front of the camera. She'd had a few on camera spots with KNOP during her time there, but nothing more than a couple of minutes. The idea of hosting an hour-long show had her stomach in knots.

He nodded. "We can spin that. She'll go anywhere, do anything to get the story. It's like the Bride's Best Friend meets Lois Lane." His smile signaled he was pleased with himself for the retro reference. He turned to a young man sitting behind him. "Go ahead and start working on a tagline using that theme." When the young man nodded but stayed put, Stuart motioned rapidly with his hands. "Now!" As the young man scurried out the door, he shouted after him, "And send someone up from wardrobe."

Roxanne looked down at her outfit and then back up at the appraising eyes of Mr. Bossypants Lofton. This was so not what she'd bargained for, but before she could respond, Nancy stood and Rodney rose with her.

"You're in good hands with Stuart. The contract's already in your inbox. This is going to be fantastic."

Nancy and her minion had barely cleared the door when Roxanne stood, intent on following. "I'm not sure this is for me," she said, directing her comment to Stuart. "Let's leave the on-camera work to someone else." She started to walk to the door, but Stuart called out to her.

"The stats on your blog are good, but people ultimately want to see a face. A face they like, a face that says 'hey, trust me to tell you all about xyz.' Not everyone who dispenses advice has that kind of face. Those who don't go on radio or write blogs, but those who do, like you, have a duty to show up and let their followers see the person who's leading them to their better life. You think you have a lot of followers now? You have no idea of the kind of reach you are capable of. Trust me. Together we can do great things."

Roxanne searched his eyes for sincerity, but found only a trace of it, which was fine. She wasn't naive enough to believe Stuart really thought the purpose of the show was to change people's lives, but she did and maybe that was all that mattered. She'd been looking for a bigger platform, and maybe it wasn't in the package she'd expected, but lately life had been throwing her unexpected surprises—Abby being a prime example. She'd blown her opportunity there, but now she had a chance to take a risk on launching her career in a new direction. Was she going to blow it out of fear or because it wasn't the direction she'd expected?

No. No, she wasn't.

"Okay," she said. "I'm in. Let's do this."

❖

Abby stood in front of her kitchen counter and willed the coffee pot to be faster. Much faster. What she really wanted to do was hop back on a plane to PV and dive back into the laid-back life she'd called her own for a week. But maybe this time she'd only stay a long weekend. A week had been too long because it had allowed her to become way too comfortable with sandy beaches, the sound of ocean waves, and pretty women. Make that pretty woman. Singular.

Roxanne had had the right idea—stay a few days, make the most of them, and dash away before things could take an ugly romantic turn. She laughed at the irony. She was the one who never stayed the night, never made promises about the future, never stuck around for the afterglow. But she'd done all of those things with Roxanne only to have her dash off just when they were getting close.

She shook her head. Time to stop thinking about the girl who got away and focus on work. She had a meeting with Tommy's siblings and their lawyer tomorrow, and she was spending all day today finishing up her presentation to outline potential options for the business. She poured what she imagined would be the first cup of many and fired up her laptop, but before she could open her email, her phone rang. A quick glance at the screen showed her mother's number on the display. Abby groaned but answered anyway. "Hi, Mom, I've only got a few minutes to talk. Big case. Lots of work."

Unaffected by the curt tone, her mother sighed into the phone. "It's Sunday, Abigail. Maybe take a weekend off now and then or you'll turn into a stick-in-the-mud like you know who."

Abby resisted the urge to correct her mother's use of her full name, and instead focused on not snapping back about the thinly veiled reference to her estranged father, two husbands past. "I'll take it under advisement." She took a deep breath. "What can I do for you?"

"You can make time for your mother. Today at eleven. Brunch at Moonshine. I picked it because it's your favorite, so don't let me down. I have important news. See you there."

"Mom, Mom…" Abby stared at the phone in her hand, but she knew her mother had already disconnected in her usual dramatic exit kind of way. Ugh. She had two choices. Ignore the pseudo invitation to brunch or rearrange her day to accommodate her mother's whims. Why did she have to pick one of her favorite brunch spots? And how could she have known that she was starving?

*Because she's your mother, duh.* Abby checked her email and guzzled her coffee. By the time she was finished, her stomach was rumbling, and she decided since she had to eat anyway, she may as well meet her mother and have a nice brunch doing it. She'd try to resume normal, post-vacation eating habits next week.

An hour and a half later, Abby pulled up to the restaurant and left her convertible BMW with the valet, noting his whistle of admiration for her sweet ride. She'd owned the car for a year, but it wasn't until she left her old firm in Dallas that she had time to drive it. Now she rode around with the top down as much as she could. She tucked the claim check in her purse, went inside, and glanced around for her mother.

She didn't have to look long. Donna Wheeler always stood out in a crowd, and not for the first time Abby admired her mother's tall, trim form and ageless face and prayed she'd inherited those genes. Otherwise, they'd have nothing in common.

"I thought you'd never get here," her mother said, sweeping her hand through the air with dramatic flair. "I'm famished."

"Thank goodness, since I'm pretty sure they can take care of that here." Abby asked the hostess for a table on the patio. Once they were seated, she said, "I'm kind of mystified about why you chose this place."

"What's that supposed to mean?"

"Last time we talked you were replicating some movie star diet of warm water and lemon. Chicken and waffles loaded with butter and syrup doesn't really seem like your thing."

Her mother scoffed. "Show's how much you know. I have eclectic dining habits. Besides, I seem to recall you love this restaurant."

Warning bells went off in Abby's head. "Are you about to ruin my appetite with some bad news?"

"Not in the least."

"Great. Let's get in line." Abby didn't wait for a response before standing and motioning to the closest buffet line. She knew better than to think this was nothing more than a friendly mother-daughter brunch, but if a shoe was going to drop, it could wait until she had a full stomach.

Once she'd loaded up on food. She met her mother back at the table and shook her head when she saw all she put on her plate was a salad. "Is that all you're going to eat?"

"I can always get more," her mother said. "How was your trip?"

"It was nice."

"Nice is boring. Was it really boring?"

Abby sighed. "It wasn't boring. I swam, I snorkeled, I parasailed, and I hooked up with the hottest woman at the resort. We had tons of sex."

Her mother lifted her coffee cup and took a long sip. "I got over you trying to shock me when you were in high school. That sounds way better than nice."

Abby sighed. "It was, but alas, I'm back to the real world now. I played hard, now it's time to work hard."

"You're going to grow old alone if all you do is work. I thought you girls started your own firm so you would have more freedom."

"Mom, you've got to stop calling us girls. It's disrespectful. And we do have more freedom. I wouldn't have been able to take an off the grid vacation if I was still at my old firm, but we're still in the start-up phase so when I'm not on a beach, I'm working hard. At least I'm working toward my own future instead of lining other people's pockets."

"Are you going to see her again?"

"Who?"

"The hot girl, uh, woman. The one from the resort."

Abby knew she shouldn't be surprised at her mother's one-track mind, but fashion, shopping, and relationships were the trinity of her life, and that was probably never going to change. "It was a vacation. It was amazing while it lasted, but we're back to real life now." She tucked into a bit of waffle to signal the conversation was over, but her mother picked at her salad and pressed on.

"Are you seeing anyone here then?"

Abby set her fork down. "Why the interrogation about my dating life?" It wasn't new, but it did seem out of context.

"I may be having a special event soon and I thought you might need a date."

Angst wound its way up Abby's spine and her stomach soured. She set her fork down and took a deep breath. "Tell me."

"You don't have to sound like you're dreading what I'm about to say."

Abby forced a smile and a fake lilt to her tone. "Just excited to hear what you have to announce."

Her mother cocked her head like she was assessing the lay of the land and then reached into her purse and pulled out a small box. She took her time easing it open and slowly slipped the ring with the massive diamond on her ring finger. "It's gorgeous, isn't it? I said it was way too big, but Russell insisted. Go big *and* go home, he said. Get it?"

Abby got it all right. Husband number four was lined up and ready to go. "When's the big day?"

"You're mad."

"I'm not mad, Mother."

"You only call me Mother when you're mad." She folded her arms. "I thought you liked Russell."

"I met him once. Frankly, he didn't seem like your type." Abby recalled the quick meeting less than a month ago when her mother brought a housewarming gift by her condo with her new boyfriend, Russell, in tow. Abby recalled he had some kind of government job and drove a Ford pickup. She didn't have any issues with either, but since her mother usually went for trust fund types who drove fancy cars, Abby figured Russell wasn't long for her world.

"I don't have a type."

"Sure. Right. Look, Mom, I like all the guys who fund your way of life, but that doesn't mean you have to marry them in quick succession."

"Well!"

Abby wished she could reel the words back in, but they were out there, and she'd actually meant them, so there was that. "I'm sorry for being a jerk about it, but I'll never understand why you keep feeling the need to take a vow to spend the rest of your life with someone when you know full well it's not going to play out that way."

"Is that so?" Her mom looked like she was about to cry. "I take leaps, big, risky jumps to see what happens next. At least I'm willing to make commitments."

"What's that supposed to mean?" Abby kept her voice to a whisper, but she could tell the people at the tables near them were starting to listen in.

"Do I really have to say it?"

"Since when has that ever stopped you?"

Her mother made a show of setting down her fork and leaning forward. "I'm going to ignore your bitchy tone and tell you exactly what you're too scared to admit. You are afraid to find someone and settle down and that's why you criticize everyone else who does."

"'Settling down'? Is that what you call the few years you spend with 'insert name here' until you're ready for the next?"

Abby was barely finished speaking when her mother stood and tossed her napkin on the table. "Abigail Keaton, you're out of line, and just for that you can pay for brunch. You're invited to the wedding, but I'm begging you not to come if you can't show up with a better attitude. I love you, but I won't have your toxic take on love ruining my special day."

She finished her speech and strode off, leaving Abby sitting at the table stunned into silence, acutely aware that everyone at the tables around them had heard the exchange. What just happened? Had the queen of serial monogamy just called her out for failing to commit? As if. She committed to plenty of things way more important than a romantic relationship. She was committed to her work, her friends, her independence. Falling in love was the kind of thing that derailed all that other stuff.

She looked down at her chicken and waffles. She wasn't hungry anymore and the food she'd eaten so far was like a lead weight in her stomach, and to top it all off, her mother had stuck her with the bill. She tossed a few twenties on the table to compensate for the scene and slunk out of the restaurant. At least her mother's abrupt end to the meal meant she had more time to work. Too bad the case she was working on was just a bunch more angry brides-to-be. More proof marriage wasn't the fluffy, sweet wonder it was promised to be.

## CHAPTER EIGHT

R oxanne reached up to brush away a strand of hair, but the man standing over her swatted her hand away.

"No touching until I'm done," he said.

"That's what she said."

"Very funny." Luther, the stylist for *Best Day Ever*, gently stroked a brush along the edge of her hair, and then stood back with his hands on his hips. "Okay, we're done. And I lied before. No touching period. You'll be tempted to fool with my masterpiece, but don't do it. What we have here is a delicate balance, and one unskilled move and it will all fall to pieces. Understood?"

"Did you just call me unskilled?"

"I may have. Am I wrong?" He whirled her chair around so that she was now facing the brightly lit mirror. "Behold!"

Roxanne sucked in a breath. Plenty of people had told her she was attractive, and she knew she'd been blessed with good genes, but she barely recognized the reflection in the mirror. "Wow. Just wow. You, sir, are a miracle worker."

Luther shook his head. "Hardly. You were gorgeous when you walked in here. I just added a little pop here and there."

Roxanne couldn't tear her eyes away. Luther's version of pop included a new hairstyle and makeup color combinations she would've never considered on her own. When she rolled out of bed this Monday morning, she'd never imagined she'd be transformed into a beauty queen before noon. "I feel like I should buy a fancy dress and go out on the town."

"Perfect timing," a loud voice called out from across the room. Roxanne and Luther both turned toward the sound, and Roxanne groaned inwardly at the sight of Stuart Lofton heading toward them.

"Hi, Stuart," she called out. "I'm just hanging here with Luther, watching him work miracles. What do you think?"

Stuart stopped directly in front of her and surveyed her like she was a lab specimen. "Better. Much better. But now it's time to dress it up."

Did he just call me an "it"? Roxanne bit back a smart retort. Guys like Stuart thrived on generating drama with their acerbic attitudes, and she had no interest in feeding that beast, so she made a conscious decision to ignore his remark. "Talk to me. What do you have in mind?"

"This way." He turned quickly and walked toward the door, not waiting for her to follow. With a quick wave at Luther, Roxanne scurried after and followed him out of the room and down the hall, nearly smacking into his backside when he pulled up short in front of a set of double doors.

"What I'm about to show you is fashion's version of the Garden of Eden. You may look, but do not touch. If there's something you want to try on, you may point to it, but I will make the ultimate decision. Understood?"

She nodded, scared if she spoke out loud, her tone would border on sarcastic. Seriously, what a control freak. Apparently satisfied she was going to obey, he threw open the doors with a flourish. She half expected him to say "ta-da," but he merely stepped to the side and waved her in. When she stepped over the threshold, she gasped. "Oh my God."

"I know," Stuart said with as much of a smile as she'd seen from him. "It's a lot to take in your first time. Go slow and look around. I have some things in mind, but it's important that you are invested in the sense of style you will be projecting."

Roxanne nodded, but she wasn't really listening since every last bit of her focus was trained on rack after rack of stunning garments worthy of a runway. And the shoes! She practically swooned at the sight of half a dozen racks loaded with pair after pair, each one costing more than her car payment. "This is the mythical fashion closet, isn't it?" She reached out to touch a Jimmy Choo rust metallic lizard print pump she'd seen advertised in last month's issue of *Best Day Ever*, but pulled back when Stuart cleared his throat. "Sorry. I was blinded by the bling."

Stuart crossed his arms. "Fashion closet, yes. Mythical, no." He let loose a slight grin. "I came through earlier and set aside a few things for you to try on, but I'm open to seeing if there is anything that calls out to you. Take a few minutes and then point out what catches your fancy and we'll go from there."

He wandered off for a moment, and she took advantage of being out from under his watchful eyes to run her hands along a Christian Siriano dress. Nothing in the room was anything that could be purchased off the rack, but every clothing store in the country carried designs inspired by these one of a kind pieces. She fired off a quick text to her sister. *You'll never guess where I am. 3 tries.*

*In a coal mine. In a boat off the coast of Spain. At the farmer's market.*

*Wrong. Wrong. Wrong. Fashion closet at Best Day Ever. About to be wardrobed for the big gig.* She heard the door open. *Gotta go. Drinks later and I'll tell all.*

"Well?" Stuart asked as she slipped her phone surreptitiously into her purse. "Anything catch your eye?"

"Everything caught my eye." She pointed to a trench-style dress. "Love this. Totally my style, just, you know, at the knock-off of a knock-off price."

"There's nothing like the genuine article."

"There is if you want to eat," she said. "Don't get me wrong, my blog has become very successful, but it's only in the last year that I've started to accumulate sponsorships, and most of those have gone toward paying down the debt I accumulated writing on spec." She stopped when she realized Stuart, dressed in his custom-made suit and Prada shoes, couldn't possibly relate to her situation. "Anyway, I like the dress and," she pointed to a floral print Etro suit hanging nearby, "the cut on that suit is perfection."

He gathered the garments and held them at arm's length. "You have a good eye and you know your own style, so you're already ahead of the game. You favor lighter colors, but I'd like to push you a bit outside your box if you're okay with that. Do you trust me?"

"Yes." She didn't have to think about her answer. She expected men like Stuart were accustomed to telling, not asking, and the fact that he was letting her have any input at all was a big overture on his part. "What do you recommend?"

"I've got an outfit in mind for today's appearance that should have everyone talking. Let's get you fitted for that and then we'll meet back here tomorrow and go over the other things I've selected." He clapped his hands, and magically, a duo of minions appeared at the door. "Here's your team. Get her dressed and ready to go in two hours. Go!"

Roxanne barely saw him leave the room as she was surrounded by two young men taking measurements and discussing various details to get her camera-ready. "Uh, guys?" She pointed at herself. "I'm right here. Would someone mind showing me what you're measuring me for?"

The taller of the two stepped back, smiled, and pulled a garment bag off a nearby rack. He started lowering the zipper. "Ready?"

"Ready." She watched intently as he quickly lowered the rest of the zipper and eased out the hanger. She stared at the deep crimson sheath dress with an asymmetrical neckline. It was classically simple and breathtakingly beautiful. Guaranteed to make a statement. "I'm so ready."

❖

Abby stood at the head of the conference room table, gritting her teeth. With the exception of the aborted brunch on Sunday, she'd spent the entire weekend working on an array of contingency plans for Barclay's Bridal, but the twins and their contentious lawyer, Sam Thedford, had shot down every alternative.

"We're wasting our time here," Sam said. "Sadie and Phillip no longer want to be in the bridal business. They've communicated this desire to Tommy time and time again. He can buy them out if he wants to reopen."

"With what?" Tommy asked, shrugging off Abby's hand on his arm. "Seriously, since Mom and Dad died you've shown no interest in trying to turn the business around."

"Because we never wanted to be in the business in the first place," Sadie said. "This is your dream, not ours. Why can't you get your investor for the online business to give you the money to reopen the stores?"

Abby caught Tommy's eye and shook her head. They'd discussed this option, but the investor wasn't interested in brick-and-mortar stores, only an online presence, and he didn't want to buy in to that unless he could be assured there would be no lingering lawsuits against the Barclay name, which left them at an impasse. "Two separate issues," she said. "We're here to discuss options for Barclay's Bridal."

Sadie folded her arms across her chest. "We made a decision to close the stores and that's it."

"Exactly," Phillip chimed in. "This is all a waste of time. And money." He turned to Tommy. "Quit trying to reopen the stores. Either buy us out or liquidate the assets at auction, and save the money we're all having to pay on lawyers. How much is she charging?"

Abby focused on keeping her breathing calm and steady. "What I'm charging is a drop in the bucket compared to what you'll be paying in lawsuits for all the contracts you're violating with your suppliers and customers, but I'm sure Sam here has explained that to you," she said, not at all confident he had. "If you'd come to me before you made the decision to close, we could have worked out a structured bankruptcy arrangement, but now we're faced with back-dooring everything and it's not going to be pretty. Simply liquidating the assets isn't going to save you from lawsuits for violating contracts or the loss of goodwill." She pointed to the flow chart she'd written on the board. "We do have a few options to cut your losses, but we need to settle on one fast. In case you haven't noticed, there's a big media campaign brewing designed to stir these women up. No one really cares about manufacturers and distributors not being paid, but angry brides-to-be are apparently a hot item right now."

"It's all those stupid reality shows focused on everything wedding. They encourage everyone to have unrealistic expectations," Sadie said.

"Those shows kept our business afloat," Tommy said. "Do you know how many people think it's okay to buy a wedding dress online nowadays? Mom and Dad would be rolling over in their graves at the idea of UPS tossing a box stuffed full of chiffon on someone's porch. Reality wedding shows are one of the primary reasons women still shop at our stores."

"That's pretty hypocritical, coming from you. Aren't you trying to take the business online?"

"To complement the existing business, not destroy it."

"Mom and Dad's failure to be forward thinking is what got us into this mess in the first place," Phillip said.

"Quit pretending you were ever interested in this business," Tommy said. "Either of you. All you ever cared about was its ability to fund the lifestyles you've become accustomed to. Mom and Dad would've loved for you to show an interest when they were alive, but the minute it became hard, you both decided to bail, and it's not okay."

Sam looked up from his phone. "Counselor, I think you need to tell your client to dial it back a notch."

Abby wanted to punch him and his clients in the throat, but instead she mentally counted to ten. "Let's take a breath. I get you all have lots of emotions around what should happen to the family business, and I want you to process all of those, but we have some hard decisions to make, and the more willing you all are to give a little, the more likely you'll all be able to walk away with something other than hurt feelings. Okay?"

Before any of them could answer, Graham burst through the door. "I'm sorry," he gasped, clearly out of breath.

Abby wanted to be mad, but she couldn't remember ever seeing him look anything other than perfectly composed. "What is it?"

"The blogger. I saw her on the news over the weekend, and now she's in the parking lot. The Bride's Best Friend. It's really her, although I suppose it could be anyone because no one knows who she really is, or at least they didn't until now."

He wasn't making any sense. "Take a breath." She glanced over at Sam and the twins who were looking impatient. "Who's outside?"

"The Bride's Best Friend. She's a wedding blogger. Very well known. *Best Day Ever* carries her blog. She was at the downtown Barclay's on Thursday, and since then her video has gone viral on YouTube." He dropped his voice, and said, "I sent it to you yesterday through your Leaderboard account."

Her stomach sank with the realization she was behind the curve. She'd seen the red dot alerting her to a new message, but she'd ignored her social media accounts in favor of prepping for this meeting. Her only solace was that the Barclays didn't seem to know about the video. She turned back to Graham. "So, what's going on now?"

"Now she's out front with a bigger crowd, and news crews are everywhere. They're blocking the door and the crowds are getting bigger by the minute."

*Crap. Crap. Crappity crap.* Abby fixed a determined smile on her face for Sam and the Barclays, but what she wanted to do was slink out the door. Her first instinct was to call the cops to clear out the lot, but with the press camped outside, she knew cops showing up to put would-be brides in handcuffs would be a public relations nightmare. "How bad is the video?"

"It's compelling."

Ugh. Were those tiny tears at the edges of Graham's eyes? She pushed away the thought. She couldn't afford to feel sorry for these women over what was essentially a few yards of fabric. "Let's see it."

He pursed his lips and slowly handed over his phone. Abby scrolled to the Leaderboard video app and started to punch play, when Campbell appeared in the doorway.

"Hey, I was just mobbed by a bunch of women in the parking lot," she said. "They have signs and everything."

Abby shoved Graham's phone back in his hand. "I got this. Save that." She pointed at the phone. "For evidence of what sent me over the edge." She waved at Tommy. "I'll be right back."

She strode out of the conference room ready to do battle when she remembered there were cameras trained on the front door. She paused for a second and fixed a determined smile on her face, ready to dispatch the crowd with poise and grace. She swung open the door and was temporarily blinded by the sunlight. When her vision finally cleared and she was able to focus, her determination lasted about three seconds.

Standing not six feet from her was Roxanne. She was turned slightly away, but Abby knew it was her. She was dressed to the nines and she looked amazing. Roxanne had been gorgeous in casual resort wear, but today she looked like she'd stepped from the pages of a fashion magazine, camera ready and perfectly coiffed. The only thing wrong with her was that she was holding a microphone.

"You deserve to have your special day be everything you planned it to be," Roxanne said to the veiled woman standing in front of her who merely nodded sadly in response. "You deserve justice."

"I do," the woman replied, her voice tentative at first then followed by a firm, "I do."

"Of course you do," Roxanne said, nodding eagerly. "All of you do. Don't you?"

It started slowly at first with just a few voices, but then the chant grew. "I do, I do, I do."

"You do what?"

A loud chorus of "I do deserve my special day!" answered her back.

Abby barely suppressed a groan. This was the cheesiest display of protest she'd ever seen. A bunch of women wearing makeshift wedding veils chanting "I do." Seriously?

"Isn't that her?"

Abby heard the voice, but she didn't register the woman shouting the question was talking about her until the crowd pivoted in her direction. She purposefully made eye contact with the women in front in an attempt to dispel the notion she was some big, bad lawyer out to steal their dreams. When she was satisfied she'd connected with the leaders of this assembly, she turned and faced Roxanne head-on. "What are you doing here?"

## Chapter Nine

R oxanne walked through the parking lot of Clark, Keane, and Maldonado, certain she was about to break an ankle and wishing she'd ignored Stuart's choice of shoes. She loved her a high-heeled designer shoe, but this was her first official foray into the world of TV, and she wasn't keen on breaking a limb on camera. Frankly, she should've spent more time researching this law firm rather than her wardrobe, but this whole fiasco had been Stuart's idea for her debut before the *Best Day Ever* cameras.

When she reached the front door, she was surprised to see how many brides-to-be were already assembled—the number had quadrupled since her viral video from Friday. Maybe Stuart was on to something. She had to admit there was definitely a synergy about meeting her readers in person, and as if to prove her point, the women started crowding around her.

"You're the BBF, aren't you?"

"I've been reading your blogs since before I even met my fiancé. You have such good advice."

"Way to show up for your peeps. We're counting on you to lead the fray."

Whoa, wait. Roxanne felt the big smile she'd been wearing a moment ago start to collapse into a frown. She wasn't here to be a participant, only a documentarian. She wasn't a gossip columnist bent on whipping up a frenzy to garner ratings, and now was the perfect time to clarify her role.

"Ladies, I'm here for you. To document and report your stand here today and make sure your voices are heard, but the protest? That's all you. Don't let anyone take away your power, including me. If you want to confront the attorneys who are earning big bucks to help Barclay's ruin your special day with their careless disregard for your life plans, then you should do that on your own. What better way to impart your message than with the most personal of touches. Am I right?"

She looked across the parking lot, dismayed to see the cameras rolling. Stuart had agreed she could have some time to find her footing before they started shooting for real. She probably should've clarified exactly how she would convey that she was ready to film, but she supposed jumping right in wasn't the worst idea.

"Hey, there's one of them now," one of the women shouted, motioning to the area across the parking lot. Roxanne turned in the direction she was pointing and immediately spotted a beautiful woman wearing a business suit, headed directly for the front doors of the law firm. Determined to get this over with as quickly as possible, Roxanne rushed to her side.

"Good morning, my name is Roxanne Daly, but you may know me as the Bride's Best Friend or BBF. Do you have anything to say to these lovely brides-to-be who've been left without dresses on the eve of their special day?"

The woman offered a hesitant smile as she edged away. "I'm afraid I can't help you out, but best of luck to your bridal posse." And just like that, she was gone. Roxanne watched the door to the firm close behind her as the on-scene producer, Jake Tillson, came over to stand beside her.

"I think you're going to need to be a little more aggressive if we're going to get some good footage," Jake said.

She dropped her voice to a whisper. "This isn't really my thing."

"Being on camera or getting in people's faces?"

"Both. The camera I can get used to. I'm looking forward to getting in front of a whole new audience, but the aggressive part doesn't exactly scream happy wedding blogger, in my opinion."

"I guess, but this show isn't going to sell itself. You need a hook, and your willingness to stand up for brides who've been ripped off is a good one. Without an advocate, the only resource these women have is to hire lawyers of their own who'll take even more of their money. Imagine how good it will feel to help them cut their losses and suit up for their special day."

Roxanne nodded while she contemplated his assessment. He was right, of course, and what better use for this platform than to provide real, concrete assistance to the women who'd been loyal readers for the long haul? She glanced around to take in the situation. Brides to the left and the law firm to the right with the Barclay family inside, plotting their next move. Time to bridge the gap in whatever way she could.

The door to the law firm opened and she nudged Jake's arm. "Start rolling. We might have good footage on the way." She waved at the crowd of brides and motioned toward the front of the law firm, smiling when they started up the "I do" chant again. She started walking toward the door, shoulders squared, ready to do whatever it took to show *Best Day Ever* she had what it took to dominate the wedding market, but she was barely three steps into her march when she stopped dead in her tracks at the sight of Abby standing in front of her with her hands on her hips.

"What are you doing here?" Abby asked.

Roxanne's heart beat faster and her eyes locked on Abby's kissable lips pursed into a frown. She wanted to ask the same thing, but words failed her as she had apparently lost the ability to speak or string together complete sentences. She motioned to Jake to stop filming, but he merely shook his head. Exasperated, she turned away from him and stepped closer to Abby. A rush of heat swept between them, but she told herself it was Abby's obvious anger fueling the fire and not the simmering attraction that had once been full boil.

"I could ask you the same thing," she said.

Abby's eyes narrowed. "This is my office. I belong here." She gestured toward the crowd. "Are you really with these people?"

Roxanne slowly digested the tidbit of information. Abby worked here. At this office. Was she? Could she be? She had to know. "You represent Barclay's? Say it isn't so."

"Don't pretend you didn't know."

Roxanne crossed her heart. "Swear. I had no idea. How would I? No shop talk on the island, remember?" She watched as Abby's eyes darkened the way they had when they'd made love. *Made love.* Roxanne shuddered and reframed the thought. They'd had sex. Excellent, mind-blowing sex, but that's all it had been. "If you'd called, maybe we could've talked about current events, like how your clients are ruining the hopes and dreams of hundreds of women on the eve of their special day."

Abby cocked her head, looking puzzled for a second before her angry face returned. "If I hear the words 'special day' one more time, I'm going to blow. Exchanging jewelry, eating cake, and dancing the night away may make for a great party, but it doesn't mean anything beyond that, especially when the percentage of couples who don't actually make it far outweighs those who do. This"—she gestured again, but wildly this time to encompass the entire crowd—"this is a big show designed to convince people that if they spend enough money, they can guarantee future happiness, but the only guarantee they can really get is that they'll wake up the morning after, legally bound to another person who probably doesn't look as shiny and new anymore once they're out of the wedding day spotlight."

Even through her anger at Abby's tirade, Roxanne saw the pain in Abby's eyes, and she almost forgot where she was and what she was doing long enough to pull Abby into her arms and hold her until the hurt subsided. But the camera was rolling, and her big break depended on turning moments like these into TV gold. Could she be that heartless? She looked over her shoulder and saw that the camera was still trained on them and every one of the BTBs was listening in.

"Excuse me, ma'am?"

It took a moment, but the authoritative voice shook Roxanne from her dilemma. She looked up to see a policewoman standing beside Abby with a firm expression. "What seems to be the problem, Officer?" she asked, unable to resist the easy line.

"Do you have a permit to be demonstrating on this property?"

*Damn.* "I think you already know the answer, but just for the record, I do not."

"Wait here, I'll be right back." As the officer walked away, Roxanne leaned in close to Abby. "I can't believe you called the police."

"Really? You can't believe that a place of business, one that isn't nor ever has sold bridal dresses, might not want to be mobbed by a bunch of angry brides."

"Brides-to-be."

Abby waved her off. "Whatever."

"Don't whatever me. It makes a difference. Some of these women have been planning their…" she paused and then spoke with emphasis, "*special day* for a very long time. Just because it doesn't mean anything to you doesn't mean it's not meaningful to them. Are you going to say that it's just a dress? Because your clients have made their living off those dresses. But I guess they no longer care about the Barclay's brand." She clipped off her words as the cop walked back over.

The cop pointed at the cameraman. "Obviously, you can be here to report on this, but I don't think any one of us wants a scene, and these women don't have permission to be here. Maybe you can do something to get them to move off this private property?" She lowered her voice. "I mean you're the BBF, right?"

Roxanne smiled brightly at the officer. "Yes, ma'am, I am." She thought fast. "I might be inclined to ask these women to move if I could get an exclusive interview with the attorney for Barclay's." She turned to Abby and offered an even bigger smile. "What do you say, counselor?"

❖

After she hustled the Barclays and Sam out the back door, Abby met Grace and Wynne in the conference room where they didn't waste any time grilling her about her encounter with Roxanne.

"Why exactly did you agree to an interview with a gossip columnist?" Grace asked.

"She's not a gossip columnist," Abby said, knowing she wasn't really answering the question.

Grace folded her arms and shook her head. "Seems fraught with danger to me."

"Don't say words like 'fraught.' It makes you sound like a little old lady."

"Don't change the subject. I'd expect a crazy idea from Campbell, but you're usually not this impulsive." Grace glanced at Wynne who'd been sitting quietly up to this point. "Sorry."

Wynne shook her head. "Don't tone things down on my account. It's going to be really awkward working for you all part-time if you have to worry about how I'll react any time you mention Campbell."

"Who's mentioning me?" Campbell stuck her head in the door. "Are we having a meeting about the crazy wedding blogger and her herd of dressless brides?"

"Brides-to-be," Abby said before she caught herself. She saw Campbell arch an eyebrow. "Never mind. The point is we've got a problem." She hesitated, but then decided it would be better to come clean now rather than later. "Make that two problems."

Campbell held up a finger. "Problem one."

"Problem one is these women aren't going away," Abby said. "The twins hired Sam Thedford to represent them and they are prepared to fight. They aren't budging on keeping the stores closed, which leaves Tommy without a lot of options short of going to court to try to force them to act, and I don't like our odds."

"Okay, we can discuss some other options. What's problem two?"

Abby paused. There were so many reasons why she didn't want to share how she knew Roxanne. Embarrassment topped the list, but an underlying motivation was a desire to keep private the intimacy they'd shared back in fantasyland. If she talked about it now, all her happy memories would be sullied by the real world and the conflict facing them right now.

But this was the real world and she owed her friends the truth. "You have to promise not to react." She waited for a second as they all nodded. "Okay, so the BBF? She's the woman from Puerto Vallarta."

"Private beach woman? Sexy, private beach woman?" Campbell exclaimed. "You weren't kidding when you said she's gorgeous. What are the chances she'd be leading a protest at your office?"

"Slim, but apparently the odds were stacked against me," Abby replied.

"Well, this seems easy," Grace said. "You have the perfect in to ask her to back off. Invite her to dinner, reconnect over a couple of martinis, and smooth her over. You got this."

Abby nodded, wishing it were that easy. Martinis made her think of drinks, and for a second, she daydreamed she was back on the beach with Roxanne sipping fruity, umbrella-laden beverages while soaking up the sun and each other.

But they weren't on the beach anymore. This Roxanne was the one who'd left the resort, leading her to believe she was going home when in fact she was headed somewhere else on the island to have fun, probably with another unsuspecting tourist. "Yeah, I don't know."

"Come on, Abby," Campbell cajoled, swiping away Wynne who was shaking her head. "It'll be fine. I don't know anyone more persuasive than you when it comes to pleading a case. Just get her to tone things down for a bit until you get things worked out between the Barclays. I predict the women will have their dresses in no time and everything will be back to normal. You never know, maybe you and the BBF can hook back up where you left off post-paradise."

Abby started to let the assumption stand, but she just couldn't. "Things didn't quite end on a happy note." She paused for a second and then pressed on. "Roxanne was only at Azure for a few days. When she left, I thought she was headed home, but apparently, she had other rendezvous planned in PV. I saw her at the airport when we landed back in Austin."

Campbell nodded. "Okay, so you assume she left you to have a play date with someone else?"

"I don't know." Abby felt silly for bringing it up. "I guess."

"Later we'll talk about why you're suddenly caring that a fling flaked on you, but right now you need to be all business and do some damage control. You got this?"

Ugh. Now her friends thought she was upset because Roxanne had effectively dumped her. *But aren't you?* She shoved away the thought. "Fine. I'll give it a go, but I don't want her to think this is a date. Because it's not. Whatever happened in PV isn't happening here."

"Fine, Ms. No Commitment," Campbell said. "Get Graham to set up dinner like it's a work meeting."

"You know if you post the fact you're having a meeting with her on Leaderboard, your ranking is going to skyrocket," Wynne chimed in. "The BBF is hugely popular right now."

"For precisely the wrong reasons," Abby said. "I don't need to feed that beast. She's churning out plenty of bad publicity for Barclay's all on her own. The last thing I need her to do is turn her focus on us."

"Looked to me like her focus was already on you," Grace said. "But I agree. Keeping your meeting under wraps is a good idea. At least until you know what direction it's going to take. There's that new place on Sixth, lots of secluded booths. Get Graham to pull some strings and get you in there tonight."

"Anyone else want to micromanage my evening?" Abby asked, her tone harsher than she meant it to be, but for real this whole conversation was wearing her out. The prospect of sitting across a table from Roxanne was enough to send her over the edge, but the pressure of keeping her cool about being blown off in PV and then ambushed back at home had her pretty riled. "Sorry, I know you're just trying to help. I think I need a few minutes to decompress." She edged toward the door. "I'll be in my office if you need me."

Once she was in her office, she took a few deep breaths and fired up her computer. Everyone else seemed to know the BBF, and it was time she did too. Her first search returned dozens of hits, and she scrolled through the results, taking in the tidbits as they displayed on her screen. According to her self-penned bio, Roxanne had gotten her start working the social beat at KNOP. After a stint covering a bunch of high-profile weddings for the news outlet, she was inspired to use what she'd learned to start a blog about weddings in general with a focus on offering advice to brides looking to maximize their time and money for the greatest effect. Her blog went into syndication last year and had been picked up by *Best Day Ever*'s online content division.

Abby checked out *Best Day Ever*'s website. The front page boasted teaser clips for the upcoming premiere of a new cable program by the same name on the GAL network, starring none other than Roxanne Daly. That explained Roxanne's desire to whip these brides into a frenzy. All that drama made for excellent television and would no doubt drive up *Best Day Ever*'s numbers.

Well, no matter what they'd shared in PV, if Roxanne thought she was going to ruin her reputation or Tommy's over a bunch of whiny brides who didn't get the dresses they wanted, then she was in for a big surprise.

## CHAPTER TEN

Roxanne stepped out of the car and took a ticket from the valet. Abby had certainly picked a fancy place. Of course, it was possible Abby didn't have anything to do with the choice; perhaps that overly formal, ultra polite guy who'd called from Abby's firm had made the reservation. Either way, this place screamed date, and Roxanne wasn't sure how to take that.

She didn't understand why Abby hadn't called her since they'd gotten back home. It was possible she'd imagined the connection they'd shared, but she didn't think so, and if the smoldering look Abby had given her this afternoon when she thought she wasn't looking was any indication, then she was probably right. But something was holding Abby back, and she intended to find out what it was before they finished their "meeting" tonight.

"Sorry I'm late."

Roxanne turned around to find Abby standing behind her, looking stunning in a fitted pinstripe suit, and she was struck by the fact that Lawyer Abby was as beautiful as Beach Abby. The only thing wrong was the frown on her face. "It's okay. I just got here. Are you that unhappy to see me?"

"What? No. I'd like to talk to you, and I thought it might be better to do it here than in front of a bunch of women ready to stab me with their empty dress hangers," Abby said.

"I want to talk to you too," Roxanne said, injecting a trace of desire in her voice. This might be a business meeting, but she wished it could be more. It was hard to tell in the waning light, but Roxanne was pretty sure Abby blushed. Maybe Abby was happy to see her after all. The thought gave Roxanne hope and she decided to capitalize on it. "Then let's get a table so we can do just that. Is the reservation under your name?" She started walking toward the hostess stand.

"Yes, but—"

"But what?" Roxanne said, on the move. "But here in the real world, you're used to taking the lead? But you changed your mind and don't want to have dinner with me? But you wish you'd picked a place that wasn't this romantic?" She smiled to soften her interrogation and strode up to the hostess before she lost her nerve or Abby could respond. Maybe Abby didn't really want to have this meeting, but even if it was the last time they saw each other, they needed some kind of closure, and she needed a chance to explain why she'd had to leave their idyllic paradise so abruptly.

"Table for two. We have a reservation. Abby Keane." She turned back in time to see Abby raise her eyebrows. "Yep, now I know your last name and all kinds of other tidbits that Google was willing to offer. Tell me you haven't done the same."

"Right this way," said the hostess, saving Abby from having to respond. Roxanne followed her across the restaurant to a cozy booth tucked into a secluded spot, hyperaware that Abby was mere feet behind her. Lit candles bounced sweet shadows along the sides of the booth, giving off a warm ambience. The hostess stepped back to let them in before handing them menus.

"Our specials tonight include glazed duck and a chateaubriand for two—"

"We're good, thanks. If you could let our server know I'd like an extra dirty martini and a…" She motioned to Roxanne who nodded. "Make that two. Thanks." Abby's words were clipped, but the hostess handled the brush-off with grace and glided back to the front of the restaurant.

"That was a little abrupt."

Abby pointed to the inside of the menu. "The specials are printed right here."

"I seem to recall you enjoying having the specials read to you."

"That was vacation, this is a business dinner. A lot has changed since we were at Azure."

Roxanne took a breath to keep her temper down, but Abby was really pissing her off. This brusk woman was not at all the same person she'd shared a bed with in PV. "I can see why you needed a vacation. Your job must be really stressful."

"What?" Abby shook her head. "My job is fine. I help protect people from other people who want to steal their dreams."

"Hmmm, sounds like we're in the same line of work."

"Hardly. Your job is to stir things up to increase your readership. Apparently, it's working, because word is you're getting your own show. Congratulations on your upcoming debut."

Roxanne started to argue, but there was some truth in Abby's statement. Plus, she didn't want to argue. She wanted to find a way past this and back to the Abby who drank fruity drinks and plowed her way through breakfast buffets. "I guess you looked me up too. Was it just so you could better represent your clients, or can I hope that some small part of you wanted to see me again?"

"I think you're forgetting how this went down. You're the one who slipped away in the early morning without a word about where you were going. I didn't know your last name, where you lived, or what you did for a living. For all I knew, you never wanted to see me again."

The waiter appeared with their drinks, saving Roxanne from having to answer. She watched as Abby sipped her martini and gave a tiny moan of pleasure. She'd missed watching Abby experience pleasure, but not enough to put up with her being a jerk for the rest of the evening. They both ordered, and when the waiter left, Roxanne launched in. "I want to explain something about PV."

Abby waved her off. "Nothing to explain."

"Sure there is. I didn't want to leave, but I'd never planned to stay the full week. I was there on a work trip and had two other resorts to review. I had hotel and restaurant reservations that could not be rescheduled. I should've told you from the start, but we'd agreed not to talk about work or anything to do with the real world." She crossed her hands on the table and sighed. "When you didn't call, I figured you were mad. I wanted to explain at the airport, but you rushed off."

"Wait a minute," Abby said. "That's the second time you've mentioned me not calling. How was I supposed to call you? A, I didn't know your number, and B, I didn't know your last name, and C, I didn't have a clue where you were."

Roxanne grinned. "Do you always argue in outline form?"

Abby narrowed her eyes as if she was trying to figure out whether she was teasing, and then burst into a laugh. "Probably. Occupational hazard."

"Fair enough. I have only one answer. I left my number on the bookmark in the novel on your nightstand. I figured since you'd have a lot of free time on your hands you'd probably be reading and that might be the first thing you'd see."

Abby laughed again. "Except after a few nights of incredible sex only to be abruptly dumped, reading a romance novel was the last thing I wanted to do. I shoved that book in my suitcase and haven't looked at it since. You mean we could've been having phone sex the rest of the week?"

Roxanne returned the smile. The banter between them felt good, and natural, and familiar, and she didn't want it to end. "Absolutely. And it would've been hot. Not as hot as in person, but definitely steamy." She waved her hand in front of her face to ward off faux flames.

"You know, *you* knew exactly where I was. You could've called me."

Roxanne stared into Abby's eyes, surprised and happy to see the vulnerable, tender woman she recognized from the resort. She liked the in-charge version of Abby, but she suspected the softer version was one not many people got to see, and she treasured the trust. "You're absolutely right, and if I had it to do over again, I definitely would've called. Hell, I might've quit my job just for a few more days on that beach with you."

The admission slipped out before she could stop it, but once she'd said the words, she had no regrets. She liked Abby. She liked her a lot. She might have bungled things back in PV, but now they were home and she had a second chance. And this was better because if they felt the same way about each other here, then it was more real and had more possibilities. Possibilities she was ready and willing to explore.

"We did have fun, didn't we?"

Abby's tone was wistful, and Roxanne took a ray of hope that maybe tonight could be the start of something more.

Their food came and it was like they'd never been apart. Abby stole food from her plate, and she pretended to fight her for every forkful. They ordered another round of drinks and relaxed into the careless comfort of the evening. When the check came, Abby insisted on paying and handed her card to the waiter, and they bantered about life in Austin and how strange it was they'd had to travel to another country to run into each other for the first time. Then Abby circled back around to the reason for their meeting.

"I was kind of a jerk to you about the whole bride thing. I get it's just your job, and you don't really have a choice."

Roxanne rolled the words over in her head for a few minutes. Something about the way Abby tossed off the "it's just your job" phrase bothered her, but she should just let it go. Right? Why ruin a perfect evening over semantics? Before she could stop herself, she said, "Well, it's not just my job and I did have a choice."

The waiter brought Abby's credit card with the receipt and set it between them, but neither one acknowledged him, as their eyes were locked. Abby broke the connection first. "I didn't mean anything by it. I just meant, it's not like you're one of those whacko brides, excuse me, brides-to-be, unable to let go of the fact they might have to be flexible about what to wear on their *special day*." She added air quotes to the last two words.

"Who are you right now?" Roxanne asked, unable to contain her frustration. "Never mind. I know who you are. You're Career Abby. I was just having dinner with Resort Abby and I'd like her back, thank you very much."

"You're hilarious," Abby said without a trace of mirth in her voice.

"How about you? I swear for a little while here I thought you really were the sensitive woman I met in PV, but now I'm thinking Career Abby is the real you and the whole laid-back vibe you were giving off was only an act to get women. Could it be your problem with all this wedding nonsense, as you call it, is that you're scared you're never going to have one?"

Abby tossed her napkin on the table. "I have absolutely no desire to get married, and I don't need to do anything to get women." She leaned in closer. "Believe it or not, you're not the first fling I've ever had."

Roxanne resisted the urge to recoil at the clear smackdown, but her insides went hollow and she wanted to slink away. She stood quickly, desperate to put as much distance as possible between them. "Well, the fling is over, and I couldn't be happier about it."

Abby gave the valet a generous tip and roared her engine out of the parking lot. Instead of smoothing things over as Grace had suggested, she feared she'd only stirred things up not just between her and Roxanne, but internally as well. Sitting across from Roxanne without completely lapsing back into vacation mode had been hard enough, but watching Roxanne stalk off was even harder.

And Roxanne's reaction to her declaration that she never planned to marry? She'd practically deflated. Seriously? What was it with everyone being so sappy about weddings? People like Roxanne pumped up everyone's expectations, and no good could come of that. Did she really buy into the hype?

If she did, then they were better off not getting involved. Too bad, since Abby had held out hope when things were going so well at dinner that maybe they could resume vacation mode back here in the states.

When she got home, she parked in the garage and wandered into her condo. Even though it had been months since she'd moved from Dallas, she still hadn't quite finished unpacking except for the important stuff like her books and her clothes. She poured a glass of pinot noir and wandered over to her bookshelf where she found the book she'd abandoned reading in PV in favor of real life romance. Sure enough, Roxanne had scrawled a number and her name on Azure stationery and left it with the bookmark in what should've been a prominent, easy to find location. Underneath, she'd written "just in case." Now it seemed like an afterthought, a souvenir of a wonderful time that was over and done, leaving only a hazy memory in its wake.

She shoved the book back onto the case and flicked on the TV. She needed something to distract her thoughts. Something to fill the void. What she found was way more than she bargained for.

"The Bride's Best Friend and local lawyer clash, but is their heat full of anger or sparks signaling something more? Turning now to our correspondent in the field for her take on the altercation at the offices of Campbell, Keane, and Maldonado early today."

Abby watched as the reporter gave a blow-by-blow of the scene outside her office this morning followed by an interview with the BBF herself where Roxanne talked about how important getting the perfect dress was to the brides-to-be assembled in protest. Pretty one-sided stuff.

Damn. She'd really blown it by not taking better advantage of the opportunity to spin the situation for her client. The twins likely didn't care, since they just wanted out from under the crushing debt of Barclay's, but this was Tommy's world. As much as she didn't care about wedding stuff, he did, and it was her job to protect his interests.

Abby considered calling the reporter to see if she could get her own exclusive, but she was kind of annoyed the reporter hadn't reached out to her in the first place, which indicated she had her own angle to spin. She took a sip of wine and contemplated her options. Everyone at her old law firm would've cautioned her to stay quiet, not to rile the press and let the story blow over, but part of why she, Grace, and Campbell had started this firm was to take a different approach, custom designed for each of their clients. She knew Tommy well enough to know he would want to tackle this bad press head-on, but the reporter was only a conduit. She needed to go directly to the source. Before she let caution scare her off, she reached for the book on the shelf, fished out the bookmark with Roxanne's number, and fired off a text. *Nice interview. Score one for BTBs. How about equal time with the other side?*

Smiley face. *Didn't expect to hear from you...so soon. Equal time, huh? Want the phone number for KNOP?*

*Actually, I was hoping to get some time with the famous BBF. Perhaps get her to see my point of view. Starting with an apology for going off at dinner.*

*Hmmm. Maybe we can work something out. What do you have in mind?*

Abby paused with her thumbs over the keys as she pondered the open-ended question. She could almost see the lopsided grin on Roxanne's face as she typed. So many possible responses. She started to suggest a one-on-one live interview with her and possibly Tommy but decided to take a smaller bite for now and go from there. *Let's start with a tour of Barclay's flagship store and see where that leads.*

A moment passed. A really long moment during which Abby regretted not going bigger. She'd banked on the hope that Roxanne wanted to see her again badly enough to take a baby step, but that had been silly really since they'd passed the point of baby steps when they'd hopped into bed together back in Puerto Vallarta. She started to toss her phone to the side in the hope that ignoring it would elicit a response and, like magic, just as she let go, it buzzed in her hand.

*Does tomorrow work?*

Abby stared at the screen, tempted to wait a while to respond. Silly, really when she'd been the one to suggest the meeting. Besides, she wasn't used to holding back when she saw something she wanted. Before she could overthink it, she typed her reply. *Absolutely.*

That settled that. She set the phone down and took a deep drink from her wine, enjoying the warm glow of alcohol reaching through her veins, hoping it would relax her. Now she had a plan. So why did she feel so completely unsettled?

## Chapter Eleven

Wednesday morning, Roxanne pulled up to Val's house and parked in the drive. Dan, Val's fiancée, walked out the front door as she walked up the steps. "Hey, Dan, how's it going?"

"Great, Roxanne. I'm off to try on tuxes." He spread his hands across his abdomen. "I'm thinking powder blue cummerbund. Maybe a glitter bowtie. What do you think?"

She blew him a kiss. "You'll look great no matter what you wear."

"From your lips to Val's ears." He pointed back toward the house. "Heads up, your mom dropped by. This is your last chance to get away."

Roxanne knew he was joking, but everyone in the family, Dan included, was well aware that her mother didn't understand why she spent so much time writing about weddings instead of planning her own. She was constantly explaining she hadn't met the right person yet, to which her mother replied, "You never will if you're always working." She wondered what her mother would think of the way she'd met Abby. Of course, her mom would be so focused on the fact that Abby was a successful lawyer, she wouldn't care about anything other than getting them down the aisle.

"Thanks for the heads up," she said. "I think she's feeling a little left out of the whole process."

"I'm sure that's it." He forced a smile. "It's just one day, right? We just have to find a way to make our own dreams come true and please both our families and loved ones and serve the best damn cake money can buy. We got this."

"I promise you do. Everything will go off without a hitch, and if it doesn't, you'll have great stories to tell your grandkids."

"Slow down there, missy. I don't even have a tux yet."

"Better go take care of that then." She shooed him toward his car and made her way to the door which opened as she approached. A moment later, she was swept up into Val's arms and Val leaned close to her ear.

"Save me. Do it now."

She leaned back and nodded. Mom time was taking its toll. "On it." She strode past Val into the house and went directly to Val's room where their mother was inspecting the clothes in the closet.

"Val, you need new things for the honeymoon. None of these things is proper attire for a special resort."

"Mom, leave her alone. If the wedding goes well, she shouldn't need any clothes for the honeymoon."

"Hush your mouth, young lady." Her mother grinned as she spoke, and she and Val joined her in a good laugh. "She'll at least need to show up wearing clothes. Whatever happens next is between her and Dan."

"Can you two stop talking about my sex life?" Val asked. "You're creeping me out."

"Fine," their mother said. "But good thing Roxanne is here. She should be able to tell you exactly what to wear since she just got back from one of those swanky resorts."

"Three actually," Roxanne said. "It was a bit of a whirlwind, but my editor loved the article. It'll run with a full spread in next month's *Best Day Ever*."

"Meet any cute girls on your trip?"

"Mom, leave her alone."

Roxanne held up a hand. "It's okay, I got this. Mom, I was working. You know, activity that puts food on the table and a roof over my head. Everything's not about finding my soul mate."

"Your soul mate is not going to appear to you in a beam of light projected from the heavens. She's going to appear when you least expect it to steal your heart, but you have to be open to the possibilities if you don't want to miss out." She gestured widely. "She could be anywhere."

"When you put it that way, it sounds kind of spooky."

"Don't make fun."

"Sorry, Mom." Roxanne felt a twinge of guilt for lying to her mother, but since the alternative would result in an interrogation and insistence on meeting Abby as soon as possible, she got over her guilt pretty quickly. "I'll keep an eye out for Miss Soul Mate. I promise."

Her mother stared hard like she was trying to figure out if she was lying and then nodded once in an exaggerated motion. "Now help your sister pick out her clothes while I go fix you both something to eat."

Roxanne started to say she wasn't hungry, but her mother was out of the room before she could reply. As soon as she was out of sight, Val grabbed her arm.

"Didn't you want to tell Mom about your fling at Azure? Maybe I can fill her in on your behalf."

"Don't even think about it. I think the rulebook clearly states that if you talk about a fling, it's no longer a fling."

"Okay, so it's no longer a fling. What do you want to call it?"

"No, wait. I was just saying…You know."

"That it wasn't a fling. I heard you. What's her name?"

"Ugh. Abby. Not that it matters."

"Abby." Val nodded slowly. "Name's good. Now tell me why it's no longer a fling."

"I didn't say it wasn't." She paused, not entirely sure she wanted to share more, but it felt weird not to divulge to Val. "It's just we met up again, but it's an impossible situation."

"How so?"

"Let me see, where I should start. First of all, she's made it perfectly clear she is not interested in a relationship."

"We knew that going in."

"We?" Roxanne play-punched Val's shoulder. "And second, did you see the segment on KNOP yesterday?"

"Sure."

"Did you happen to notice the footage of the hot but temperamental attorney?"

Val whistled low. "That was her?"

"Indeed."

"The anchor was playing it like you two were a thing. And there were definitely sparks."

"Yes, the kind when you hit metal with a sledgehammer. Trust me, there's nothing happening. Not anymore at least."

"What's the matter? Your vacation rendezvous is too much for the real world? Seriously, Rox, she's super hot."

"You mentioned that." Roxanne sank onto the bed. "She's exactly the person I thought she was before our first 'date.' Not remotely interested in anything other than a few causal nights in paradise."

"Then do her again and get it out of your system."

Roxanne shook her head both to signal a no and to try to banish the image of Abby naked in her bed. "I never should've 'done her' in the first place. I knew she wasn't for me."

"You're allowed to have fun on your quest for your soul mate." Val used air quotes around the words "soul mate."

"Does Dan know you're making fun of his undying love for you?"

"It's not that I'm making fun. It's more of a reality thing." She handed a ruffled blouse to Roxanne. "Grandma gave this to me last year. Hide it before mom decides I should be wearing more ruffles." She sat on the bed next to Roxanne. "Is Dan the guy I want to spend the rest of my life with? Absolutely, but the whole idea of a soul mate, someone destined to complete you and fit together in every way is a bit more than I can wrap my head around. That's not only daunting, it's pretty impractical. I mean, what if you never meet this person? Say, you're supposed to meet them on a plane, but your connecting flight gets delayed? What's fate telling you then?"

"It doesn't work like that," Roxanne said. "I'm pretty sure if you're destined to be with someone, the universe isn't going to give you just one slim chance to meet them."

"Then maybe you should start paying attention to the fact the universe has just thrown you back in contact with hot lawyer lady."

"Don't call her that, and this has nothing to do with fate. Trust me. If it did, then she wouldn't be such a hater when it came to the idea of relationships. She clearly only wanted a few nights on an island. Running into me again, under these or any circumstances, wasn't part of her plan at all."

"Maybe. Doesn't matter. Maybe you'll meet someone at the wedding. Weddings are perfect for finding soul mates. The ceremony gets everyone all dreamy-eyed and looking for romance. Plus, there's cake. Can't really beat that for a perfect atmosphere. Didn't you write an article about that?"

"I did indeed. A woman even replied that she started crashing weddings in an attempt to find the love of her life, but I'm not entirely sure the idea came from me. It's a pretty well recognized trope, but it doesn't apply in this case since I'll be way too busy at your wedding making sure you have everything you need for your…" Roxanne paused as her tongue tripped over the word "special," and she quickly adjusted. "For you to have a seamless day." Okay, so maybe "special day" was overused, but that didn't mean Abby had to mock her for it. Weddings were special days and there was absolutely no reason to apologize for that fact. When she saw Abby, she'd tell her that to her face. A quick look at her watch warned her that would be soon. "Val, I've got to go."

"But Mom's fixing lunch."

"As tempting as it is to eat whatever giant sandwich she's whipping up, I'm going to pass. You know how they say the camera adds ten pounds? Well, double that. Besides, I can't bear to hear more about how unlucky I am in love." This was the perfect time to tell Val she was on her way to meet up with Abby, but instead she held back, unsure why. "Give me a shout if you run into trouble. Love you." She called out the last two words as she was on her way out the door, bypassing their usual hug for a quick getaway.

As she drove away from her sister's house, she focused on telling herself that her rush had more to do with avoiding her mother than eagerness to get to the Barclays' store where Abby was waiting.

❖

Abby paced the lobby of Barclay's flagship store wondering if Roxanne was standing her up. Being casual about appointments had been the custom in Puerto Vallarta, but she'd expected that when Roxanne was back in the real world, she'd be back to a routine that involved keeping appointments and being punctual. Abby knew she was being an ass, but she had every right since, unlike PV, this wasn't a vacation—it was her client's livelihood.

A few minutes later, she nearly jumped at the sound of a rap on the glass door and turned to see Roxanne standing on the sidewalk outside. Abby took a moment to assess the woman leading the charge against her client. Dressed in well-worn jeans, an Austin City Limits T-shirt, and dark Ray-Bans, Roxanne looked more like one of the hipsters who hung out on South Congress than a social media bully. All Abby had to do was ignore how hot she was, and she could crush her campaign against Barclay's like a bug. She breathed deep and opened the door. "Come on in."

"Thanks." Roxanne touched the door as she walked in, grazing Abby's fingers. "I appreciate you meeting with me."

Abby focused on not reacting to the tingle that swept up her arm at Roxanne's touch. "And I appreciate you not showing up with cameras and a bevy of brides-to-be."

"Bevy?" Roxanne grinned. "How long did it take you to come up with that line because it sounds like you practiced it."

Abby couldn't help but return the grin. "Maybe I'm just going for your level of alliteration, Ms. BBF. It seems to work for you."

"True. Although I never expected it to work this well."

Abby wanted to ask her what she meant, but it felt awkward to get into a big discussion standing in the lobby of the store. "How about I show you around and then we can talk?"

"Sounds great. You lead, I'll follow."

Abby heard a suggestive tone but chose not to respond in kind. This was a professional meeting, an opportunity for her to sway an influencer to have sympathy for her client. If she was successful, then maybe it would take some of the heat off of the business long enough for Tommy to either work something out with the twins or to close the deal with the investor who was funding his online business. If she wasn't, then Tommy and the twins would probably spend a lot of money in court battles, which would generate fees for her firm, but might cause them to lose future business from Tommy down the road. He wouldn't be hiring lawyers for his new business if he lost it all on this litigation. The key for today was focus. If she let her libido take over, she'd lose her edge.

"I don't know how much you know about Barclay's history, but this is the flagship store and it was opened by Alice and Mike Barclay when Tommy, their oldest son, was in first grade. The entire family worked in the store. The kids put in hours before and after school, helping with inventory and waiting on customers. Alice and Mike put their hearts and souls into making the experience of selecting and purchasing bridal gowns an intimate and custom affair for every bride-to-be who walked through their doors.

"About five years ago, they were approached by investors who had noticed the success and wanted to start a chain of stores to go national. The Barclays were reluctant at first. Barclay's Bridal had always been grounded in providing a personal experience, and Alice and Mike weren't certain they could maintain the same level of service on a large scale, but after a ton of research and assurances from the investors that they would not interfere with the basic business model, they agreed to the financing as long as the company remained privately owned."

"Interesting," Roxanne said. "Of course, I knew this Barclay's has been around forever, but I didn't know how they got into the national market."

"Are we off the record?" Abby asked. "For real."

Roxanne crossed her heart. "Promise."

"It was a mistake."

"Really? They opened a ton of stores. I figured they were doing great."

"It's almost impossible to replicate personal service like the kind they provided their customers on such a large scale. They were successful at keeping the same attention to detail when they expanded within Texas, but it just didn't translate nationwide. Too many different markets with different expectations, and they ran into issues where they were competing with stores who offered the same kind of personal experience they'd created here, but now they were the big box store coming in to dull the experience. Customers who weren't familiar with the brand automatically assumed they couldn't or wouldn't offer the same personal touches, and their attempts to show them otherwise were viewed as pushy and overbearing."

"Sounds like they had a messaging problem."

"Definitely. And the investors' solution was to push them to purchase expensive ad buys, when what they should've done was utilize as many free and low-cost alternatives like social media and influencers, like you, as they could reach."

"I remember last year Barclay's had a huge spread in *Best Day Ever*," Roxanne said. "That must've cost a fortune."

Abby nodded. "It's hard to know how to stop the bleeding. This place was Alice and Mike's dream, and when they died, it was their legacy. I think the twins would've sold on the spot, but Tommy was raised right here in this building. He used to do his homework in the office in the back and, as a teenager, he made deliveries and helped with the books. He's built his entire adult life around the wedding industry, and if you ruin him in the court of public opinion, you'll be thwarting not only his dreams, but his parents' legacy."

"No pressure there." Roxanne shook her head. "You make it sound like it's my fault your clients decided to shut their doors and deny these women who paid for the dresses they counted on. What about their hopes and dreams?"

"Tommy is doing everything he can to make good on their agreements, but if all this publicity keeps ramping up, then his only option is to walk away. Nobody gets their dresses, nobody gets their money back, nobody's dreams come true. Is that what you want?"

"What exactly do you want me to do?"

Abby prayed Roxanne was asking because she really wanted to help, and she adopted her most earnest and imploring tone. "I want you to drop this story. If the BBF moves on to some other topic, everyone else will too, including the women who are lining up to protest. Give me some cover, and I'll do my best to work things out so that we find a compromise that suits everyone."

Roxanne bit her bottom lip, a sign Abby recognized as her thinking face. When had she started to pick up on such subtle clues, and what did that mean? She pushed the thought away. It didn't mean anything other than they'd spent time together and it was only natural to start to notice things about each other. Like the way Roxanne's new hairstyle accentuated her eyes. And how her jeans hugged her hips in the sexiest way possible, which made Abby want to tug her right out of them, and...

"Okay."

"What?" Abby wasn't sure she'd heard.

"Okay. I'll give you some cover, but I can't promise I'll hold off for long."

Relief swept through Abby. "Thank you. You won't regret it." Abby took Roxanne's hands in her own. "How about dinner on me? You pick the place this time."

Roxanne eased out of her grip and stepped backward, her expression unreadable. "Uh, that's okay. I'm really swamped right now. Let's talk later." She started walking toward the door. "Thanks for the behind the scenes."

Abby watched her go, barely resisting the urge to follow. What just happened? It was like she'd made a connection, managed to get Roxanne to see things her way, but then Roxanne took off like she couldn't wait to get away from her. She should be happy, she'd gotten what she wanted out of this meeting, but all she felt was empty.

## Chapter Twelve

R oxanne rushed into the lobby of *Best Day Ever*, late for her meeting with Stuart to go over notes for the pilot. She was bent on bypassing Sylvia, the steely receptionist, but she was a mere two steps from the elevator when Sylvia called her name. She watched the elevator doors close and turned back to the desk where Sylvia was waving a hand, urging her to come back.

"I'm late for a meeting with Stuart. Do I need a hall pass to ride the elevator now?"

Sylvia cocked her head. "Hall pass?"

Roxanne shook her head, not remotely interested in explaining the reference. "Never mind. What do you need?"

Sylvia shoved a vase of flowers across the desk. "These came for you."

The arrangement, centered around a bird-of-paradise, was gorgeous, simple and elegant, and Roxanne's first thought was that Stuart had sent them as a congratulations on the upcoming launch of the show. She took the vase and wandered over to one of the tables scattered throughout the lobby, set it down, and tore open the envelope.

*Thanks for the meeting. The dinner invite is open. Call me whenever.*

She stared at the arrangement, and it took her back to Azure where there had been a bird-of-paradise on Abby's deck that they'd both admired. She reread the card and recognized Abby's handwriting from the many times she'd scrawled it on checks for incidentals at Azure, which meant Abby had taken the time to select the flowers herself, a thoughtful touch that spoke volumes. Roxanne tapped the card against her hand while she processed her mixed reaction.

Since she'd scrambled out of Barclay's earlier, she'd been second-guessing her decision to turn down Abby's dinner invitation, but she couldn't help but think Abby had only made the gesture as payment for her agreement to lay off the whole give the brides their dresses chant for a bit. And maybe she shouldn't have agreed to lay off the story since her objectivity was clearly in question.

She felt a tap on her shoulder and looked up to see one of the juice girls from her last meeting. Myra or Mira—something like that. "Hey, we're waiting for you upstairs. Are you coming?"

"Yes, sorry." She stood and contemplated what to do with the vase of flowers. It looked nice on the table where it was, and for a moment, she considered leaving it there since it would be easier than explaining why she was toting around a big bouquet. But as she started to turn away, she was drawn back to the flowers—a sweet, thoughtful gesture on Abby's part. Roxanne summoned her inner diva and shoved the vase toward juice girl. "Please find a place for these until the meeting is over. I can find my way upstairs on my own. Thanks."

Stuart gave her a slow clap as she walked into the room, and she could feel the burn of a blush start to creep across her face. "I guess you were happy with the footage so far," she said as she took her seat across from Stuart and Jake.

"Beyond happy. It's a fantastic start. The chemistry between you and angry lawyer lady was off the charts, and I can't wait for you to stoke some more of that for the camera."

"About that." Roxanne cleared her throat to give her time to think. She should've anticipated his reaction and prepared a response, but she hadn't so it was time to improvise. "I think we should broaden the story and take a look at some other stories of wedding-related business closings across the industry and how that impacts a bride's ability to plan. Talk about the importance of having contingencies in place for every situation."

Stuart closed his eyes. "Snoozefest," he uttered between snoring sounds.

Roxanne smiled to cover a strong desire to smack him. "I promise we'll make it interesting. I have some ideas."

Stuart exchanged a look with Jake who barely hid a slight eye roll. "I'm sure you do," Stuart said. "But so do we. Trust me, TV is not the same as print. You can take your time building a story on your blog, but you'll have one hour to sell this story, this entire show." He started snapping his fingers. "Things are happening fast and now. We have to plunge right in and riff off what works. And when something is working, we capitalize on it, we don't back away. You feel me?"

She did and she didn't like where it was going. "Yes. I, uh, feel you. But the blog has never been about me. I'm the Bride's Best friend. You know, the offstage helper who makes sure things go smoothly, but never steals the spotlight from the star of the show—the Bride. If you start to make the story about me, it changes everything."

"Welcome to showbiz. You are the star. Our test group ratings for the segment are well beyond expectations, and their comments say they want to see more of you clashing with what's her name, so we're sticking with that."

"Abby," Roxanne muttered under her breath.

"What?"

"Nothing." No sense giving him fuel for the fire. "Tell you what. I'll write up the next segment with a small piece to follow up on the dressless brides, but then we pivot to my idea about contingency planning. If you hate it, we'll regroup. I'll get you the script tomorrow." She flashed him a big smile. "I promise I know how to get my readers to transition into viewers. You can trust the bride's best friend—she'll never let you down." She nearly gagged at the sickly sweet tone, but the satisfied look on Stuart's face told her it was working.

"Fine. We'll meet to go through it tomorrow. If anyone even looks like they're dozing during the read, we're back to my plan."

"Deal. Anything else?"

"Yes. I've booked you on the morning show circuit for later in the week." He pointed over her shoulder, where juice girl suddenly appeared as if she'd teleported from the lobby. "Mira will get you all the details. And, Mira, she's going to need more clothes and shoes. Lots of shoes. Nothing sensible, no matter what she says." Stuart turned back to Roxanne. "Don't think I didn't notice you wobbling in those Jimmy Choos. Practice at home if you want, but brides want their best friend to have impeccable fashion sense. Do you feel me?"

She suppressed a groan both for her feet and his continued lame attempts to sound hip. "Oh, I feel you all right."

"Great." Stuart started toward the door. "I'm out of here. I've got a photo shoot with the star of that new prime time talent show, and believe it or not, she's as difficult to manage as they say." He placed a finger over his lips. "Shh, don't tell anyone I said that."

He was gone before she could reply, but she doubted he cared what she had to say, which was turning into a theme here. Oh well, she hadn't expected her rise to stardom to be easy, but she'd had enough for today. She stood to leave, but Mira tapped her on the arm.

"Ready to go to the fashion closet?"

She should be. Who wouldn't want to explore all the runway fashion money couldn't buy? But she didn't want to do it with Stuart's lackey in tow. "I'd love to, but I have an appointment across town. How about tomorrow?"

"I guess that would be okay."

"Hey, Mira, you get to decide what's okay. Stuart put you in charge of my new look, right?"

Her eyes lit up. "Right. Tomorrow it is."

"Perfect." She walked to the door, turning back right before she left the room. "Oh, and, Mira?"

"Yes?"

"I'm bringing my sister, Val, along to help with my wardrobe. You'll get her a visitor's pass, right?" She followed her question, not really a question, with a strong stare while she nodded her head. One, two, three seconds passed, and then Mira started nodding too.

"Of course. Leave her name with Sylvia."

Roxanne grinned as she waited for the elevator. She might be a small star, but apparently, small stars were bright enough to get benefits, and she may as well make the most of it.

Abby looked up at the knock on her office door to find Graham standing ramrod straight at attention. "At ease, Graham. What's up?"

"There's a woman on the phone. She asked to speak to you, but I told her you were not to be disturbed."

"Yet here you are disturbing me."

"I'm sorry, but she was cryptic, and I thought it might be best to consult with you before dismissing her outright."

"What did she say?"

"She wouldn't give her name, but she said to tell you thanks for the flowers. And then something about tiny umbrellas. I believe it might have been code."

Abby laughed. "Go ahead and put her through." Graham disappeared quickly, and a moment later Abby saw the flashing green light telling her she had a call waiting. She'd spent the last few hours wondering if she'd made a mistake sending flowers to Roxanne. It wasn't like she'd never sent flowers to a woman before, but they'd always been whatever the bloom of the day had been, never anything personal or referencing a shared experience. She wasn't sure what had possessed her or why she was so hell-bent on getting Roxanne to have dinner with her. She told herself it was so she could continue to plead for Barclay's case, but she suspected it was more than that, and her suspicions signaled danger lay ahead.

She punched the button and picked up the line. "BBF? I have a question."

"Shoot."

"Is it acceptable to have a cash bar for the reception?"

"Hmm. That's a sticky one. I completely understand the desire to limit costs, but do you really want your guests to have to remember to stop by the ATM on the way to the wedding? If you want to serve alcohol at your wedding, make it as seamless as possible. If cost is an issue, offer only beer and wine or a signature cocktail, and then they can pay if they want to order off menu."

"Are you always this prepared with spontaneous answers to wedding related questions?"

"Well, it's kind of my job, so yes."

"I like a woman who's good at her job," Abby said, and then winced. "Sorry, that didn't come out the way I intended."

"Would you like to explain what you really meant? Perhaps over dinner?"

Abby sighed with relief. "I'd love to. I know a really good place down near South Congress, and I bet I can get a table on the fly. Shall I pick you up at seven?"

"Actually, I was thinking of something a little more low profile. Like Chez Roxanne. It's not fancy, but I can promise there won't be any BTBs or press around."

Abby took a second to register that Roxanne was inviting her over. To her house. Just the two of them. Was this some kind of thinly veiled method of recapturing what they'd shared in PV? The prospect excited her, and she answered before she let her natural instinct to shy away from this kind of intimacy take over. "Sounds perfect."

"Great. Give me your cell and I'll text you the address."

"Can I bring anything?"

"Just you and your appetite."

When they hung up, Roxanne's words lingered. Abby had an appetite for sure, but she wasn't thinking about food. She spent the rest of the afternoon pretending to work when she was really daydreaming about the evening ahead. Negative billable hours later, she'd made little headway in her work when Grace and Campbell showed up in her doorway.

"We're quitting early," Campbell said. "Come with us to Charlie's. Partners meeting."

"Can't." Abby pointed at her computer. "I have to finish this research."

"Says who?" Grace asked. "Your boss? Because last time I checked, that's you."

"Exactly. And if I don't do what I say, then I don't get paid. Seriously, you two go."

Campbell marched over to her and stood in front of her computer. "Nope. We're a team. If you don't bring home the bacon, none of us get to eat."

"And now all I can think about is a BLT. Thanks for that."

"Happy to help." Campbell grabbed her bag and held it just out of reach. "Come on, we can brainstorm ideas together."

Abby considered for a moment. It was four o'clock and she wasn't supposed to be at Roxanne's place until seven. And she really could use Grace and Campbell's help. One drink plus three brains thinking together might equal a plausible solution to help Tommy out. "Okay, I'm in, but only for one drink and I'm taking my own car because I have to leave by six thirty. I have a thing."

Grace winked at her and nudged Campbell. "She has a 'thing.' Looks like Abby's back in business. Now I can live vicariously again. You and Wynne with your coupled-up coziness aren't doing it for me anymore."

"Speaking of Wynne," Abby said, "Is she around? I was going to ask her about some of this research."

"She's meeting her parents for dinner to talk about her dad's case. I offered to come with, but we both figured he might feel more comfortable not having this talk in front of the girlfriend."

Abby nodded. Wynne had shared with them that her parents were grifters and her dad had been arrested a few months ago for working at an illegal gaming room in town. "I get it." She looped her arm through Campbell's. "So, it's the three of us on the town for happy hour. Perfection."

The bar was crowded, but Campbell, who knew someone everywhere they went, managed to coax the hostess into letting them sit at one of the tables that was marked reserved. They slid into their seats, and Abby asked, "What did you say to her?"

"I merely explained that empty tables made the bar look like a dud of a place, and people who were cool enough to have reserved tables weren't going to show up this early. We warm the seats and bail before the VIPs arrive and it's a win for everyone." Campbell waved at a cocktail waitress passing nearby and they ordered a round of their usual drinks, which appeared at the table with lightning speed.

Abby raised her martini glass. "Here's to early bird VIPs."

Grace and Campbell both said "I'll drink to that" at the same time.

After the toast, Campbell set her tequila on the table. "I'd like to call this meeting to order. First item, Barclay's. Ms. Keane, you're up."

Abby cleared her throat. "We've got a problem. The twins are refusing to budge on reopening the stores, and every day that goes by with the stores closed is damaging Barclay's reputation and value."

"Does Tommy really want the stores reopened?" Grace asked.

"Yes. Maybe. Kind of." Abby took another sip of her martini. "He definitely wants to stay in the industry, but he gets that brick-and-mortar may not be where it's at anymore. He's got an investor lined up to fund a new online wedding dress enterprise that combines the best of both worlds with easy back and forth shipping for custom fits and virtual tailoring. But what he wants in the short-term is to reopen long enough to satisfy Barclay's existing obligations to try to keep his reputation intact. If Barclay's is synonymous with ruining everyone's 'special day,' then any new business venture is dead before it starts. The twins are convinced it's a trick, and once he gets them to reopen, they'll start incurring even more debt."

"What's your plan?" Campbell asked.

"Wynne and I think our best shot is a minority shareholder oppression suit. Basically, we say that even though the twins have the majority interest, they acted in bad faith by calling a shareholder meeting when they knew Tommy wouldn't be around to argue his case, and we ask for an injunction, allowing for some limited reopening long enough for Tommy to take care of any customers with a current order." Abby noted their skeptical expressions. "Long shot, I know, but Tommy wants to go for it, and if nothing else, it shows he's trying to do the right thing."

Campbell, ever the optimist, raised her glass. "To brides and their dresses."

The three of them toasted. "I think this might be the best martini I've ever had," Abby said, munching on the edges of one of the blue cheese stuffed olives.

"A good warm-up for your date," Grace said

"It's not a date."

"But I thought you said…" Grace scrunched her brow like she was mentally replaying the conversation. "Now that I think about it, you were purposefully vague. If it's not a date, then where do you have to take off to?"

"I'm having dinner with Roxanne Daly." She waited a beat, but neither Grace nor Campbell seemed to click. "The Bride's Best Friend."

Grace turned to Campbell. "Sounds like a date to me."

"Me too." Campbell ticked points off on her hand. "It's dinner. They've had sex before. And it's preplanned. Yep, it's a date. Do you think we need to caution her about fraternizing with the enemy?"

"Yes," Grace said, "But I should be the one to do it since you fell in love with the competition last time this was an issue." She swiveled in her chair until she was staring right at Abby. "Be careful. I know things were wonderful when you two were in paradise, but Roxanne's got a job to do just like you do, and the juicy story is to keep all those brides whipped into a frenzy."

"Please. I got this. You two can sit here and ponder my personal life all you want, but I'm headed out to perform some very important public relations with a blogger to keep her from trashing our client." Abby swallowed the rest of her drink and stood. "Business. Meeting." She ignored their knowing smiles and left the bar.

It was a perfect night for driving with the top down and she took full advantage, enjoying the way the breeze blew through her hair, and telling herself if this really was a date, she'd be more concerned about arriving carefully coiffed than enjoying the ride. She arrived in minutes and found Roxanne's place was a charming little house with a cute front porch. She put the top up on her car and walked to the door, suddenly wishing she wasn't showing up empty-handed, but she quickly pushed the thought away as too date-like. This was a business meeting. Business. Meeting.

When Roxanne opened the door, any pretense at business was swept away. She wore a midnight blue floral print maxi dress with a really high slit up the side, and Abby fumbled for words. "You look amazing, but I thought we were staying in."

Roxanne reached for her arm and tugged her inside. "We are, but there's no reason not to look nice, am I right?"

"You are indeed right, but I'm afraid I didn't get the memo." Abby looked down at her own outfit. "I came straight from a meeting with my partners and didn't think to change out of my lawyer drag."

"You're perfect." She led the way farther into the house. "After seeing you in a swimsuit and then nothing at all in PV, it's fun to witness the other side of you. If you'd told me then that you wore a business suit every day, I'd never have believed it. You were the consummate resort rat."

Abby wanted to respond, but she was stuck on the word naked, and for the first time she could remember, words failed her. Instead she sniffed the air. "Is that dinner? It smells amazing."

"Yes, there's been a bit of a battle, but I'm hoping I won the war."

They walked into the kitchen. It was small and cozy, and every available surface was covered in pots and pans and bowls. Roxanne wrinkled her nose. "A mess, I know, but the recipe called for no less than a million ingredients, all cooked separately. Things got a little out of hand."

Abby laughed. "Thank God. By the smell of things, I figured you were secretly a gourmet chef and I wouldn't be able to pronounce anything we were having."

"I confess I'm more of a drive-thru gal, but I spotted this recipe for duck confit risotto in this month's magazine, and it sounded amazing. Apparently, this is a dish the bride-to-be should make to impress her new in-laws."

"Are you trying to impress me?"

Roxanne play-swatted her with a spatula. "Maybe. If you don't die from my cooking, I expect you to be fully impressed."

Abby peeked under the lid of one of the saucepans. "It doesn't look deadly. Actually, it looks amazing."

"Do you cook?"

"Not at all. I do have every restaurant delivery app there is, but a home cooked meal is a special treat. Are cooking tips part of the whole wedding blogger thing?"

"Hmmm. I'm guessing you haven't checked out my blog."

Abby raised her hands. "I have actually, but you have a lot of posts. Most of what I saw had to do with the day itself, not deep background."

"You don't know the first thing about weddings, do you?"

"I know some. My mom's about to have her fourth. In my experience, there are flowers and cake and bridesmaids and rings. I'm sure there's more to it, but that's more than I ever wanted to know."

Roxanne handed her the spatula and motioned for her to stir the vegetables she was sautéing. "And here you are, having dinner with a wedding blogger."

"More than a blogger now. You're going to be a TV star."

"Star? Hardly."

"How did you get into it? I mean I read about how you covered weddings and social events when you worked for KNOP, but have you been married before?"

"Me? No."

"Was that such a strange question?" Abby asked.

"No. I mean yes, but you're not the first person who's asked. Here's the deal, I'm not sure being married really qualifies anyone for being an expert on weddings. I mean that's like saying because I ate out at one restaurant, I can be a restaurant critic. I learned a lot about engagements and weddings, covering both for the news, and I don't mind saying I was one of those little girls who used to think about having my own big, beautiful, fairy-tale wedding someday." She pointed at the vegetables Abby had stopped stirring. "Those are done if you want to put them in that bowl. Since we're on the subject, what made you decide to become a lawyer?"

"Lots of time spent at lawyers' offices with my mother while she worked out the terms of her many divorces?" Abby watched for a smile on Roxanne's face, but all she saw reflected back was surprise and maybe a little pity. "Sorry, that was crass, but it's not far off the mark. My mother is a serial bride, but no matter how many times she tries, she doesn't get any better at it."

"The allure of the wedding is strong." Roxanne grinned and pointed to the cabinet near her head. "Why don't you grab a couple of plates and some wine glasses. I have a nice pinot noir breathing, but I can open something else if you have a preference."

"Pinot sounds great." Abby shrugged out of her suit jacket and hung it over the back of one of the dining room chairs, rolled up her sleeves, and reached into the cabinet to grab the dishes. She maneuvered around Roxanne and made her way to the far counter and poured them each a glass of wine before taking a sip. "This is delicious." As she handed Roxanne her glass, she was suddenly struck by how very domestic this whole situation was and how it felt...nice. No, it was way better than nice. She'd never spent time with a date cooking dinner, and there was something very easy and comfortable about the whole experience.

Date. There was that word again—it just kept popping up. She took another sip of wine and brushed away her concerns. This wasn't the first or last time she'd have a business meeting with food. Get over it.

"Are you okay?" Roxanne asked. "You look like you're deep in thought."

"Would it be weird if I said I wished we were back in Puerto Vallarta?" Abby blurted out the question before she could think, not realizing until she spoke the words that she'd even been thinking about PV.

"No. Azure was the perfect spot."

"The resort was nice, but I wasn't talking about that."

Roxanne put down the knife in her hand and stared intently into her eyes. "I know."

"You could've told me you were there for work."

"Maybe I should've. It just seemed strange. I'm used to being totally anonymous when I review venues, and after you were so adamant about being anti-wedding, announcing what I did for a living seemed like it might be a huge buzzkill." She stepped closer and purred the next words. "And I didn't want to kill the buzz."

Warmth coursed through Abby's body at Roxanne's declaration, and flashes of her naked blurred her ability to think about dinner or Barclay's or even her own name. She reached her hands around Roxanne's waist and leaned in close. "The buzz? It's still going. It hasn't stopped. You make me crazy."

"How hungry are you?"

"Pretty damn hungry, but dinner can wait." Abby captured Roxanne's lips in her own and moaned with pleasure at the familiar feel of her mouth. "You taste so good."

"You. You do," Roxanne murmured. "Wait here and don't move."

She eased away and Abby watched her deftly flick off all the burners and turn the knob on the oven to warm. A second later, Roxanne was at her side again. "This way."

Abby's head swirled. She shouldn't follow Roxanne because she was here for business, but she had no choice. She hadn't been lying when she told Roxanne the buzz had never gone away. It had been a low hum in the background ever since she'd returned from PV, distracting her with its temptation. She would give in eventually—why not go ahead and get it out of her system? Then she could focus on her job and her client. It was just sex and she'd done this dozens of times before with other women whose names she didn't even remember. That Roxanne's name and face were firmly implanted in her memory was a small obstacle in the path to pleasure and she wasn't about to let it trip her up.

## CHAPTER THIRTEEN

From the moment Abby had walked through the door, Roxanne had been off-kilter. In a good way. If she'd had doubts about inviting her here, they'd been swept away while she watched Abby roam around the kitchen in her go-to-court suit, being all domestic and stuff. The juxtaposition was hot, and all Roxanne could think about was the time they'd spent together in PV and how much time they'd wasted since.

She paused in the hall and looked back, locking eyes with Abby. The air between them was smoldering, but was it enough for Abby to follow her all the way? She held out her hand and waited. One, two…On three, Abby stepped closer and grasped her hand, raising it to her lips. Within seconds, they were locked in an embrace, hands roaming over each other's bodies, all the first date jitters lost in the familiarity of knowing each other's bodies so well.

"So many clothes," Roxanne gasped.

"Definitely different than beachwear."

"We could remedy that." Roxanne ducked her head to get a good look into Abby's eyes. "If you want."

"I want." Abby's answer was quick and steady.

"Good, because it's all I've thought about since I had to leave you in PV."

Roxanne instantly wished she hadn't made the declaration out loud for fear she'd scare Abby away. She started to qualify the declaration, but Abby placed a finger over her lips.

"Me too. But it's different now. Better. No surprises, no expectations." She ran her hand up under the seam of Roxanne's blouse and whispered into her ear. "Right?"

"Right." Roxanne spoke the words without considering what Abby meant because the way Abby was touching her blocked any ability to process thought. She arched into Abby's touch and submersed her prior hesitancy in a big vat of feels good right now where all she cared about was being naked and being with Abby, and nothing was going to get in the way.

"Bedroom?" Abby asked, her voice a ragged whisper in her ear.

Roxanne answered by taking her hand again and leading her down the hall, relieved she'd straightened every room in the house in anticipation of Abby's visit. *You hoped this would happen.*

It was true, she had. Business dinners were for restaurants, not in her house with home-cooked meals abandoned on the stovetop. But when it came to Abby, business and pleasure were all jumbled up in one big ball of I-should-be-asking-her-questions-but-I-just-want-to-rip-off-her-clothes. It was useless—she'd lost all sense of control. Roxanne looked up into Abby's eyes, which had gone from caramel to deep, dark brown. Abby, the high-powered attorney, was clearly used to being in control, directing the action, getting what she wanted. Okay then. She'd give Abby what she wanted, but she was going to be the one in control tonight. "Take off your clothes."

Abby's eyes went even darker, and a slow smile spread across her face. Roxanne sat on the edge of the bed and watched while Abby slowly unbuttoned her blouse. When it hung loose and open, she reached back and unzipped her skirt and let it fall to the floor. Roxanne sucked in a breath at the sight of Abby standing in the middle of her room, wearing nothing but a jet-black, sexy matching set of bra and panties, but she resisted letting arousal rush things along. "All of your clothes," she said.

Abby complied, even slower now, each movement a delicious but excruciating delay. When she was finally completely naked, Roxanne crooked her finger and motioned her to the bed. "Lie down."

Abby complied, easing around her to lie back against the pillows, deliberately brushing her leg along the way. Roxanne shuddered at the touch. She was so turned on right now, but determination to remain in charge kept her from giving in to the desire to fall into Abby's arms. She inched out of Abby's reach and pulled her dress up over her head and dropped it to the floor, enjoying the gasp of pleasure she received in response. Abby reached for her, but she caught her wrist and tugged Abby's arms above her head while she bent down to take Abby's breasts in her mouth, one after the other, over and over, lavishing them with her tongue until Abby writhed beneath her and began to beg. "Feel how wet you make me."

Roxanne slid her hand down and ran a finger along Abby's thigh, deliberately skirting the space between her legs, trailing it back up her abdomen. Abby quaked beneath her. "Do you want me to touch you there?"

"Please, yes."

Roxanne heard the raw need in Abby's voice, and her resolve to stay in control started to slip. She wanted nothing more than to give Abby the release she sought, and her own body thrummed with the need to give in to the pleasure they both craved. Pretending she had the power to resist the pull of Abby's allure was nothing more than an act, and she decided in that moment control was overrated. She captured Abby's lips between her own and slid her fingers into her wet, hot center, determined to make her come again and again. Her last thought before she gave in to Abby's desire was crystal clear. Abby had captured her heart from the very first night.

❖

Abby shot awake and scrambled to sit up in bed. Instinct told her something was wrong, but it took a moment for her to realize morning light was peeping through the blinds, so she'd either forgotten to lower her blackout shades or she wasn't at home. She squinted at the mahogany footboard of the sleigh bed. She didn't have a footboard and she definitely didn't have anything as sentimental as a sleigh bed. This meant trouble. She patted the space next to her, and her palm touched silky hair which, once her eyes adjusted to the light, she could see was fanned out on the pillow beside her. *Damn.*

Last night had been amazing, and she'd enjoyed every second she and Roxanne had spent exploring each other's bodies, but she'd never meant to stay over. Staying over was the kind of thing that girlfriends or people trying out for the role of girlfriends did, and no matter how great the sex had been, this was not that.

*You didn't mind sleepovers with Roxanne when you were on vacation.*

Abby couldn't deny her inner voice was right, but she wasn't on vacation anymore. This was real life, and she'd already broken too many of her standard rules. She looked around for something to tell her the time and spied an old school digital alarm clock on the nightstand just inches from Roxanne's head. Seven a.m. If she hurried, she could sneak out before the sun fully illuminated her departure. She eased back the sheets and gently swung her legs over the side of the bed, wincing at the creak of the springs.

"Are you trying to make a break for it?"

Abby froze in place at the sound of Roxanne's groggy but very much awake voice. "No. I mean, I should go. Because work and stuff." Damn. Way to be articulate. She turned so that she was facing Roxanne, completely unprepared for how the sight of her naked body tousled in the bedsheets might weaken her resolve. "I had a great time last night."

Roxanne reached over and wove her fingers through hers. "Me too. Do you really have to go or are you just scared if you don't, I'll make more out of this than you intended?"

Abby wanted to lie and give some plausible reason why she needed to rush off. The possibilities were endless. An early court setting, a meeting with a client, but she couldn't manage to pull together the strings of a lie when Roxanne so clearly deserved the truth. She settled on a singular admission. "I'm sorry."

Roxanne raised her hand and kissed it softly, trailing her lips up to Abby's wrist. Abby sucked in a breath as the tug of arousal held her in place.

"There's no need to be sorry. I'm a big girl and I know where things stand. It doesn't mean I don't want to spend the rest of the morning continuing where we left off, but if you really have to go, it's all good. Either way, I'm not going to freak out on you."

"Now I feel like a real jerk."

Roxanne pulled her closer and ran her hand up the side of her waist. She let it linger for a moment just under Abby's breast, teasing a finger back and forth in super slow motion. Abby could feel her chest tighten and the air in the room constrict. Twin needs—escape and surrender—fought for dominance, and she wasn't sure which to cheer on.

"You don't feel like a jerk to me. You feel like maybe you're not quite ready to leave."

Roxanne barely got the last words out before Abby pulled her into a kiss. A hot, searing kiss that was supposed to sate her, but instead it merely stoked the fire. She stroked Roxanne's tongue with her own until she was forced to pull back for air. When she caught her breath, she said, "You might be the best kisser. Ever."

"You are," Roxanne said between gasps. "It's like we've kissed a thousand times before. Like we practice on the daily. Like we're world kissing champions vying for the title."

Abby laughed. "Can't we both win?"

"I guess, if we're playing for the same team. Or maybe we just tie."

Abby ran a finger along Roxanne's breast. "Oh, I think we're playing for the same team."

"Then let's play."

Abby leaned back against the bed frame. She didn't have any early meetings. She didn't have to be in court. She was her own boss. If she wanted to stay and fool around with Roxanne all morning, there was nothing stopping her. The only reason she had for leaving right now was to keep Roxanne from thinking this was something more than it was, but she'd already said she didn't.

Too much thinking was threatening to dampen the mood. Time to enjoy the here and now and not worry about how either of them would feel later today, tomorrow, or when they next faced off over Barclay's. "Yes, let's."

## Chapter Fourteen

Abby strolled into the office at two p.m., feeling absolutely no guilt about spending the better part of the day naked in Roxanne's bed. She smiled and waved at Graham. "Happy Friday, Graham. What's shaking?"

"Campbell and Wynne are waiting in the conference room as you requested. Will you be needing refreshments for your meeting?"

Abby considered telling him they would like tea and crumpets but worried he might take her seriously and spend the afternoon scouring the city to find legit crumpets. "No. Thanks though. As always, your attention to detail is most appreciated."

She stopped by her office long enough to stow her purse, and then headed to the conference room where she strode through the door and announced, "I've decided what we need to do," but stopped short when she spotted Campbell and Wynne hastily hiding something on the table.

"What's up?" she asked, surprised at the guilty expressions they both wore. "You look like you're plotting world domination. Or did Campbell make another extravagant purchase for the firm? What's going on?"

Campbell stood and scooted over making it impossible for Abby to see what was on the table behind her. She crossed her heart. "No world domination in the works, and no extravagant purchase. Not for the firm, anyway."

Abby maneuvered to try to see what Campbell was hiding, but Campbell kept shifting to block her view. After a couple of seconds of this, Wynne gently pushed Campbell to the side. "We have a confession to make," Wynne said. She reached behind Campbell's back and held up a stack of magazines. "We've become obsessed with all things wedding."

Abby stared at the stack of bridal magazines in Wynne's hand and then at her friends. They were wearing big smiles, and it was pretty clear reading bridal magazines was something they were actually enjoying rather than an onerous by-product of client representation. It took a full minute, but finally the puzzle pieces fell into place. "Oh, wow. You're getting married?"

Campbell's smile faded. "Try not to act like we just told you the world was ending."

"It's not." Abby fumbled for words. "I mean, I'm happy for you. That's exciting news." She forced a smile, hoping it looked slightly authentic and searched her mind for how normal people would respond to such news. "Who proposed? How did it go? When's the big day?"

"Wynne surprised me with a ring in a box of Kate's donuts," Campbell said. "Remember how I said I thought she had a lot on her mind lately? Well, apparently, asking me to marry her was top of the list."

"It's true. Everyone thinks Campbell's the big romantic. I wanted to show her I've got moves of my own." Wynne set the magazines back on the table. "We haven't set a date yet. We're in the very early stages. And this is not the way Campbell wanted to tell you."

"Have you told Grace yet?" Abby asked, wishing Grace were here because she would know what other questions a person was supposed to ask in this situation.

"Nope," Campbell said. "I was planning a thing to tell you both at the same time."

Knowing Campbell, the "thing" was going to be some grand reveal, and now Abby had completely blown it both by discovering them planning and by her less than enthusiastic reaction. She summoned reserves of empathy and pulled Campbell into a hug. "I'm sorry I spoiled the surprise. I'm a big jerk, but I'm happy for you both." She winked. "I bet I can get you a nice discount on a couple of wedding dresses."

Campbell punched her in the arm. "You're a normal-sized jerk, but I forgive you." She pointed to the magazines. "You know, the BBF has a lot of great ideas about weddings. Maybe you should keep her around so we could use her as a consultant."

"About that…I may have spent the night with her."

"May have?"

"Okay, I did."

Campbell turned to Wynne. "Abby's not a stay the night kind of date."

"Hey!"

"I speak only the truth. I'm just trying to give Wynne some context."

Abby sighed. "She's right. There's something about her though."

"I know exactly what it is," Campbell said.

"Spill it, wise one."

"It's the lure of the forbidden. You know that nothing can come of it, so it's perfectly okay to take risks."

Wynne placed her hand on Campbell's arm. "Honey," she said with a warning tone.

"It's okay," Campbell said. "She knows I'm right. It's a vicious cycle. BBF is off limits for anything more than a hook-up because she's trying to take down Abby's client, but the fact that she's off limits makes the idea of being with her even more exciting. There's really no risk because neither one of them can get involved. The brides-to-be would turn on BBF if they knew she was sleeping with the lawyer of the company that stole their dresses, and Tommy and the twins would have a fit if they knew Abby was giving it up for the other side."

Abby stood frozen in place as Campbell's words landed like sharp darts penetrating the armor she wore to protect her heart. Was Campbell right? Was she that predictable and that much of a player? Pre-PV, she would've proudly worn that badge, but something about the way Campbell was describing her now made her feel empty and shallow. When had things changed? Or was she merely so wrapped up in all things wedding that she viewed her own cynicism through a different lens?

She closed her eyes for a second and relived this morning. Not the part where she tried to sneak away before Roxanne woke up part, but the part where Roxanne had made pancakes and they'd sat naked in bed, scarfing up every last bite before one more round of sex. The time they'd spent had been like the mornings they'd shared in PV, and completely at odds with her usual fare. The truth was she liked this better, but admitting it out loud called into question so many facets of her life, she wasn't ready to go there for fear her entire sense of self would come tumbling down. Besides, if Campbell was right, Roxanne probably wasn't any more interested in anything more than casual sex either. Why should she put herself out there if there was nothing to gain from doing so?

"You're right, as usual," she said. "Nothing to see here except sex so wild I fell asleep from the exertion before I could drive home." She forced a laugh. "She did agree to back off the story long enough for us to make some progress with Barclay's, plus she's going to interview Tommy to give some perspective to the story. My goal is to get her to do the interview and tease it on her blog before we get a hearing on the injunction on the minority oppression issue. I've got the motion almost ready to go."

"Hmm," Campbell said. "Have you ever handled one of those before?"

"No, but I bet your fiancée has," Abby said and they both looked at Wynne.

"I have. Once. They're not common and they aren't usually successful." Wynne inclined her head. "But you've got the right facts to support it. You've got an inherited family business and the majority shareholders are reluctant owners. They didn't include Tommy in the decision to close the stores, and shutting down the way they did is causing damage to his reputation and affecting his ability to form another business." She folded her arms and nodded. "With all the bad PR Barclay's has been getting, we won't have any issues proving harm. It's as good a case for minority shareholder oppression as I've seen. If nothing else, filing a suit, may get the twins to see reason and settle. What does Tommy want out of all this?"

"Ideally, he would like the stores to reopen and undergo some kind of reorganization, but he doesn't have the resources to sustain the stores under the current circumstances. The big thing is retaining his reputation. It might be too late to keep the existing stores open. If you were a bride looking for a dress, would you go to Barclay's?" Abby laughed. "I guess you two are uniquely situated to answer that question now."

"We're so not there yet," Campbell said. "And quit bringing up wedding plans in front of Wynne because she's already mad at me for blowing the big reveal."

"Only because I know how much you wanted it to be a thing," Wynne said. "My parents got married in front of the justice of the peace when I was seven. I have no perspective when it comes to all things wedding."

"You will," Campbell said. "Trust me. I got this."

Abby watched them gaze into each other's eyes and resisted her usual eye roll at any overt show of emotion, especially the lovey-dovey kind. Was everyone but her wired like this? Even her mother, who had every reason to believe that relationships would never work out, kept up her quest for the perfect man, the perfect happily ever after. Why couldn't she muster a glimmer of hope for the same?

Her phone buzzed with a text and she glanced at the screen. A picture of an empty plate sat next to a bottle of maple syrup. The caption read: *Best breakfast ever.* She smiled and a flood of warmth coursed through her at the memory of Roxanne putting the last forkful of pancakes in her mouth and saying she was glad Abby had stayed to play. She was glad too, but play was all it was. They both knew that and that was okay because play was all she had the capacity to handle no matter how much she wondered if something more might be possible. Sex and pancakes. Who needed anything else?

Her phone buzzed again, and she smiled at the anticipation of another message from Roxanne, but this text was from her mother and it was a bombshell.

*Having the wedding this weekend. I can count on you to be there, right? XOXO*

Abby's stomach fell and she dropped the phone like it was full of poison. If she'd needed a reminder relationships were doomed, the news her mother was rushing to the altar for the fourth time was right on schedule.

Friday morning, Roxanne paced outside Stuart's office, ignoring the glaring looks from Sylvia. It wasn't her fault Stuart had waited until just now to read the show script she'd sent over yesterday. Perhaps it was a good thing for her to catch him on the fly. If he had too much time to think about it, he was likely to reject her concept completely out of hand.

By the time he opened his office door and motioned for her to come in she'd worn a trail in the carpet. She shot a glare of her own at Sylvia and followed Stuart into his inner sanctum. He sat down behind his desk, but she remained standing, not wanting to presume.

"Go ahead and sit. I loved the script and we're going to try out your plan with just a few tweaks."

"That's great news," Roxanne said, her mind flooded with relief. She wasn't sure how she would've broken the news to Abby if the network had decided they wanted to focus the full episode on the Barclay's closing.

"We'll see. If the teasers don't play well, be prepared for us to take a very different approach. Understood?"

"Fair enough."

"Excellent. You said you wanted to start with the piece on Barclay's at the top of the show and then move on from there, so I think we should film the opening on location at one of their stores. Sound good to you?"

"Sounds perfect. Oh, and I landed an interview with one of the owners, Tommy Barclay."

"Really?"

"Yes." Roxanne resisted telling him it had actually been Abby's idea, over pancakes no less. She suddenly had an idea of her own. "And I'm pretty sure we can get him to let us film the interview inside their flagship store. I don't think it would hurt to give the viewers an inside glimpse of what all the protest is about, but just for setting, not like some exposé."

Stuart held his hands in the air. "Who said anything about an exposé?"

"Uh-huh." Roxanne wasn't sure she could trust him, but her burgeoning idea would give her an excuse to call Abby. "Now that I know you're on board, I'll make a couple of calls and get back to you this afternoon for scheduling."

Roxanne barely waited until she'd left the building before calling Abby who picked up on the first ring.

"Is this the Pancake Hotline?" Abby asked.

"I think you're supposed to call a hotline, it's not supposed to call you."

"I guess that's true, but a girl can hope."

"A girl can indeed," Roxanne said. "Speaking of things a girl can hope for, I have a favor to ask."

"Funny, I do too."

"You go first."

"Okay, please promise you'll hear me out until the end."

"I promise." Roxanne braced for impact. "What's up?"

"Will you go to a wedding with me?"

Well, that wasn't what she'd been expecting. "Are you serious?"

"Dead serious. It's sudden and annoying and I don't want to go, but I figured you might actually enjoy it seeing as how you like all things wedding, and if I was with someone who wanted to be there, I might not be tempted to stab anyone in the wedding party or any of the other guests." Abby paused for a moment, and then rushed on. "Oh, wait. That was incredibly inconsiderate. Of course you don't want to go to a wedding—that's work for you…Are you still there?"

Roxanne laughed. "I figured you'd run out of breath eventually. Are you done having this conversation by yourself?"

"Yes, but forget I said anything."

"Who's getting married?"

"My mother. For the nine hundredth time. She's convinced this one is going to take."

Roxanne heard the edge beneath Abby's joking tone and remembered Abby's earlier reference to her mother's many nuptials. She wanted to ask more but decided this was a conversation better had in person. "What day?"

"Pardon?"

"What day is she getting married?"

"Saturday night. It's pretty thrown together, so it's not going to be anything like what you're used to—"

"Stop." Roxanne waited until she was sure she had Abby's attention. "I'd be honored to go to a wedding with you. I have only one question."

"Spill."

"Will there be cake?"

"Of course," Abby said. "I think it might be against the law not to have cake at a wedding."

"Well, it wouldn't do to violate the law, especially not with a lawyer present. Text me the details and I'll meet you there."

"We should plan to be there about six. How about I pick you up at five fifteen?"

"I can meet you there. Won't you have wedding stuff to do?"

"Oh, no. Not me. Been there, done that. I'm showing up and that's all I've got in me for this one."

For a second, Roxanne wondered what she'd gotten herself into, but she wasn't about to back out now and miss the opportunity to meet one of the primary reasons Abby was so anti-marriage. "Great. Five fifteen sounds perfect." She paused. It felt weird to bring up her favor now, but it was the perfect time to see how into reciprocity Abby was feeling. "Now, about why I called."

"Of course. Sorry to sidetrack you."

"No worries. We're going to open our first show with a piece on Barclay's, including the interview with Tommy, you know, to give the audience a glimpse of the other perspective, and I'd like to use the flagship store as a backdrop."

"Nothing stopping you there. It's not like there are cars lined up in the parking lot."

"The inside. I'd like to use the inside."

"Oh."

Roxanne felt the mood change and wished she'd waited to broach the topic to put some distance between the personal and professional. "Never mind. It was a dumb idea. I was thinking if you want to show more of an objective view of things, you could do for our viewers what you did for me and let Tommy give them an inside look, but I totally get why that might complicate things with the protests and all."

"Wait," Abby said. "Actually, I think you might be on to something. I guess I'm just trying to figure out why you would want to balance out the perspectives when it seems like your strategy so far has been to stoke the fury of the brides-to-be."

Roxanne conceded she had a point. "Maybe sharing pancakes with the lawyer for the other side has persuaded me there's more than one angle to this story. The lawyer was very persuasive, after all."

"She's glad to hear that. Tell you what, I'll talk to Tommy and see what I can work out."

"Perfect." They spent the next few minutes discussing Abby's mother's impromptu wedding before Roxanne reluctantly ended the call. She walked the rest of the way to her car with a skip in her step, confident Abby would come through. In any case, they were going to a wedding together, and she was certain that meant more than Abby had been willing to imply. Weddings were about love and romance and happily ever afters. For all Abby's protests that she didn't believe in any of those things, her actions implied differently, and Roxanne was convinced that whatever happened this weekend would reveal Abby's true self. And she could not wait.

## CHAPTER FIFTEEN

A bby walked toward Roxanne's door suddenly nervous about the evening ahead. She'd spent the last couple of days working this whole scenario out in her head, and it went something like this: frustrated daughter of repeat bride attends wedding of mother with popular wedding blogger in tow to have an opportunity to dish about all the things wrong with the current nuptials. Because daughter was working on a case about bridal wear that her date happened to be embroiled in as well, expenses related to attendance might qualify as a tax write-off, but at a minimum the field trip might help her understand the irrational anger of her client's "victims."

Not likely. If her mother could throw together a ceremony and reception in less than a week, then these whiny brides had no room to speak about losing only one aspect of their "big day," with plenty of advance notice about the road ahead.

She knocked and waited, trying to quell her nerves and second-guesses about having invited Roxanne to attend. What had she been thinking? It was bad enough that she felt compelled to go, but dragging a date?

This wasn't a date. It was a friends-with-benefits outing to discuss wedding stuff so she could get some perspective about the case she was working. And since her mother had invited Campbell and Grace to the wedding too, she figured she could count on a roundtable discussion about legal matters over the post-ceremony drinks. She only hoped that husband number four was springing for an open bar.

She looked back up at the door, and then checked the time. What was taking so long? Had Roxanne bailed on her? She reached up to knock again, but the door flew open and Roxanne stood in the doorway looking disconcerted and devastatingly beautiful in a skin-hugging aubergine dress. Abby gulped for breath. "Wow. Just wow. You look amazing, but you also look like you want to run away. Did you change your mind about going?"

"No, but I have a problem." Roxanne grabbed her arm and tugged her into the house. She pointed at her neck. "The zipper's stuck and therefore so am I. It won't go up or down, and I can't show up at a wedding with my dress half open."

Abby stepped around her so she could get a better view of the difficulty. "I see. That is a problem. Mind if I give it a try?"

Roxanne grimaced. "If it breaks you're going to have to cut me out of this dress and I don't own it and I fear it's worth like a million dollars because it's one of a kind I *borrowed* from the fashion closet at *Best Day Ever*."

Abby laughed. "Are you confessing that you stole this dress? Because I'm not that kind of lawyer, although I might have an in with the prosecutor who's running for district attorney."

Roxanne reached back and started to fiddle with the zipper. "Stole is a strong word, but I do need to return it in one piece, and preferably without anyone knowing." She sighed. "Seriously, I think it might be a lost cause."

"Hold still." Abby play-swiped at her hand. "I have mad wardrobe skills. Let me work." She carefully tugged at the zipper and gently eased it loose. "Are we going for zip up or down because I know which way I would vote." She leaned in close and left a trail of light kisses along Roxanne's neck.

Roxanne turned into Abby's embrace. "How about up now and down later? I don't want to be the one responsible for you no-showing at your mother's…"

"You were going to say 'special day' weren't you?" She laughed. "I guess a person can have a bunch of special days. It's not like they mean anything anymore." She reached behind Roxanne and zipped up her dress. "You're all set."

Roxanne's expression was hard to read, but Abby thought she detected a trace of disappointment. "I'm sorry we can't skip, but I promise I'll work my zipper magic in the right direction when we're done."

It took a moment, but Roxanne nodded. "Sounds perfect."

The tone was off, and Abby wasn't sure what had changed between them, but if they didn't leave now they would be late, so she filed it away to discuss later. Or not. If things went her way, this wedding would be over quickly and they'd be back here, sans zippers and conversation, to have a consummation of their own.

Abby had the top up on her car, but it was perfect convertible weather. If only they weren't headed to an occasion where bird's nest hair would be frowned on. How much more fun would they be having if they were on their way to the lake or Barton Springs or Marble Falls or one of the many other cool destinations nearby, zooming along the highway with the top down? She started to ask Roxanne if she'd be interested in taking a day trip with her next weekend but stopped short. Having Roxanne accompany her to the wedding as kind of a wingwoman was one thing, but a road trip was an entirely different circumstance. It was a step beyond dating, and she wasn't ready to commit to that.

Or was she? She'd seen more of Roxanne than any other woman she'd slept with. Ever. And despite their professional differences and outlook on relationships, she enjoyed spending time with her, enjoyed her company. What did it matter if they both had different ideas about where relationships should end up? They were at the beginning, not the end. The end could take care of itself when it happened. For now, she wanted to live in the moment and enjoy the ride.

She reached over and squeezed Roxanne's hand. "I appreciate this."

"This?"

"Attending other people's weddings probably isn't the most fun you could have on a date."

"Oh, so this is a date? I thought it was a business meeting."

Abby was certain she heard a trace of a tease in Roxanne's voice, but was there an edge of truth as well? "I suppose it can be if that's what you want. My law partners are going to be there."

Roxanne grinned. "I'm kidding. Let's make a deal and agree not to talk about your case or my show. We'll act like we're still in PV and nothing intervened to change the fact we enjoy each other's company and that I find you wildly attractive."

"You do?"

Roxanne placed a hand over her heart. "Truth. Now let's go find the fun side of this wedding. I know you don't care for weddings, but I promise you there's always a fun side."

"I'm always up for finding the fun side." She pointed to a big sign on the side of the road, Moonlight Ranch. "I don't see any buildings, but I guess this is it."

"Moonlight is a beautiful venue," Roxanne said. "Simple and rustic, yet full of charm."

Rustic and simple were two words Abby would never have associated with her mother, but she was certain she'd read the email invite correctly. Abby drove down the gravel road, pulled into the parking lot, and parked in one of the few paved spaces she could find. She got out and met Roxanne on the other side of the car. She looked up at the large barn, lit with twinkling lights. "This is not at all what I expected."

"Surprises can be nice."

Abby smiled. "True. And for the record, I find you wildly attractive too." She punctuated her remark with a kiss, taking a moment to savor the sweet taste of Roxanne's lips and the heady way the touch made her feel. Everything about Roxanne was more than she'd bargained for, more than she thought she wanted, but for once in her life, her natural instinct to flee wasn't rearing its protective head, and she was content to let things be. No, she was more than content. She was happy and she liked it. So happy, it took her a moment to register someone was calling her name.

"Hey, Abby, are you kissing the woman who's trying to take down our client?"

Abby froze at the sound of Grace's voice, and she felt Roxanne pull away. She instantly registered and regretted the lost contact, but it was probably for the best since Grace, and Campbell, and Wynne were all walking toward them. "Look, the gang's all here."

"Your mom isn't one to take no for an answer," Campbell called out. "Although, I think this was a ruse for her to finally meet Wynne."

"You could be right," Abby said, "But it could also be a ruse to fill seats on the bride's side. Mom doesn't like it when the groom has more guests. Trust me, it's happened and it's not pretty."

"Be nice," Grace said. "It's your mom's—"

Abby held up a hand. "Please, please don't say it."

"Special day," Grace said with an evil grin. "Sorry, I couldn't resist." She reached a hand toward Roxanne. "Sorry Abby is being so rude. I'm Grace, and this is Campbell Clark and Wynne Garrity."

"Nice to meet you," Roxanne said. "And by the way, I'm only on the side of all things wedding." She raised her hands. "No agenda here."

Grace gave her a long, appraising look. "I will keep that in mind and reserve judgment. For now."

Campbell edged her away. "Down, Grace. Roxanne, it's great to meet you. I've been following your blog for a while now. I like how you offer practical advice for brides, and not a bunch of extravagant ideas."

"I guess you do," Grace said with a knowing grin.

"You know?" Abby asked.

"Once we told you," Campbell said, "it was impossible to keep it a secret any longer." She turned toward Roxanne. "Wynne and I are engaged. It's brand new."

"Congratulations."

"Careful," Abby said. "She's going to start asking for advice."

"I'll buy her a drink first," Campbell said. "Don't worry, Roxanne, I'll wait until the reception to bother you with my questions."

"Where there will probably be an open bar," Abby teased her. "As much as I hate to say this, we should probably get inside or we're going to miss the solemn occasion of my mother making her fourth trip down the aisle." She barely resisted the urge to take Roxanne's hand as they walked toward the big barn, unsure where the impulse had come from in the first place. Weddings did funny things to people. Campbell was more cheerful than usual, and even prickly Grace was laughing and joking with Roxanne. But she kept a level head. Weddings lasted a day, and in that one day, romance ruled, and everyone was happy, but nothing about it was real. In a week or two when all the cake and flowers and champagne were gone and the honeymoon was over, her mother and what's his name would be back to their real lives without champagne toasts and dancing and receiving lines. It would just be the two of them, spending day after day together, and just like the others, their happily ever after wouldn't last.

She glanced back in time to catch Roxanne looking at Campbell and Wynne who were huddled together, smiling and sharing whispered conversation, and some of her sour mood abated. She wanted her friends to be happy, and if they felt like they needed a special day of their own to make it work, then who was she to be a killjoy?

"You ready to go in?" she asked Roxanne.

"Are you?" Roxanne asked in a whispered voice, her brow narrowed in concern. "If you want to make a dash for it, I'm here for you."

Abby smiled. "As much as I'd love to be anywhere else right now, I think Mom might notice if I take most of the bride's side with me. Besides, Campbell and Wynne are pretty giddy about weddings these days. I'd hate to rob them of the experience."

Roxanne took her hand and squeezed. She started to let go, but Abby held on, suddenly not caring about her reputation or what her friends might say. She laced her fingers through Roxanne's, surprised at how natural it felt. "Let's do this."

As they approached the door to the barn, Roxanne asked, "Are you sure you don't need to do anything for your mom before the ceremony gets started?"

Abby brushed away the creep of annoyance and guilt at Roxanne's question. She knew Roxanne didn't mean any harm, and normally daughters would want to be at their mother's side for all the wedding stuff. But it wasn't normal for mothers to marry everyone they met, so there was that. She stared into Roxanne's eyes and saw only genuine concern and sincerity. "I'm not even sure what I would do."

"I doubt you have to 'do' anything. I bet checking in with her would be enough, you know, just to let her know you're here to support her even if you don't necessarily agree with her decision." Roxanne grinned. "It's like your roles are reversed for the day. You get to be the grown-up, the functional one. It's like a gift you get to give yourself."

"Crap."

"What?"

"I didn't get her a gift."

"Oops."

"Not only did I not get her a gift, but I showed up with the goddess of all things wedding so it's not like I can even pretend I didn't know you had to bring a gift to your mother's twentieth wedding." She could feel panic rising in her chest. Why did she all of the sudden care about what was expected? Besides, what in the world was she supposed to buy since her mother had already acquired all the usual stuff from her past nuptials. Still, she felt like a heel for forgetting entirely. Roxanne reached out and squeezed her hand.

"It's okay. Send her something after the fact. She'll get so many gifts today, receiving one later will really stand out."

Abby nodded. "I think I will go see her before the ceremony starts. You sure you don't mind if I leave you here alone?"

Roxanne glanced around at the crowd of people packing into the venue. "I think I'll be fine."

Abby stood and edged her way down the row past her friends who shot her curious looks, but she didn't stop to explain. She made her way across the room to a woman wielding a clipboard who looked like she might be in charge. "Hi, can you help me find the bride? I'm—"

Without looking up, the woman snapped, "The bride is indisposed. You'll see her when everyone else does."

Abby bristled at the rebuke. "I'm not angling for a special feature. Believe me, I've seen it before." She pointed to a door to the left. "I'm betting she's in there. Am I right?"

The woman responded by finally looking up. She narrowed her eyes like she was trying to assess the threat level Abby posed. "Family?"

"Yes." Abby was used to everyone thinking she and her mother were sisters, in fact she joked sometimes that her mother married rich so she could afford the really expensive moisturizer. "Can you get me in? I'd appreciate it. I'm her daughter."

The woman raised a tiny walkie-talkie to her lips and whispered, "Daughter to see bride. Stat." She pointed. "Go through that door and follow the hallway to the second door on the right. She'll be waiting for you." She shook her pen in Abby's direction. "We're on a tight schedule here, so you only have three minutes. Go."

Abby didn't need the urging to leave control freak's space, and on her way down the hall she wondered what Roxanne would think of her tactics. This had gotten to be a habit—wondering what Roxanne thought. She probably wouldn't be strolling down this hall to wish her mother well were it not for Roxanne's coaxing. And despite it being the exact opposite of what she wanted to do, she knew that Roxanne was right, and checking in with her mom would make her feel better about herself. She filed the realization under things to examine later and knocked on the slightly ajar door.

"Is that you, Francine? I promise I'm almost ready, I just can't seem to fasten this last button."

"You shouldn't have to do that yourself," Abby said as she walked through the door to see her mom standing with her arms contorted behind her neck, trying to reach the last button of her dress. "Here let me."

"Thank you, dear. I wasn't sure you were coming."

Abby reached up and fastened the stray button. "Why would you think that? Just because you decided to accelerate this ceremony and only gave a week's notice, by text no less?"

"It couldn't be helped. Russell's work is taking him overseas and we don't know when he will be back."

"Right. So you had no other choice but to marry him. Mom, it's not World War II. You can hop a flight whenever you want, and there are things like phones and Skype and email."

"It's complicated," her mother said. "There's the issue of a visa and he'll be on a base and he may be there for a while. I've waited all my life to find him. I don't want to waste another moment. Plus, we wanted to get married here with our friends and family. Mostly you." She shook her head. "I know you don't understand, but I'm glad you came."

Abby couldn't quite process her mother's emotional reveal, so she resorted to the tried and true. "I haven't missed one yet."

"Abigail?"

"Yes?"

"Russell is the one."

"Sure, right." The walls started to close in, and Abby edged toward the door. "Well, I'm sure you'll have a happy life."

Her mother touched her arm. "Look, I know you have no reason to believe me, but I love Russell and he loves me. It's not about money or status, things I used to think mattered. Russell is a good man." She waved a hand. "The others—I thought they meant more than they did. I'm old enough to admit when I was wrong, but I'm not wrong this time."

Abby started to change the subject, but a nagging question burrowed its way to her lips. "How do you know?"

"It's hard to explain."

"Never mind." Abby started toward the door. "Forget I asked. Come on. You don't want to be late for your own wedding, do you?"

"Abigail, wait."

Abby paused, but she wanted to run. Why had she even started down this road? She'd heard it all before. A few years would go by and her mother would tire of the same routine and start seeking more. It was an endless cycle doomed to be repeated because her mother would always seek to fill the void.

But she refused to follow the same path. It might be lonely sometimes to accept that she had only herself to rely on for her own happiness, but ultimately, she was better off never suffering the disappointment of other people and endings that would always come. "It's okay, Mom. He's the one for you. I'm cool with that. We better go. You've got a room full of people waiting for you out there."

"Let them wait. They're all here for the cake and there won't be any cake until I say, 'I do.'" She pointed at a couple of chairs. "Sit."

Abby let go of her resistance and sank into the nearest chair. "Only because it's your special day. Spill."

"Russell is a good man and I don't deserve him, but he loves me anyway. All the others? They didn't love me, and I knew it at the time, but I traded security for love. All I had to do was be arm candy, and I never wanted for anything. Except someone to love me for who I am."

"And Russell is different how?"

"It's hard to explain."

"Well, you better try and fast since no one's getting cake until you walk down the aisle. If I were Russell, I'd start thinking of an exit strategy right about now."

"When you meet the one you love, exit strategies go out the window. Trust me, Abigail. You'll know when it happens for you, but you have to be open to it."

"I'll take your word for it, but I'm good just the way I am."

"You can be independent without being lonely. Don't forget that."

Abby stood and helped fluff her mother's dress, avoiding her steady gaze. "Okay. He's the one. You're happy. I get it." She pointed to the door where the control freak with the clipboard was probably listening in. "It's time. Do you have someone waiting to walk you down the aisle?"

"Are you offering?"

She hadn't been and she started to say so, but then she caught the misty look in her mother's eyes. She'd seen similar looks from her mother before, but this time felt different, genuine. Who was she to judge? Letting her mother have this moment didn't mean she had to change anything about herself. The realization brought with it a sense of freedom, and she held out her hand. "Let's get you your special day."

## CHAPTER SIXTEEN

R oxanne pulled a Kleenex from her purse and dabbed at the corners of her eyes. After Abby's descriptions of her mother's marital exploits, she'd been expecting an impersonal ceremony, but while short and simple, the exchange of self-written vows in this charming venue was one of the most heartfelt she'd ever witnessed. She even thought she'd seen Abby get a little misty at one point while her mother was pledging her future to the bald, plain-looking man beside her.

It was the way he looked at his new wife that sealed it. With absolute adoration, like there was nothing she could do wrong, nothing that could make him love her less. It was the same way Dan looked at Val, and the thing she would hold out for because there was no substitute for that kind of love.

After the preacher pronounced them duly married, the newlyweds practically skipped down the aisle. Roxanne glanced over at Abby who, instead of looking at her mother and her new husband, was staring intently at her. She stared back for a moment, conscious she was smiling like a loon. "What?"

Abby grinned. "You have the best smile."

"I bet you say that to all the girls."

"Hmmm, well, I might have told some they had a great smile, but 'the best'? Nope."

"All right then, compliment accepted. Now, I believe you promised cake. Please tell me there's cake."

Grace appeared at Abby's side. "There better be."

"I second that," Campbell said as she and Wynne popped up next to Grace. "And tequila. How about it, BBF, is tequila appropriate for an evening wedding reception?" She squeezed Wynne's arm. "Inquiring minds want to know."

Roxanne looked between her and Wynne. "Am I wading into a Jose Cuervo-sized conflict here or are you just asking for fun?"

Wynne shook her head. "Tequila is happening when we tie the knot. I'm resigned to the fact. Campbell's the pro when it comes to all things spirit." She leaned into Campbell's touch and they locked arms. "In fact, I'm certain she has at least one of those airline-sized bottles in her bag right now just in case the bar isn't stocked with her favorite brand."

Campbell play-protested, and Roxanne watched their easy affection with admiration and a trace of longing until Abby whispered in her ear. "Shall we?"

A sign outside the barn announced the reception was set up at the other end of the property, and the woman with the clipboard was directing everyone to board a shuttle waiting at the entrance to the ranch. Grace, Campbell, and Wynne dutifully lined up, but Abby led her around the line, back to the parking lot. "You have an aversion to buses?"

"I have an aversion to being trapped somewhere without the means to make a quick getaway. We'll follow the shuttle—I promise." She opened Roxanne's door and waited for her to climb inside.

Once Abby was behind the wheel, Roxanne asked, "I'm guessing your visit with your mother didn't go so well."

Abby pulled in her lower lip and appeared to be giving the question hard thought. "It was...different. Not bad." She shook her head. "I don't know."

"The ceremony was nice. I liked that they wrote their own vows."

"Uh-huh."

Roxanne wondered what Abby was thinking. She'd seemed to be doing fine until she'd brought up her mother. If they were going to have fun this evening, perhaps the best thing she could do was change the subject. "Your law partners seem more like best friends than co-workers."

Abby smiled. "They are my best friends. Grace and Campbell have known each other for years and I met them in law school. We instantly hit it off and were inseparable until we graduated, then we all got job offers in different cities and got so caught up working our asses off to try to make partner, we hardly ever saw each other. Last spring, we had our five-year reunion, and after a few shots of tequila, Campbell gets this big idea that we should quit our jobs and start our own firm. So, we did."

"Wow. Just like that?" Roxanne didn't try to hide her admiration for Abby's daring move.

"Yes. I was living in Dallas at the time. I marched into the senior partner's office the next Monday and gave my notice. They cut off my network access and had security watch me pack that day."

"Harsh."

"Yes, but I'm sure they thought I was going to try to steal client info. It happens all the time. Some of the clients I worked with did follow me to our new firm, but I didn't talk them into it."

"Was Barclay's one of them?"

"Yes. I've known Tommy since we were kids. There was no way he would've stayed with a firm that I'd left. He was pretty happy that I moved back to Austin."

"What does Wynne do?"

Abby hesitated before answering. "She's a lawyer too. She's doing some contract work for us, but she's kind of in-between regular gigs right now. We met her earlier this year."

"Feels like there's something you're not telling me. Is she on the lam?"

Abby laughed. "No, but we did meet her when we were working on a case for Leaderboard. She was working for Worth Ingram and competing with Campbell for the client's business."

"But Campbell won?" Roxanne still felt like Abby was holding something back.

"I guess they both won since they fell in love with each other."

"Aw. What a great story." She play-punched Abby. "Why were you so hesitant to tell me that? Is it because the story has a happy ending and you don't believe in those?"

Abby followed the shuttle into a parking lot near a large outdoor structure with tiny white lights hanging from the rafters that lit up the entire area. Roxanne loved the magical effect and wondered what else the bride and groom had in store for the reception, but right now she was waiting for Abby to answer her question.

"It is pretty," Abby said, following her gaze at the venue. She turned off the car and shifted in her seat. "I may not believe in marriage, but I wish the best for Campbell and Wynne. As long as they're happy now, who cares about forever, right?"

Roxanne wanted to argue the point, say that now was only temporary and people needed a future they could count on and someone to share it with, but she couldn't deny Abby's logic. If they all got hit by a bus tomorrow, the love they had today might be the only thing that mattered, commitment or not. "You sold me. Let's go enjoy the now."

The reception venue was a picture-perfect display of simplicity at its best. In addition to the lights hanging from the rafters, twinkling fairy lights in Mason jars were strewn through the trees. They were greeted by a server dressed in jeans, boots, and a crisp white button-down carrying a tray of highball glasses.

"Would you like to try the bride and groom's signature drink?" he said. "It's called Perfect Thyming. A blend of bourbon, with lemon and thyme-infused simple syrup."

Abby took two and handed one to her. "Didn't you do a blog with signature drink recipes a few months ago?"

Roxanne paused mid-sip. "I did." She cocked her head. "How many of my blogs have you read?"

"Plenty." Abby grinned. "Research. It's my job to know the competition."

"It's not competing if you want the same thing." Roxanne let the words roll out without censor, hoping they didn't send Abby running. She needn't have worried since Abby's only reaction was a smoldering gaze.

"Tell you what though," Abby said. "I haven't seen a blog that explores a very important issue that's been on my mind."

"Well, good thing you have the expert right here so she can answer all your questions. Spill."

"What's the minimum amount of time a daughter needs to stay at her mother's fourth wedding before it's considered rude for her to leave?"

"You are incorrigible." Roxanne pointed toward an arbor a few feet away. "There's cake over there and I'm not leaving until I get the piece I was promised. Understood?"

"Understood, but in the meantime…" Abby took her hand and led her around the corner to a gazebo on the ridge with a perfect view of the setting sun. When they were tucked away, all alone, Abby placed her hands on either side of Roxanne's waist and leaned in close. "I've been waiting to do this since I picked you up tonight."

Abby's lips were soft, grazing hers at first before pressing firmly against her mouth. Roxanne surrendered to the surreal pleasure of Abby's deepening kiss, no longer caring that they were standing yards away from where wedding guests were gathering to celebrate the nuptials.

Abby did this to her every single time—it didn't matter that she resolved to keep her at arm's length, Abby showed up with the compliments and the kisses and the fiery passion and made her forget she was unavailable and not even remotely interested in anything beyond sex. And the sex was amazing, but it wasn't enough to make her compromise on the whole package. She wondered if she'd come to this wedding with Abby to assess exactly how relationship averse Abby was in real life. It was one thing to say you weren't interested in the long-term, but who could resist the pull when you witnessed the walk down the aisle and the vows and the sealing it with a kiss? If Abby showed no signs of sentimentality after a full evening in the presence of all these triggers, then Roxanne would have her answer. But maybe…

She heard a voice calling out and barely registered Abby's name in a seriously unfortunate déjà vu. She felt their connection break and instantly felt Abby stiffen in her arms. Damn. Just when she thought she was making progress.

❖

Abby groaned at the interruption. She stepped to the side and looked up, expecting to see Grace or Campbell, but instead it was her mother headed toward her in full bridal regalia. "Crap," she muttered under her breath, wishing she were a million miles away. "Mother, shouldn't you be throwing a bouquet or having a first dance or something?"

"Abigail, don't be rude. Introduce me to your friend."

Resigned to this formality, Abby did the honors. "Mom, meet Roxanne Daly. Roxanne, this is my mother, Donna Wheeler."

"It's a pleasure to meet you, Roxanne." Abby's mom narrowed her eyes. "You look awfully familiar, but I can't place where we might have met."

Roxanne stretched out a hand. "I have that kind of face. Girl nextdoor and all."

Abby started to say no you don't, but her mother beat her to it. "No, wait. I know. I saw an ad for your new show. You're the BBF!"

"It's true," Roxanne said. "I'm not used to being recognized in public. I spent years writing my blog without anyone ever knowing it was me. I wanted it to be all about the brides and not a personality thing, but the network seems to think it's better to put a face to it now that we're filming."

"Abigail, I can't believe you didn't tell me you were bringing a wedding expert to my wedding. Now, I'm all self-conscious about whether we have our act together."

"Well, you have had a lot of practice," Abby said, but a quick look at Roxanne's furrowed brow prompted her to soften her words. "I'm sure you've checked all the boxes."

"Actually," Roxanne said. "My favorite thing about this evening is how outside the box it is. So many great touches, from the lights in the trees, the gorgeous setting, and," she raised her glass, "this drink is my new fav. If you don't mind, I may mention some of these touches in my next blog post."

"Go right ahead. Russell was involved in every aspect, and I'd love for you to meet him. Join us over by the donut bar?"

"Absolutely," Roxanne said without any hesitation.

Her mother started walking off, but Abby stayed in place for a second while she tried to imagine her slim, calorie conscious mother ordering a donut bar for her wedding. "Did she say donut bar?"

Roxanne grinned. "I hope so. Come on."

Abby suddenly found herself following Roxanne and her mother toward a display of donuts in all shapes and sizes. While the array of sugary food was tempting, Abby couldn't help but wonder how she'd gone from kissing a beautiful woman to being under her mother's tow. When they drew up to the table, Russell greeted them with open arms.

"My wife," he exclaimed. "I don't think I'll ever get tired of saying that."

"You better not," Abby's mom said with a play-stern tone. "Those vows are legally binding."

This was where Abby would usually crack a joke about how laws were made to be broken, take it from a lawyer, but she was mesmerized by the way her mother and Russell stared into each other's eyes like there was no one else around. When she finally recovered her voice, she blurted out, "Cake."

"Pardon?" her mother asked.

"Cake. I promised Roxanne cake. Is there going to be cake?" Everyone was looking at her like she'd grown an extra head. "What? Did I say something wrong?"

Grace stepped forward. "Hey, Abby, I need to talk to you for a sec." She didn't wait for an answer before grabbing Abby by the arm and pulling her a few feet away. "What's up with you?"

"I don't know what you're talking about."

"First off, you brought a date to your mother's wedding." She shook a finger for emphasis. "A date, Keane."

"You don't like her?"

"What's not to like? She seems smart and nice, and she's very personable, not to mention pretty, but I expected you to show up, get liquored up, and go home with someone you met here. BYOD isn't really your style. I get you not wanting to show up all by yourself, but you could've come with me."

Abby sighed. "You're right. It's just…" She trailed off unable to finish the sentence because she didn't have an explanation for her out of character actions lately. "You said 'first off.' What else is wrong?"

"Well, how about the fact that if you are going to date someone for the first time since I've known you, you don't pick a woman who's trying to take down your client."

Abby waved her off. "Oh, I've got that covered. She's going to include Barclay's side of the story in her next show."

"If you say so."

Abby heard the edge, and an irrationally disproportionate response sprung to her lips. "I do say so. I've been doing this as long as you have, Grace. I think I know what I'm doing."

"I guess it depends on what the 'this' is you're talking about. Is it representing shareholders in hostile situations, or falling for women who don't have your best interests, professional or personal, at heart?"

Abby started to say she wasn't falling for Roxanne, but the words halted in her brain. Was she?

No, and it was silly to think so. They had a short and sweet history and they'd reconnected. End of story. Besides, she knew Grace well enough to know she was only looking out for her. She started to say look at Campbell and Wynne and how things had turned out for them, but the comparison crash-landed before she could say it out loud. Campbell and Wynne were in love. Hell, they were engaged. She and Roxanne weren't that; they weren't even a couple. Which begged the question, what was going on between them?

She spotted Roxanne across the way, still talking to her mother and Russell. Campbell and Wynne had joined them, and they all appeared to be engaged in a spirited conversation. Her mother obviously liked Roxanne—she could tell by the way she smiled at her and inclined her head when Roxanne was talking. And now Wynne and Campbell were laughing in response to something Roxanne said, and Abby wondered if she was regaling them with one of her wedding tales. Even all business Grace admitted Roxanne was personable, smart, and nice—grudging praise, but praise nevertheless. If she were going to date someone on the regular, Roxanne checked all the boxes, not that she'd ever considered checking boxes an important thing to do.

Maybe it was time to think inside the box.

## CHAPTER SEVENTEEN

A bby strode through the lobby of her firm on Monday morning determined to make it to the coffee machine before she did anything else. The universe had other plans.

"Ms. Keane, Ms. Garrity and Ms. Maldonado are in the conference room and they have requested an audience with you, and Mr. Thomas Barclay is holding on the telephone."

Normally, the onslaught of demands pre-caffeine would put her on edge, but after spending Saturday night and Sunday in Roxanne's bed, complete with lots of sex and pancakes, she was ready to tackle anything this week had to deliver, including an employee with oddly formal behavior. "Graham, thank you for the detailed update. Please tell Mr. Barclay I will call him back forthwith, and let the ladies Garrity and Maldonado know that I require caffeination and then I will grant them an audience."

He nodded and picked up the line. As much as she wanted to hear him repeat her exact words, she wanted coffee more. Grace was standing at the espresso machine when she walked into the kitchen. "Good morning," Abby said. "Graham thinks you're in the conference room."

"I was, but for some reason I'm having trouble waking up this morning." Grace pointed at the machine. "You want a cup? It's just as easy to pull two shots as one."

"My kingdom for a cup. I'm dying here."

"Rough weekend?"

A flash of Roxanne trailing hot, wet kisses down her torso made her weak at the knees, but she wasn't about to tell Grace that, especially after her reaction to bringing Roxanne to the wedding. "You could say that."

Grace handed her a cup of espresso. "Listen, I'm sorry about what I said at the reception. I was being a jerk."

"A little."

"I know you would never compromise a case over a casual thing."

It was on the tip of Abby's tongue to object to the word casual, but she bit her lip. It was a casual thing, but not in the way that Grace thought. She definitely had feelings for Roxanne. Friendship feelings, which made her different from all the other women she'd slept with before. It was kind of nice, but she wasn't ready to parse these new feelings and definitely not out loud and definitely not in front of Grace who'd already questioned her objectivity. To divert the conversation, she changed the subject. "Is Wynne still in the conference room?"

"Yes, she said Judge Abel set a hearing date on your injunction, and she's waiting to go over it with you. My trial got reset, so she asked me to join, if that's okay?"

Abby heard the hesitancy in Grace's voice, and she looped her arm through hers. "Of course. We can use all the help we can get. And you and me? We're all good." She felt Grace relax at her declaration, and knew she'd said the right thing. Her friendships were everything, and she would never let anything come between her and Grace and Campbell.

But what about her new friendship with Roxanne?

She filed the thought under things to be dealt with later and led the way to the conference room where Wynne had her head buried in her laptop. "Hey, Wynne, word is we have a hearing date?"

Wynne looked up, her expression unusually frazzled. "We do. Tomorrow morning. Guess when we asked the judge to fast-track it, she took us seriously."

"That's great news. It means she's taking our allegation that every day the store remains closed is causing damage claim to heart."

"Yes, but it means we're going to be working solid until then to prepare."

"Uh," Abby hesitated. "Tommy has an interview with *Best Day Ever* today. We scheduled it last week, and they have a filming crew scheduled to be at Barclay's at noon. I don't think it'll take too long, but we could use the PR right about now."

"Definitely," Wynne said. "Not a problem. We'll meet back here after the interview and work late."

Abby sighed with relief until she spotted Grace wearing a frown. "Spill, Grace. I can tell you have something on your mind."

Grace crossed and then uncrossed her arms. "Nothing you haven't heard before. Just be careful. Don't let Tommy say anything that could be detrimental to the hearing."

"Roger that." Abby resisted adding that she'd done this before and knew how to handle herself. Grace was just being Grace— overly cautious and managerial. Normally, those qualities were ones she admired, and they were the reason she and Campbell had voted to make Grace the managing partner, but Grace needed to learn to trust that she knew what she was doing. If she weren't so happy from all the sex with Roxanne, she might've told her so. Instead, she focused on the hearing prep which went by at a glacial pace until it was time for her to leave for Barclay's.

On the drive over, she called Roxanne who answered on the first ring.

"Pancake Hotline. How can I help you?"

"So that's how it's supposed to work," Abby said. "This is nice. What are my options?"

"Hmmm, there are so many. Do you like toppings?"

"Yes, but I think letting the other woman have control is just as fun."

Roxanne laughed. "You're impossible."

"Not even. I'm absolutely possible."

"Great. I'm going to take you up on that. What are you doing tonight?"

Abby's daydream about what she'd like to do with Roxanne came to a screeching halt. "Tonight's bad."

"Oh. Okay."

She registered the disappointment in Roxanne's voice and instantly wanted to erase it. "Only because I have to work. We have a hearing about Barclay's tomorrow." She could hear Grace's voice in her head, urging her to keep her mouth shut about the hearing. "Are we off the record?"

"I think you forget I'm on a show about weddings, not legal exposés. Yes, we're off the record."

"Sorry. Anyway, we filed a suit asking the judge to overturn the decision Tommy's siblings made to close the store. The lawsuit will take a while, so we're asking the judge to keep the stores open until things play out."

"Got it. You're prepping for the hearing tonight."

"Yes, exactly. We didn't get a lot of notice, but it's a good thing the judge set it so quickly. I think it means she thinks we have a case."

"That's great news. And I promise I won't tell anyone, but let me know how it turns out. I'll be thinking about you tonight and tomorrow when you're in court being all lawyerly, but in the meantime, I'll see you in just a few."

"Definitely. I'm on my way."

"I'll be waiting."

Abby clicked off the line, and wished she were about to be seeing Roxanne in non-work-related circumstances. Maybe after this case was over, they could take a road trip and spend an entire weekend curled up in a hotel bed or one of the B&Bs in the hill country. She let her mind fill with images of the two of them eating pancakes and then going back to bed until lunchtime when they'd venture to town to stroll the square, browsing for antiques.

She shook her head. Breakfast and road trips and antiquing? She never used to think about anything other than the bed part.

What was happening to her? And more importantly, why did it feel so right?

❖

For the tenth time in as many minutes, Roxanne swatted at the stylist Jake had insisted on bringing on location. She was anxious about the interview with Tommy Barclay, and it didn't help that the *Best Day Ever* van was crowded with the crew for the filming.

"Sit still and let Trixie do her job," he said. "The lights will wash you out. You don't want to look like you're filming this on a selfie-stick, do you?"

He was right, but she didn't want to be stuck in a chair with a smock tied around her neck when Abby showed up, which would be any minute. Besides, this stylist didn't have Luther's touch and she'd had her hair pulled one too many times. She made a mental note to add a provision to the contract to have her styling done exclusively by Luther. Abby worked with contracts all the time; maybe she would handle that for her.

*Think again. She's not your lawyer. She's not even your girlfriend, even though you want her to be.* The thoughts were iron weights on the happy balloon feelings she'd let soar lately. As it should be. She might not be doing exposés here on *Best Day Ever*, but she did have a responsibility to be the objective voice BBF readers had come to expect over the years, and that meant not swooning over Abby Keane and wishing what they had was something more, no matter how right it felt. She was about to interview Abby's client and she would be totally professional. But later? Later, she was going to jump Abby's bones, and try not to worry about what happened next.

Jake's phone chimed and he announced that Abby and Tommy Barclay had arrived. The stylist sprayed a full can of hairspray on her head and pronounced her ready. Too bad she wasn't reporting on a hurricane, because she was certain every hair would stay in place, wind shear be damned. She tossed off the smock and rushed to get out of the van.

Abby, wearing a double-breasted black suit that hugged her curves, looked like she'd walked off the pages of a fashion magazine. Likely all without the aid of a professional stylist, and Roxanne wanted to jump in her car and drive away with her. Instead, she took a deep breath and walked over to Abby who was standing next to a tall, imposing man, who she recognized from her research as Tommy Barclay. Abby looked up as she approached, and Roxanne was certain she caught a glimpse of desire in her expression before it settled into a neutral smile.

"Ms. Keane, good to see you again," Roxanne said before sticking out her hand to Tommy. "Mr. Barclay? I'm Roxanne Daly. Thanks for agreeing to this interview and special thanks for letting us do it here at your store."

"Nice to meet you. Thank Abby," he said. "I've been following her advice since we were kids. No reason to stop now."

At the mention of Abby's name, Roxanne flicked a glance her way and found Abby staring at her with what she recognized as a simmering desire. So much for neutrality. Her own breath became shallow, and for a few seconds, everything else—the camera crew, Stuart, Tommy Barclay—faded into the background and it was just her and Abby, in the shuttle on the way to Azure, sharing breakfast in bed, making love until dawn.

Whoa, making love wasn't part of this thing between them. Abby had been clear from the start that sex with no strings was all she was in for, and for better or worse, she'd tacitly agreed to those terms. But all she could think about now was what a future with Abby would be like, and every single thought on the subject told her it would be good. No, it would be fantastic.

"Are we ready to get started?"

Roxanne looked over to see Tommy staring at the two of them with a knowing smile. She cleared her throat to stall. "Absolutely. Right this way. We have a stylist who's going to do a little magic to keep the lights from washing you out, and while you're with her, perhaps Ms. Keane could let me in so we can go ahead and set up."

"Sure, but I hope by 'magic' you don't mean makeup, because I take pride in my natural look," Tommy said with a grin.

Roxanne was instantly charmed. "Trust me, I feel exactly the same way, but I promise if you don't get a tiny bit of enhancing, you'll look anything but natural. The lighting will make you into a ghost." She handed him off to Trixie and followed Abby inside Barclay's, but her hope for a few minutes alone with her was shattered when Jake came running up behind them.

"Let's get a backdrop with racks of dresses." He looked at Abby. "You can show us that, right?" Turning back to Roxanne, he added, "Micah's waiting to do a sound check. Meet you back here in five and let's get started. Stuart wants to see film this afternoon."

Roxanne caught Abby's eye and telegraphed her regret for the interruption with a frown, but it was probably for the best that everything about this shoot stayed professional, and a few minutes alone with Abby likely would've blown that all to hell.

The sound check was a breeze, and a few minutes later, she was seated across from Tommy Barclay and they were both surrounded by a sea of bridal gowns. Abby was standing off to the side, a few feet out of her sight line, but simply knowing she was there gave her a charge. Focus. Focus.

Tommy fiddled with the mic on his collar and drank an unusually large amount of water from one of the glasses Micah had set on the table between them. "I haven't done many of these interviews either," Roxanne whispered.

"Then I guess asking you for advice about how to stay calm would be a bad idea?"

"Probably. I do know one thing. I'm pretty good at one-on-one conversation. I plan to forget about the cameras and what will ultimately happen with the footage they'll be taking today. It's just you and me, talking about the business you love and have known all your life. Nothing more."

"When you put it that way, it sounds easy."

Roxanne picked up the other water glass and tilted it toward the one in Tommy's hand. "Here's to good conversation."

Tommy clinked his glass against hers and they both drank. Over the rim of her glass, Roxanne sought out Abby across the room and found her staring in her direction, wearing a flirty grin. She recognized the desire in Abby's eyes, and took pleasure in knowing it was directed at her. For someone who insisted she was only interested in sex and friendship at most, Abby sure was attentive and sweet and thoughtful—several of the exact qualities Roxanne would like to find in whoever she chose to share her happily ever after. The problem was that more and more, she couldn't think of anyone else she wanted to have that happily ever after with.

## CHAPTER EIGHTEEN

Abby downed her espresso and pointed at Wynne's empty cup on the conference room table between them. "You want another?"

"I'm good," Wynne said. "Are you having another?"

"You say that like it's a bad thing."

"Well, you've already had two and it's still early. At this rate, you may peak and crash before we ever get to the hearing."

Wynne had a point. They'd met at the office early to go over last-minute prep for the court appearance, but Abby was more focused on staying awake than on the papers in front of her. "You're probably right, but I didn't sleep well last night, and I want to make sure I'm fully caffeinated for whatever the twins' attorney decides to throw our way this morning."

"Is everything okay?"

Abby paused before answering. The truth was last night was the first time since the long weekend with Roxanne that she'd spent the night by herself, and it reminded her of how she'd felt after Roxanne had left her alone in Azure. Funny how you spend your whole life sleeping alone and a few nights with a certain someone and suddenly you start tossing and turning like it's the night before the bar exam. Hopefully, tonight she and Roxanne would be celebrating a victory for Tommy and the brides-to-be, and tomorrow morning she'd wake up refreshed and ready to take on the next challenge. "Everything will be great once Judge Abel grants this injunction. We should probably start packing up. I'll drive."

The phone on the conference room table buzzed and Abby pressed the intercom button. "Good morning, Graham. What's up?"

"Mr. Barclay is on line two with a matter of great urgency. And you should leave in five minutes to allow adequate time to traverse the distance to the courthouse."

Abby barely suppressed a laugh at the word "traverse." "Certainly. We shall leave post-haste. Please put Mr. Barclay through immediately." She hung up the line and when it buzzed again, she punched the intercom button. "Hi, Tommy. Is everything okay?"

"Everything's fine, or it will be once the judge rules in our favor. I just wanted to make sure you don't need me to bring anything. I've got the prospectus and investment package for the online store in case you need it."

Abby looked over at Wynne who nodded. "Go ahead and bring it. I'm not sure the judge will let us get into your other business plans, but it's better to be prepared. We're about to leave for the courthouse now. See you there?"

"You bet. Oh, and do you happen to know when the interview with *Best Day Ever*'s going to air? I was telling this woman I'm dating about it and I don't think she believed me. Of course, the camera adds ten pounds, so I'm not sure I want her to see it. By the way, the chemistry between you and Roxanne is off the charts. How long have you been dating?"

Abby nearly fell out of her chair in her rush to take the phone off speaker, but she could see by the knowing grin on Wynne's face, it was way too late for damage control. "Hey, Tommy, I have another call coming in that I have to take before we leave. I'll see you in a few." She disconnected the call and slumped back in her chair. "Well, shit."

"It's not the end of the world to be dating a smart and pretty woman you know."

"We're not dating."

"Okaaay."

"You sound just like Campbell."

"I guess we've been dating too long then."

"Just long enough," Abby said. "Besides, is it still called dating if you're engaged?"

"That sounds like a question for the BBF."

"It does, doesn't it?"

"Totally. You should ask her on your next date."

Abby laughed. "Clever. Very clever." She decided to do exactly that, but in the meantime, it was time to get off this subject before she confessed out loud that she probably, kind of was dating Roxanne, and she actually liked it.

The courthouse was in downtown Austin, only a few miles from their office, but Austin traffic was a bear on a good day, and it took thirty minutes to crawl the distance. As Abby made the turn in front of the building, she urged Wynne to start looking for an open parking meter. "I hate parking in that big lot. Someone always parks right up against my door and then I have to pretzel my way out of the car. Last time, someone dinged both sides. At least when you park on the street—"

"Abby, look to your right. Right now." Wynne pointed out the window and shook her finger for emphasis.

Wynne's tone was ominous, and Abby followed the line of her hand. It took a few seconds to register what she was seeing, but then she realized she'd seen it before, outside her office building—a crowd of women dressed normally except they were all wearing wedding veils and carrying signs. Except at her office there had been a few dozen women, tops. There were at least a hundred women marching in front of the courthouse right now. She narrowed her eyes and focused on the woman closest to her who carried a sign that read. *I bought a wedding dress from Barclay's and all I got was sore from holding this sign.* Not the most original, but who needs original when you've got volume, and these brides-to-be had a ton of that. "This can't be happening."

"I'm afraid it is," Wynne said. "Don't suppose you know a secret way into the building?"

"Just the usual. I don't understand why they are all whipped up again. I thought they'd calm down once Roxanne stopped posting about the store closing."

"Good question," Wynne said, pulling out her phone. "Maybe there's something in the news that got these women all hopped up about their MIA dresses again."

Abby drove up to the next street and turned right, determined to find a parking place well out of sight of the angry almost brides. While she idled behind a line a cars, her phone rang through the car speakers, and a glance at the dash told her it was Tommy calling. She connected the call quickly in order to warn him not to approach the building yet. "Hey, Tommy, we're outside the courthouse looking for a spot to park, but we've got a bit of a problem."

"You're damn right we do. What the hell is your girlfriend up to? Did you know she was going to twist everything I said or were you so blinded by the sex you ignored her lack of ethics."

Abby's head spun and she struggled to make sense of Tommy's harsh words. "Tommy, I don't know why you're so angry, but protests on the courthouse steps are a thing. and this is not any different from the protests outside your stores. We'll simply walk by these women with our heads held high, looking straight ahead."

"You think I'm talking about a bunch of women wearing veils and carrying signs? How petty do you think I am? I'm talking about the interview you talked me into doing. My investor sent me the link just now. It's a complete disaster. I didn't say those things and you know it."

"Tommy, I'll call you right back." Abby disconnected the call and looked at Wynne. "I don't know what he's talking about. The interview isn't supposed to air until the premiere of the show. What's happening?"

Wynne was already typing on her phone, and Abby pulled over into a no parking zone, not caring at this point if she got a ticket. As soon as she put the car in park, Wynne handed her the phone. "There's a commercial for the show on *Best Day Ever*'s website."

Abby tapped the play button and the screen filled with the image of Roxanne seated next to Tommy, while an off-screen voice said, "What if you say yes to the dress, but the dressmaker says no to you? Tune in next week to see the Bride's Best Friend take on the disgraced owner of Barclay's Bridal over the scandal that has brides across the country reeling."

"Okay," she said turning down the volume. "It's a little sensational, but the interview went very well. I'm not happy about the way it's being billed, but networks pull this crap all the time to get people to tune in. I can't even count how many times I've watched a *Dateline* episode because the commercial said it was going to rock my world, and it was a dud."

Wynne pointed at the screen. "Wait, it's still going."

Roxanne was nodding at something Tommy said, and then she said, "I see." Abby backed the video up to see what she'd missed. When she hit a spot where Roxanne was talking, she stopped and let it play.

"I know that Barclay's has taken pride in personalized customer service, but some people say the store closing was all about money."

While the camera panned row after row of dresses, Tommy's voice could be heard in the background. "Yes, it is about the money." The camera cut back to Tommy's face and the off-screen voice cut in. "You'll hear astounding admissions." The camera focused back on Tommy from a different angle to catch him saying, "Brides can get their dresses somewhere else."

"Well, that sounds bad," Wynne said.

"It does. But that's not what he said." Abby backed the video up again and jabbed a finger at the screen. "Right here, where he mentions the money? What he actually said was in response to her question about his decision to open an online dress business. He said that it is about the money because if he has to use funds to fight this court battle, he wouldn't be able to fund the reopening of the store. And the part about they could get their dresses elsewhere? He followed that up with, they will never receive the level of service and care that we can provide and that we believe every bride deserves. They've chopped up all the questions and answers and rearranged them to make it seem like Tommy's a total jerk."

"There's more," Wynne said, pointing to the progress bar on the video. Together they watched while the disembodied voice promised further reveals and teased a couple more out of context quotes.

Abby shook her head and stared at her phone. "I need to call him back, but I don't know what to say. It's my fault he gave that interview in the first place. I never thought she'd..." She couldn't complete the thought because talking about Roxanne right now burned, and not in a good way. She'd gone her whole life without getting attached to another woman, and the first time she let her guard down, bam! Grace sure had called this one.

She heard a ring and looked at her phone, thinking Tommy was probably calling to find out what was going on, but Wynne held up her phone and signaled for her to stay quiet.

"Wynne Garrity," she said. "Yes, Your Honor. We did see them. Yes. I know. I understand. We'll wait to hear from you. Yes. Thanks for the call." Wynne set her phone down. "Guess you figured out who that was."

"Judge Abel. Let me guess, she's pissed about the brides."

"She's not happy. Apparently, there are just as many inside the courthouse as outside. She said they have the security lines completely jammed up and jurors reporting for duty can't get through. She sent out her bailiff to announce the hearing has been postponed to get them to go away."

Abby wasn't quite registering. "Are we supposed to sneak in later for the hearing?"

"No, it might actually be postponed. She said she'd review the motion and response again and if she needs to hear from either side, she'll reschedule, but it's likely she'll just rule on the pleadings we filed. She said to expect to hear from her office in a few days."

"So much for our imminent harm argument. If she's not in a rush anymore, it probably means she's going to rule against us."

"Or it could mean she wants to take a breath and make sure she considers all the angles."

Under other circumstances, Abby would appreciate Wynne's optimism, but right now she felt too defeated for it to make a difference. She glanced down at the console and stared at her phone which was blowing up with texts from Tommy. She wished she could just text him that the hearing had been postponed and leave it at that, but he deserved a call, and the sooner she got it over with, the better. She reached for the phone and scrolled through the messages. In between the increasingly angry texts from Tommy were a couple of seemingly innocent requests from Roxanne for her to call when she was done with court. As if.

Abby started to put the phone down, but as she did, another text alert rolled down from the top of the screen.

*I'm worried you're angry with me. Please know that wasn't supposed to happen.*

Abby read the text several times. "That wasn't supposed to happen" pretty much summed up her life from the moment she'd met Roxanne at the airport in PV. She couldn't do anything to erase the past, but she could keep it from happening again. She placed her thumb over the text from Roxanne and slowly slid it to the left until the bright red delete button appeared, and then she quickly hit the delete confirmation with her other thumb before she could change her mind. She wasn't sure what she expected to happen next—relief, release—but she was completely unprepared for the empty, hollow feeling in the pit of her stomach and the strong sense of loss at the idea that whatever she'd had with Roxanne was over, finished. Done for good.

❖

Roxanne watched the teaser for the premier of *Best Day Ever* for the third time, and barely kept from jumping out of her chair and strangling Stuart with her bare hands. Stuart had summoned her to the office first thing this morning to show her a surprise. She was surprised all right.

"Do you love it?" Stuart asking, his entire face a stupid grin.

"I do not. No. Not at all. It doesn't work, on any level." She took a breath. "I hope I'm being clear, but just to make sure. You absolutely cannot run that teaser."

"Why not?"

"Because that's not at all how the interview went. It's edited to make it look like Tommy said things he didn't. It's not..." She waited a beat and then plowed forward. "It's not honest."

"We're not a pharmaceutical company peddling the next great cure. As long as everyone gives consent, there's absolutely no reason we can't mix things up a bit to garner interest."

"Can you hear yourself? You can call it what you want, but it's not honest and I've built a reputation based on giving my honest, unbiased opinions."

"Exactly. Which is why no one will question your coverage, no matter what you say."

Roxanne wanted to shout and pound her fists against his chest, but she was certain the effort would be futile. Instead she forced as much calm as she could muster. "We're not airing this teaser. Not now, not ever."

Stuart leaned back in his chair, his grin was gone, replaced by a concerned and pensive expression. "You're kidding, right?"

"Nope."

"Then you better check your contract. The talent has some say in the show topics, but you don't have the right to dictate the marketing." He pointed at the screen. "Besides, that little gem is already running on every network in town."

Roxanne bristled at being referred to as "the talent" like she was some prop in the show, but that was a battle for another day. "What do you mean it's already running? You haven't even had the interview footage for twenty-four hours."

"See how devoted we are to promoting the new show?"

She wanted to punch the grin off his face, but there was probably some other dumb provision in her contract that said she could be fired if she did. Besides, she could tell he wasn't getting it and he probably never would. She reflected back on every interaction she'd ever had with Stuart and realized she should've seen this coming. How could she have been so naive as to think getting her own show meant it would actually be hers?

What she wanted to do was tell him to fuck off and that she quit, but more pressing was the need to talk to Abby. She told Stuart she'd deal with him later and stalked out of the conference room. She pulled out her phone as she left the building, wondering if Abby was still in court and hoping like hell she hadn't seen the teaser. She sent a text, asking Abby to call, and then refreshed her phone for an irrational amount of times, hoping for a response that was anything other than "go to hell." Finally, she got in her car and started to drive, hoping the distraction would calm her nerves, but instead her mind buzzed with possible solutions. She could go to the courthouse and try to sneak Abby's phone away from her and erase her ability to access the internet. That would only be a temporary solution, but the idea wasn't half bad. The courthouse was only a few blocks away. She could go there and be waiting when Abby was done with her hearing.

She was halfway there, stopped at a light, when a news story on the radio blasted away all her other thoughts.

*Courthouse personnel estimate over a hundred women wearing bridal veils and carrying signs clogged security and put a standstill to court business for a couple of hours this morning. The women were part of the ongoing series of protests against the abrupt closing of Barclay's Bridal, and according to a few who spoke with this reporter, they turned out in force today after watching the commercial for a new show named after the best-selling bridal magazine,* Best Day Ever, *and hosted by the Bride's Best Friend, Roxanne Daly.*

Damn, damn, damn. Roxanne beat the steering wheel with her fists, pretending it was Stuart's face, until the light changed. She stopped just in time to hear the reporter, who she now recognized as her friend Mary, finish the story.

*Judge Abel was scheduled to hear a motion from one of the owners who is trying to keep the stores open long enough to fulfill their existing obligations but canceled the hearing as the result of the protest. No word yet on a new hearing date. This is Mary Fielding, reporting live for KNOP.*

No sense going to the courthouse now. Besides, the last thing she needed was to be spotted in a sea of angry brides-to-be. Then Abby would never believe this mess wasn't her fault. She pulled over long enough to send one last text, and then turned the car around and headed to Abby's office.

A few minutes later, she pushed through the doors to the lobby and breathlessly announced her name to the man behind the counter. "Roxanne Daly, here to see Abby Keane. Is she in?"

The man's eyebrows drew together at her question and he held up a hand in a clear stop signal. "Please be seated."

She considered rushing the inner doors, but decided he could probably take her, so she complied with his request and perched on the edge of one of the armchairs in the lobby and watched him pick up the phone and whisper to someone, hopefully Abby. She could barely hear him, but she did catch a few snippets. "BBF"... "No, she's right here"... "In the lobby."

A moment later, the inner door burst open and Campbell and Grace came barreling over.

"You've got some nerve coming here," Grace said. "I can't believe—"

Campbell placed a hand on Grace's arm. "What Grace means to say is, how about we talk about this somewhere more private?" She led the way to a stunning conference room and invited Roxanne to have a seat.

"Actually, I was hoping to speak to Abby. Is she here?"

"Yeah, about that," Campbell said. "I think she may need a little time before she's ready to talk."

"She's pissed and she has every right to be," Grace said. "What were you thinking? There's a good chance she could've won the injunction today, which means all those women could've gotten the dresses they're protesting about, but now Barclay's may never reopen, which tells me you were all about ratings and didn't really care about getting those women what they wanted."

"That's not true. If I could just have a chance to explain..." At that moment, Abby appeared in the doorway, wearing a fierce scowl, and the words died on her lips. She was unsure any explanation would dissipate her anger, but she had to try. "Abby, I had no idea that commercial would air today, and I certainly didn't know the producer was going to chop up the footage like he did. I was furious when I found out." She flicked a glance at Grace and Campbell and risked a request. "Is there any chance we could have a moment alone to talk?"

Abby's expression softened for a second and she appeared to be considering her question, but then her face froze back into a frown. "You can say whatever you have to say in front of my friends. You know why? Because I trust them, implicitly. You, on the other hand? Not so much. Tommy lost his investor today. His online business is over before it could even get started, and it's highly unlikely Barclay's will reopen. All those brides who were protesting? They should've been protesting you because you sold them out for ratings. For crying out loud, it's your show. If you're not to blame, who is?"

Hearing Grace say she'd betrayed everyone involved had been bad enough, but coming from Abby's lips it was unbearable. Abby was right. It was her show and while she couldn't have stopped Stuart from what he'd done, the responsibility lay with her for not refusing to completely back off the story in the first place. No one would care that she'd been trying to do the right thing by letting the public see a different perspective. Maybe she wasn't cut out for showbiz. She certainly wasn't cut out for hurting people she cared about, and she cared about Abby more than she wanted to admit, more than she'd ever cared about anyone else. Ever. The best thing she could do right now would be to walk away and hope that when Abby cooled down, she'd agree to hear the whole story and hopefully, forgive her.

She stood. "You're right. This was my fault. I could not be more sorry, not just for how it may affect your case, but because I would never intentionally hurt you. I hope that someday you can forgive me."

Roxanne waited a few beats, but her apology was met with telling silence, and she knew it was time to go. As she walked out the door of the law firm, she resisted the urge to look back. Abby had told her all along that what they had was only a fling. She should've known the end was coming because, after all, flings weren't supposed to last.

## CHAPTER NINETEEN

Rox, that's the third piece you've barely touched. It's cake for crying out loud."

Roxanne looked up and grabbed her sister's hand. "Are you seriously snapping your fingers at me?"

"Yes," Val said. "But only after you ignored my question three times. Also, you not enjoying cake is a serious sign that you might be ill. Are you ill?"

"No, Val, I'm not ill," Roxanne said.

"I think you might be a little lovesick, and I know the last thing you probably want to do right now is help me plan my wedding. If you want a pass, you've got it."

"Is everything okay?"

Roxanne turned toward the perky voice of Gia Ricci, owner of Top Tier Cakes. Roxanne had featured Top Tier on her blog a few months ago as an example of the trifecta of wedding cakes: unique designs, delicious flavor combinations, and reasonable prices. Ignoring the pointed look from Val, Roxanne replied, "Everything's great, Gia, but I think you're holding out on us. Don't you have an Italian cream cake you usually save for your special customers?" She pointed at the samples on the table. "Are we not special enough for you?"

Gia laughed. "I never bring it out first because when I used to, nobody would even try the other flavors. I wanted to let you at least sample what else we have to offer, but judging by the fact you've barely touched these, I guess my plan has been thwarted. I'll be right back."

When Gia was out of the room, Roxanne said, "Brace yourself because this Italian cream cake is to die for."

"Is this how it's going to be? We're not going to talk about your big time bust up with a certain sexy lawyer?"

"There's nothing to talk about. We had a thing. It's over. End of story."

"Uh-huh."

"Leave it alone, Val."

Val shook her head. "Nope. Can't. I'm in full on romantic wedding mode. All I see everywhere I look are white doves and red roses and lace and silk." She pushed the plate holding the lemon cake with raspberry into Roxanne's space. "I like this one. What do you think?"

Roxanne waved at the plate. "I've sampled these before. That one's good."

Val slowly lifted the fork and made a show of swooning over a forkful of cake. After she licked her lips, she said, "The sister I know would fight me for a bite of this cake. You're not yourself."

"Don't worry about me. I'm good. Let's stay focused on all things wedding."

"My focus is fractured by your obvious attempts to avoid all discussion about what happened between you and Abby. Face it, sis, you're not going to feel better until you quit acting like nothing is wrong and admit you fell for her."

Val was right about the falling for Abby part, but Roxanne was certain admitting it wasn't going to make her feel better. Nothing was going to make her feel better short of a text or call from Abby to say she forgave her and wanted to try again, but that wasn't going to happen. It had been almost a week, and the only news of Abby had been what Roxanne read in the paper about the court case. Tommy Barclay had lost the injunction against his siblings and the doors to Barclay's stores remained closed. Abby had refused to give a comment for the story, but Roxanne imagined if she had said anything, she would've pointed to the clip about her interview with Tommy as a deciding factor in why her case had blown up, and Roxanne couldn't really blame her for thinking that was true.

Roxanne had picked up her phone to reach out to Abby over a dozen times over the past week, but every time she did, she remembered the combined look of hurt and fury on Abby's face the last time she'd seen her. She'd held out hope Abby would come around, but with every day that passed, she began to fear Abby would never come around, and there was so much distance between them now, she wasn't sure it could ever be bridged. She hadn't wanted to speak her fear in case it would make it real, but she'd always been honest with Val. "It's too late."

"Bullshit."

"It's not bullshit. If I had everything to do over again, I never would've signed on to do the show, but at the very least, I should've told Stuart to shove it when I saw the commercial. I should've quit on the spot." The litany of things she wished she'd done gathered steam and she kept going. "I should've immediately put out a statement—whatever I had to do to get Abby to listen to the truth, and to let everyone know that the commercial was an irresponsible ratings grab and that I would never be part of a sleazy exposé."

"Okay, so do all those things."

"It's not that easy. I have a contract."

"Break it. It's not like you don't know a good lawyer."

Roxanne sighed. Val made it sound like walking out on her own TV show in violation of her contract was the most rational thing in the world.

*Is it any more rational to keep doing something that you know won't make you happy?* The sudden thought was followed quickly by another. *You were happier being the BBF before this TV deal came along.* And another. *You were happy when you were with Abby.*

Roxanne let the idea of walking away from *Best Day Ever* simmer for a moment and found she enjoyed the anticipation of being free from the constraints of the job. "Okay. Say I quit and risk being sued for breaking my contract. That doesn't get Abby back."

"Truth. You're going to have to take an even bigger risk to win her over."

Gia burst through the doors from the kitchen holding two plates with larger than sample size slices of Italian cream cake. She set them on the table next to the other plates, and Roxanne noticed right away how all the other samples paled in comparison, and she realized that was how it was going to be for her from now on. She'd compare every woman she met to Abby Keane, and when everyone else came up short, she'd either wind up settling or spending the rest of her life alone.

Val was right again, and Roxanne knew it. What she didn't know was how she was going to win Abby back.

Abby sat in her office staring at her computer, but she might as well have been looking at static. The judge had declined to reschedule the hearing and instead had ruled on the paperwork they'd filed. Without the emotional appeal of Tommy being able to explain his vision in person, the long shot motion had been doomed, and when the news came yesterday that Judge Abel had ruled against them, Abby wasn't surprised.

In fact, she'd ceased to be surprised by just about anything after a hundred brides crashed her hearing, and her childhood friend and longtime client threatened to sue her. Roxanne's betrayal was icing on her cake of failure.

A sharp rap on her door interrupted her moping, but before she could tell whoever it was to go away, Campbell and Grace crashed their way in. "Hey, I'm working in here—"

"You're not working, you're sulking," Grace said. "Snap out of it for a minute, because there's something you need to see." She motioned to Campbell who set the iPad she'd brought on her desk and pointed to the screen which featured a video still of Roxanne facing the camera.

"What's going on?"

"Just watch," Campbell said. She tapped the play button and Roxanne came to life.

*I've been the Bride's Best Friend for a few years now, and here's what I've learned. Life throws curves at you, and no matter how prepared you are, sudden changes in circumstance can catch you completely off guard. Whether it's the sudden closing of a bridal store, leaving you without the dress you agonized over for months or the hurricane that wipes out the beach where you planned to say your vows, every curveball leaves you with a choice. Are you going to lean in and adapt or are you going to fight the inevitable? You can do either, but I promise you, only one is a path to happiness, and the more you resist the opportunities life hands you, the more frustrated you will be.*

*You loved that dress, but for real—if you're truly in love, it doesn't matter what you're wearing. That beach seemed perfect, but its absence gives you the opportunity to find another, brighter, better venue for your special day. Live your best life by embracing the unexpected.*

*And now for a confession. Two, actually. Confession one: I met a smart, beautiful woman in a place I didn't expect at the most inopportune of times. I was working and she was playing. I'm not into flings and she wasn't into anything more serious than a fun, vacation interlude, but for a few short days we both suspended our lives outside of paradise to share one of the most intimate, exciting connections I've ever experienced. When we got back home, we found out our lives were vastly different, and but for the suspension of time and space, we probably never would've met, let alone fallen in love.*

Abby punched the pause button and sank farther into her chair. "Are you okay?" Campbell asked, placing a hand on her forehead.

"Does she have fever?" Grace stepped forward and placed her hand there as well. "You know the L word makes her queasy."

Abby pushed their hands away. She knew they were joking, but she did feel like she was falling apart, and her first instinct was to run, as fast and as far as possible. First thing though, she needed to convince her friends she was unfazed by Roxanne's declaration or they'd never leave her alone. "I'm good." She mustered a smile. "Totally."

"Excellent," Campbell said. "Because there's more." Before Abby could stop her, she hit play and the video resumed streaming with a wistful looking Roxanne, mid-sentence.

*...I don't know if she did, but a girl can hope, right?*

"Hold it," Grace said. "I think we missed something. Can you back it up?" She pointed at Campbell, who pressed the back button to rewind the video.

*Sorry, I forgot this is my confession. I can't speak for her, but I definitely fell in love. I don't know if she did, but a girl can hope, right?*

"Boom," Campbell said, slapping the table. "That's a wrap." She reached to turn off the video.

"Wait." Abby could hardly believe she'd spoken out loud, but now that she had, she knew she had to go all in. She waited until Campbell hit pause. "She said she had a second confession."

Campbell smiled "She did indeed. Let's hear it."

The video started again, and Abby was riveted to the screen. Roxanne was made up for the camera, but Abby could sense her fatigue in her slightly hoarse voice and the loss of sheen in her eyes. Had she lost sleep too?

*Second confession. I made a mistake stepping out from behind the Bride's Best Friend persona. The best friend should never eclipse the bride, never draw attention from all the special moments that lead up to and are part of her special day. The BBF's role is to be a pillar of quiet strength, giving when needed and stepping back when they've fulfilled their duties. Lately, I let the allure of a spot on TV distract me from the work I've grown to love, substituting drama for support. One day, if I'm lucky, I'll be the bride.* *When that time comes, I'll get the spotlight, but until then, I'm here for all of you, to champion your ideas, answer your questions, alleviate your stress, and advocate for your happiness.*

*The commercial that aired last week for the upcoming premiere of* Best Day Ever *was a hatchet job, depicting conversations that didn't happen, at least not the way they were depicted. Tommy Barclay was on a mission to reopen the stores and release the dresses to all the brides-to-be who'd ordered them, and his attorney, Abby Keane, was working hard to make that happen, but the careless ratings grab has killed their mission and my desire to work with* Best Day Ever *along with it. I handed in my resignation yesterday.*

*Which leads me to my first blog post after my short-lived television career.*

Roxanne took a deep breath.

*Here we go. Life doesn't happen to you; you make it happen. Remember my first confession? About falling in love? Here's the deal. I let the woman I love get away without ever telling her how I feel. Actually, it was worse than that because, based on the way things went down between us, she believes I betrayed her trust, and rather than clear up that misconception, I simply walked away, hoping circumstances would sort themselves out. No more.*

Abby sucked in a breath, as the anticipation built. She could feel Campbell's and Grace's eyes on her, but she didn't dare look away from the screen and Roxanne's earnest gaze. Something important was about to happen. Something that would change her life.

*And so I say this to the woman who captured my heart on a beach far from here: if you want to see what the future holds for us, let's meet at the place where together we watched another couple exchange vows and pledge to have a happily ever after. Don't worry, this isn't a proposal, just a simple request from the woman who is in love with you. I'll be at the gazebo tomorrow night at seven. Join me if you feel the same.*

*To all the brides-to-be watching, thanks for tuning in. Love, the BBF.*

The video faded slowly into a black screen, but Abby couldn't look away. Had that really just happened? Had Roxanne quit her job, exonerated Tommy, and made a very public declaration of love? To her?

"What are you going to do?" Grace asked.

"It's not like she has a choice," Campbell said. "She's going to Moonlight Ranch. Tomorrow night. The real question is what's she going to say when she gets there."

Abby watched the two of them banter about her future for a moment, and then she cut in. "Chill, please. This is a lot."

"Exactly. Which is why we're coming with you. Aren't we, Grace?"

"I wouldn't miss this for the world."

"I love you two," Abby said, "but you annoy the crap out of me sometimes. I haven't said I'm going."

They both stared at her like she'd lost her mind. She couldn't really blame them because she had. She'd lost her mind over Roxanne since the moment she'd met her. Roxanne, with her optimistic view of forever love and happily-ever-afters, was nothing like any other woman she'd been with, and Roxanne was also the only woman who'd ever burrowed into her heart. Of course, look how that had turned out. The question was whether she was willing to open her heart to Roxanne again.

## CHAPTER TWENTY

Roxanne sat shotgun in Val's Honda and pointed at the clock on the dashboard. "You drive like an old woman. It's already six forty. At this rate we're going to be late."

Val kept her eyes on the road. "You'll be there with time to spare, and you'll thank me for the fact you didn't have a lot of extra time to stress, although you're kinda making up for it now."

"I'm sorry," Roxanne said. "My nerves are a little shot. What if she doesn't show?"

"If she doesn't show, then I drive you home." Val drummed her fingers on the steering wheel. "You know, you didn't give her a lot of time to think about it."

"Way to make me feel better. Abby isn't the kind of woman who needs to stew over something. She knows what she wants, and in a little while, I'll know what she wants too."

Val turned into the exit for Moonlight Ranch, and Roxanne started to feel jitters, beyond the ones that had prompted her to ask Val to drive her to this rendezvous. She'd figured if things went well, she would ride off into the sunset with Abby, but if they didn't, she'd have Val to keep her company for the long ride home. The post had gone viral after she'd sent a copy to Mary at KNOP, and unless Abby had gone completely off grid, it was highly unlikely she wouldn't have seen it or at least heard about it. But what if Val was right and she hadn't given Abby enough time to think about whether she wanted to take a leap? She could see the start of her next blog post now—how about a second chance, and I really mean it this time.

No, this was it. If Abby didn't show up tonight, it would be painful and sad, but it would mean it was time to move on.

When they drew closer to the ranch, she directed Val to turn down the drive toward the ridge where Abby's mother's reception had been held, and a short while later, she spotted rows of twinkling lights. She'd spoken to the owners and arranged for them to light the gazebo, but she hadn't expected them to light the entire path along the way. She pointed to the lot where she and Abby had parked the last time they were here, and when the car stopped, she took a moment to savor the memory of that night. Everything about it had been magical. Abby had treated her like a date in front of her friends and her mother, and after a few initial jitters, she'd seemed to warm up to the romance of the evening. They'd danced and drank and stared out at the stars, and when it was time to leave, Abby drove her home and came in and spent the night like it was perfectly natural—like couples do. Tonight was about recapturing those moments, about starting over.

"You ready?" Val asked.

Roxanne breathed deep. "As I'm ever going to be."

"I'll walk you in, and then make myself scarce until you give me the all clear. And don't argue, because this is happening."

"Knowing you're here really helps." She squeezed Val's hand and reached for the door handle. "Come on. Let's do this."

Roxanne started up the path to the gazebo with Val at her side. She was only a few steps in when the twinkling lights multiplied to illuminate her path, and in the early evening dusk she was able to make out dozens of women lining both sides of the pathway, holding Mason jars filled with tiny bits of light. She recognized the light jars as ones she'd seen in the trees the last time she'd been here, but more than that, she recognized these women, many of whom had been at the Barclay's protests. As she walked toward them, they began to cheer, and she turned to Val. "What's happening?"

"I think you have a fan club."

"How did they know where I was going to be?" She'd been cryptic in her video message to Abby to keep press, especially anyone from *Best Day Ever*, from showing up.

"I may have mentioned in the comments section that if they wanted to thank you for championing them, they could send me a direct message. Emily, the woman you interviewed that day you and I went to Barclay's, emailed me and then she contacted the rest. They parked back at the main entrance to the ranch to keep this a surprise."

The raw emotion that came with knowing all these women had shown up to support her left Roxanne speechless. She managed a simple thank you and walked the rest of the path to the gazebo. The view facing west was exactly as she remembered it, and the deep red and orange sunset blazed across the sky. "I guess this is it."

"I'll wait as long as you want me to."

Roxanne considered asking her to stay close until Abby arrived. Would it be weird for Abby to find her in this very romantic spot with her sister by her side like a security blanket? Why yes, yes it would. Besides, she'd vowed to go all in and that meant risking rejection even on a grand scale. "I'm good."

Val was only a few steps away, when Roxanne felt a rush of panic. "Val?"

Val stopped and turned back to face her. "What's up?"

"What if she doesn't show?"

Val smiled. "Then she's crazy and you don't want to be with her anyway. But, Rox?"

"Yes?"

"She'll be here."

Roxanne watched Val's back until she disappeared from sight, the twinkling lights in the distance the only evidence she was not alone. She kept her gaze trained on the path. Any minute now, Abby might come into view, and Roxanne didn't want to miss seeing her arrival. Would her gait be quick, like she was excited to be here, or would she be dragging her feet, like she'd shown up only to ask to be left alone?

The minutes ticked by. Six fifty-eight, six fifty-nine, seven. Seven o-one. With each aching change of the clock, time slowed, stretching like a big rubber band that might eventually snap and smack her in the face. What if Abby didn't show? How long should she wait before admitting defeat and trudging back through the gauntlet of light bearing BTBs?

And then, suddenly, a moment of clarity cut through the rising panic. *However long it takes. Abby is the one.* If she didn't show up tonight, maybe she didn't have enough notice. Maybe she had other pressing matters. Whatever the reason, Roxanne wasn't about to concede defeat over a grand gesture gone wrong. However long it took, whether it was in this gazebo or sitting in her living room, she had to believe Abby would eventually come around, and she could and would wait. Impatience wasn't going to be the reason she missed out on the love of her life.

*Please let her show up. Please let her show up.*

Abby stared at her reflection in her bedroom mirror. She was on her third change of clothes when the doorbell rang. She debated ignoring it, but Campbell and Grace knew she was in here and she doubted they'd give up and go away, seeing as how they were hell-bent on attending what they'd named Operation Win Back the BBF. Their excitement was punctuated by three more rings of the doorbell. "I'm coming, I'm coming," she shouted as she swung open the front door to find them standing on her doorstep. Grace was holding flowers and Campbell's eyes were as bright as a kid on Christmas morning.

"Come in," Abby said, not waiting for a response before turning and walking back to the bedroom. "I'm still getting dressed."

"If we don't leave soon, you're going to be late," Campbell said, following close behind.

"I know."

"You don't sound very excited," Campbell added as they walked into Abby's bedroom. "Have you changed your mind?"

"No." Abby looked into the mirror again. "Yes." She sighed and sat down on the edge of her bed. "I don't have anything to wear. What do people wear to…whatever this is?"

"A woman made a very public, very moving profession of love for you and you're worried about what to wear?" Grace asked.

"Kind of. I mean there are a million things to worry about, but that's the only one that I can control." She cocked her head. "Why are you holding a bouquet of flowers?"

Grace looked down at the flowers and then shoved them toward her. "I didn't want you to show up empty-handed." She shrugged. "I figured girls like Roxanne like flowers."

"Girls like Roxanne like a lot of romantic things, and that's precisely what I'm worried about. I mean, she made this big, incredibly romantic declaration. To me. What if she expects me to be all gooey and romantic too?"

"Have you met you?" Campbell asked. "Because we have, and Roxanne has too. I'm guessing she already knows your unromantic, marriage-phobic self, and she loves you anyway. The hard part's over. Only thing left for you to do is show up and tell her you love her too." Campbell squinted. "You do love her, right?"

Abby took a moment to assess. She was nervous and anxious, and she wasn't prone to either. At the same time, she was both excited and oddly, already feeling satisfied. It reminded her of the moment right before she'd quit her job in Dallas to join forces with Grace and Campbell. She'd had no idea what the future would hold, but she knew it would be better than anything she'd ever experienced before, and she couldn't wait to see what happened next. Take that feeling to the tenth power and she'd get close to how she felt about Roxanne. She thought back to the night on the beach at Azure when she'd arranged for the candlelight dinner. Apparently, she did have a few romantic bones where Roxanne was concerned, and that told her all she needed to know. "I do."

"Then quit worrying about what to wear and go tell her." Grace jingled her keys. "Come on."

Once they were in the car, Grace drove like a mad woman, while Campbell watched the clock. Abby sat in the back seat staring out the window, praying they would make it to the ranch on time. Timing had been everything when it came to her relationship with Roxanne, from the chance meeting at the airport in Puerto Vallarta to the morning the commercial aired right before her hearing. Was love so fragile it could be disrupted by random circumstance?

Tommy had called a couple of hours before to tell her that when his investor saw Roxanne's video blog, he contacted him to say that he was back on board to fund the online business, and the investor thought it would be a great marketing move to help the brides who were waiting on their dresses from Barclay's when the doors closed get their orders fulfilled online. They still had to hash out the details, but Tommy was confident they could find a way to make it happen. The news gave her hope that even when things looked bleak in the moment, there might be light on the other side. She checked her watch. Seven o'clock. She leaned forward and checked the readout on the dash—six fifty-nine. "Can you drive any faster?"

Grace responded by gunning the engine and roaring into the turnoff to the ranch. Abby pointed at the side road ahead. "Take that road up there, but try not to kill us in the process."

After they survived the turn, Grace sped back up, and every bump in the road jarred Abby's already roiling stomach. She closed her eyes and prayed Roxanne wouldn't leave before she got there. "Should I text her to tell her I'm coming?"

"No!" Campbell and Grace shouted the answer. "She's in a romantic setting," Campbell said. "Waiting for the woman she loves. It's an epic scene, and no one sends a text message during an epic scene. You've got to be there, in the flesh, you know, for the kissing and saying stuff."

"Then slow the car down, because we're here." Abby pointed to a spot up ahead and Grace spun into a space next to a Honda

SUV. Abby had the door open before Grace came to a complete stop, and she jumped out.

"Go," Campbell yelled. "We'll catch up to you."

She raised her hand in acknowledgment. The sun had just set, but she could just make out the path she and Roxanne had taken the night of her mother's wedding and she ran toward it. Her heart was pounding, but she knew it was from anticipation not exertion, and adrenaline fueled her to run faster. When she reached the path, it lit up with hundreds of twinkling lights, and the sudden illumination stopped her in her tracks.

"Go, Abby!"

"You got this!"

"She's waiting for you!"

Abby slowed her pace and turned her head from side to side. Dozens of women holding jars of light lined the path, and they were cheering her on. She wanted to ask questions, find out what they were doing here, how they knew, but if the shouts she heard were right, Roxanne was waiting at the end of this path and she had to get to her.

A few seconds later, she emerged into the clearing and stopped a few feet from the gazebo. A couple of weeks ago, it had been full of people celebrating her mother's wedding with food and drink and music, but tonight there was none of that—only one solitary woman, standing near the far railing, framed by twinkling lights and staring straight at her.

"You came," Roxanne said.

Abby heard the hint of surprise in Roxanne's voice and wished she'd never given her a reason to doubt. She stepped closer until they were almost touching. "I did."

"I hoped you would."

Abby placed her hands on either side of Roxanne's face and looked deep into her eyes. "There's nowhere else I want to be. No one else I want to be with."

"I'm so sorry." Roxanne ducked her head. "For everything."

Abby placed a finger under her chin and raised it so they were eye-to-eye. "Me too. I never should've doubted you. I..." She paused, lost in the raw vulnerability she saw reflected back at her. Roxanne had taken such a leap, from the very public invitation to meet her here to the waiting and hoping she would show up. It was time for her to meet Roxanne, not just halfway, but all the way. "What you said in your video? About how you didn't know how I felt? Let me be perfectly clear. I love you, Roxanne Daly. I'm in love with you, and I know you said this wasn't a proposal, but for the first time in my life, I'm interested in finding out more about this happily ever after stuff. Do you think you could help me out with that?"

Roxanne's expression burst into a big smile. "I'll make it my top priority." She pulled Abby closer. "It starts like this."

Cheers filled the air as Roxanne's lips met hers. Campbell's and Grace's voices were the loudest, but their shouts along with the others faded into the background while every nerve ending in her body stood at attention during the long, slow, searing kiss. When they finally broke for breath, she whispered in Roxanne's ear. "Anything that starts that good, can only end really, really well. Count me in."

THE END

# About the Author

Carsen Taite is a recovering lawyer who prefers writing fiction to practicing law because she has more control of the outcome. She believes that lawyers make great lovers, which is why she includes so many of them in her novels. She is the award-winning author of over twenty novels of romance and romantic intrigue, including the Luca Bennett Bounty Hunter series, the Lone Star Law series, and the Legal Affairs romances.

# Books Available from Bold Strokes Books

**Brooklyn Summer** by Maggie Cummings. When opposites attract, can a summer of passion and adventure lead to a lifetime of love? (978-1-63555-578-3)

**City Kitty and Country Mouse** by Alyssa Linn Palmer. Pulled in two different directions, can a city kitty and country mouse fall in love and make it work? (978-1-63555-553-0)

**Elimination** by Jackie D. When a dangerous homegrown terrorist seeks refuge with the Russian mafia, the team will be put to the ultimate test. (978-1-63555-570-7)

**In the Shadow of Darkness** by Nicole Stilling. Angeline Vallencourt is a reluctant vampire who must decide what she wants more—obscurity, revenge, or the woman who makes her feel alive. (978-1-63555-624-7)

**On Second Thought** by C. Spencer. Madisen is falling hard for Rae. Even single life and co-parenting are beginning to click. At least, that is, until her ex-wife begins to have second thoughts. (978-1-63555-415-1)

**Out of Practice** by Carsen Taite. When attorney Abby Keane discovers the wedding blogger tormenting her client is the woman she had a passionate, anonymous vacation fling with, sparks and subpoenas fly. Legal Affairs: one law firm, three best friends, three chances to fall in love. (978-1-63555-359-8)

**Providence** by Leigh Hays. With every click of the shutter, photographer Rebekiah Kearns finds it harder and harder to keep Lindsey Blackwell in focus without getting too close. (978-1-63555-620-9)

**Taking a Shot at Love** by KC Richardson. When academic and athletic worlds collide, will English professor Celeste Bouchard and basketball coach Lisa Tobias ignore their attraction to achieve their professional goals? (978-1-63555-549-3)

**Flight to the Horizon** by Julie Tizard. Airline captain Kerri Sullivan and flight attendant Janine Case struggle to survive an emergency water landing and overcome dark secrets to give love a chance to fly. (978-1-63555-331-4)

**In Helen's Hands** by Nanisi Barrett D'Arnuk. As her mistress, Helen pushes Mickey to her sensual limits, delivering the pleasure only a BDSM lifestyle can provide her. (978-1-63555-639-1)

**Jamis Bachman, Ghost Hunter** by Jen Jensen. In Sage Creek, Utah, a poltergeist stirs to life and past secrets emerge. (978-1-63555-605-6)

**Moon Shadow** by Suzie Clarke. Add betrayal, season with survival, then serve revenge smokin' hot with a sharp knife. (978-1-63555-584-4)

**Spellbound** by Jean Copeland and Jackie D. When the supernatural worlds of good and evil face off, love might be what saves them all. (978-1-63555-564-6)

**Temptation** by Kris Bryant. Can experienced nanny Cassie Miller deny her growing attraction and keep her relationship with her boss professional? Or will they sidestep propriety and give in to temptation? (978-1-63555-508-0)

**The Inheritance** by Ali Vali. Family ties bring Tucker Delacroix and Willow Vernon together, but they could also tear them, and any chance they have at love, apart. (978-1-63555-303-1)

**Thief of the Heart** by MJ Williamz. Kit Hanson makes a living seducing rich women in casinos and relieving them of the expensive jewelry most won't even miss. But her streak ends when she meets beautiful FBI agent Savannah Brown. (978-1-63555-572-1)

**Date Night** by Raven Sky. Quinn and Riley are celebrating their one-year anniversary. Such an important milestone is bound to result in some extraordinary sexual adventures, but precisely how extraordinary is up to you, dear reader. (978-1-63555-655-1)

**Face Off** by PJ Trebelhorn. Hockey player Savannah Wells rarely spends more than a night with any one woman, but when photographer Madison Scott buys the house next door, she's forced to rethink what she expects out of life. (978-1-63555-480-9)

**Hot Ice** by Aurora Rey, Elle Spencer, Erin Zak. Can falling in love melt the hearts of the iciest ice queens? Join Aurora Rey, Elle Spencer, and Erin Zak to find out! (978-1-63555-513-4)

**Line of Duty** by VK Powell. Dr. Dylan Carlyle's professional and personal life is turned upside down when a tragic event at Fairview Station pits her against ambitious, handsome police officer Finley Masters. (978-1-63555-486-1)

**London Undone** by Nan Higgins. London Craft reinvents her life after reading a childhood letter to her future self and in doing so finds the love she truly wants. (978-1-63555-562-2)

**Lunar Eclipse** by Gun Brooke. Moon De Cruz lives alone on an uninhabited planet after being shipwrecked in space. Her life changes forever when Captain Beaux Lestarion's arrival threatens the planet and Moon's freedom. (978-1-63555-460-1)

**One Small Step** by Michelle Binfield. Iris and Cam discover the meaning of taking chances and following your heart, even if it means getting hurt. (978-1-63555-596-7)

**Shadows of a Dream** by Nicole Disney. Rainn has the talent to take her rock band all the way, but falling in love is a powerful distraction, and her new girlfriend's meth addiction might just take them both down. (978-1-63555-598-1)

**Someone to Love** by Jenny Frame. When Davina Trent is given an unexpected family, can she let nanny Wendy Darling teach her to open her heart to the children and to Wendy? (978-1-63555-468-7)

**Tinsel** by Kris Bryant. Did a sweet kitten show up to help Jessica Raymond and Taylor Mitchell find each other? Or is the holiday spirit to blame for their special connection? (978-1-63555-641-4)

**Uncharted** by Robyn Nyx. As Rayne Marcellus and Chase Stinsen track the legendary Golden Trinity, they must learn to put their differences aside and depend on one another to survive. (978-1-63555-325-3)

**Where We Are** by Annie McDonald. Can two women discover a way to walk on the same path together and discover the gift of staying in one spot, in time, in space, and in love? (978-1-63555-581-3)

**A Moment in Time** by Lisa Moreau. A longstanding family feud separates two women who unexpectedly fall in love at an antique clock shop in a small Louisiana town. (978-1-63555-419-9)

**Aspen in Moonlight** by Kelly Wacker. When art historian Melissa Warren meets Sula Johansen, director of a local bear conservancy, she discovers that love can come in unexpected and unusual forms. (978-1-63555-470-0)

**Back to September** by Melissa Brayden. Small bookshop owner Hannah Shepard and famous romance novelist Parker Bristow maneuver the landscape of their two very different worlds to find out if love can win out in the end. (978-1-63555-576-9)

**Changing Course** by Brey Willows. When the woman of your dreams falls from the sky, you'd better be ready to catch her. (978-1-63555-335-2)

**Cost of Honor** by Radclyffe. First Daughter Blair Powell and Homeland Security Director Cameron Roberts face adversity when their enemies stop at nothing to prevent President Andrew Powell's reelection. (978-1-63555-582-0)

**Fearless** by Tina Michele. Determined to overcome her debilitating fear through exposure therapy, Laura Carter all but fails before she's even begun until dolphin trainer Jillian Marshall dedicates herself to helping Laura defeat the nightmares of her past. (978-1-63555-495-3)

**Not Dead Enough** by J.M. Redmann. A woman who may or may not be dead drags Micky Knight into a messy con game. (978-1-63555-543-1)

**Not Since You** by Fiona Riley. When Charlotte boards her honeymoon cruise single and comes face-to-face with Lexi, the high school love she left behind, she questions every decision she has ever made. (978-1-63555-474-8)

**Not Your Average Love Spell** by Barbara Ann Wright. Four women struggle with who to love and who to hate while fighting to rid a kingdom of an evil invading force. (978-1-63555-327-7)

**Tennessee Whiskey** by Donna K. Ford. Dane Foster wants to put her life on pause and ask for a redo, a chance for something that matters. Emma Reynolds is that chance. (978-1-63555-556-1)

**30 Dates in 30 Days** by Elle Spencer. A busy lawyer tries to find love the fast way—thirty dates in thirty days. (978-1-63555-498-4)

**Finding Sky** by Cass Sellars. Skylar Addison's search for a career intersects with her new boss's search for butterflies, but Skylar can't forgive Jess's intrusion into her life. (978-1-63555-521-9)

**Hammers, Strings, and Beautiful Things** by Morgan Lee Miller. While on tour with the biggest pop star in the world, rising musician

Blair Bennett falls in love for the first time while coping with loss and depression. (978-1-63555-538-7)

**Heart of a Killer** by Yolanda Wallace. Contract killer Santana Masters's only interest is her next assignment—until a chance meeting with a beautiful stranger tempts her to change her ways. (978-1-63555-547-9)

**Leading the Witness** by Carsen Taite. When defense attorney Catherine Landauer reluctantly becomes the key witness in prosecutor Starr Rio's latest criminal trial, their hearts, careers, and lives may be at risk. (978-1-63555-512-7)

**No Experience Required** by Kimberly Cooper Griffin. Izzy Treadway has resigned herself to a life without romance because of her bipolar illness but wonders what she's gotten herself into when she agrees to write a book about love. (978-1-63555-561-5)

**One Walk in Winter** by Georgia Beers. Olivia Santini and Hayley Boyd Markham might be rivals at work, but they discover that lonely hearts often find company in the most unexpected of places. (978-1-63555-541-7)

**The Inn at Netherfield Green** by Aurora Rey. Advertising executive Lauren Montgomery and gin distiller Camden Crawley don't agree on anything except saving the Rose & Crown, the old English pub that's brought them together. (978-1-63555-445-8)

**Top of Her Game** by M. Ullrich. When it comes to life on the field and matters of the heart, losing isn't an option for pro athletes Kenzie Shaw and Sutton Flores. (978-1-63555-500-4)

**Vanished** by Eden Darry. A storm is coming, and Ellery and Loveday must find the chosen one or humanity won't survive it. (978-1-63555-437-3)